Author's Note

I grew up in a riverside town not unlike the one fictionalized in this book. It too, went through a period of decline in the seventies. Thanks to the efforts of so many people, it is thriving once again. Seeing my hometown now as an art and music mecca made writing this book more gratifying than I could have imagined.

"Hard to believe that dirty little city is down there, ain't it?"
He seemed to read her thoughts. "Everything does look better from far away."

Say Hello To Valentino

by

MIRANDA MARIN

Miranda Marin

ISBN: 978-0-9972284-1-0

Publisher: Words In The Works LLC

info@wordsintheworks.com

To Genevieve, MaryAnn, Josephine, Jean, and Lee

—Thank you.

The small dark-haired girl lay under her pink and white bedspread waiting for the unwelcome but familiar sound. A car door closed quietly outside. The key turned in the front door. A few more seconds passed. Then it came. The loose floorboard in the living room made the usual loud creak as her older sister tiptoed over it.

Then his feet hit the floor with a loud thud. Footsteps began moving swiftly through the long ranch-style house. His angry voice rang out.

"What kinda shit are you tryin' to pull, sneakin' in here after you been runnin' round with whores and bums all night? You're no damn good. You were never any good."

"Go to hell!" her sister screamed.

There were more footsteps, hard and fast toward the bathroom and the door slammed.

Her mother's throaty voice cried out raised about an octave above its normal tone.

"No, Chick, no!"

The little girl sat up in bed with her eyes opened wide. She envisioned her mother grabbing him from behind in her usual vain attempt to stop him. She knew her mother's grasp could not stop his surge of anger.

"Open the door! Open this goddamn door or I'll break it down."

"Kiss my ass!" her sister hollered.

The frightened little girl buried her head under the pillow in anticipation. There was a powerful boom and a high-pitched scream.

"Don't you ever talk to me like that again, you little…"

Before he could finish the sentence, he began to cry. The little girl pressed her hands firmly over her ears. The sound reminded her of a wounded animal. Her stomach turned.

Her sister ran into their room and locked the door behind her again, despite the lesson she had just learned. She was holding a towel up to her face as she cried. At first the girl thought it was a flowered towel but when her sister switched on the lamp, she saw it was spotted with blood.

Her father continued to cry loudly. The girl pretended to be asleep until her sister got into bed and turned out the light. As her parents argued, the girl jumped up and slipped out of the house into the night. Perched underneath her favorite tree, a tall pine with crooked branches that reached in all directions, she drew her knees up to her chin and caught her breath. Her whole body shook even though it was a warm summer night.

She knew the cure. It always worked.

She began, sweet and low at first, and then louder... *"Dedicated to the One I Love."*

The moon glow was her spotlight. She sang to the stars as they peeked through the shadowy silhouette of the pine tree. Raising her palms to the night sky, the girl swayed now, listening to the sound of her voice. It was deep, strong, and clear, not the voice of a nine-year-old. It soared over the large wheat field that paralleled her yard and through the thicket of woods behind the billowy waves of wheat. Her voice echoed back to her from the steep mountain that loomed nearby. The control she had over her voice gave her a sense of peace.

Her song was soon interrupted by the sound of her mother's voice. "Theresa! Theresa! I know you're out there. You better come in this house right now. Do you hear? Right now, I said!"

But she continued. The singing quieted her fears and dissolved the pain.

She'd let her mother call her three more times. After the fourth time, she'd go inside. That was her rule.

Chapter 1

Theresa Micelli stiffened at the sight of the flashing red lights twinkling through the dingy windows of her basement bedroom. Her first thought was the police. As her familiar surroundings came into focus, the reflections dancing on the walls seemed to shed a festive glow to her dark, dank room. Then she heard the gurney being rolled across the kitchen floor followed by the sound of her father sobbing.

In that instant she knew it was her mother.

Terri had kissed her goodnight just a few hours ago. She found her different tonight, unusually affectionate. They shared a glass or two of wine.

"C'mon, doll. Give me a kiss," her mom had beckoned just before Terri went to bed. That should have been the tipoff; that unexpected show of affection.

In the last year, her mother's health had quickly deteriorated. She had *"failed"* as Terri's aunts would say. Terri was always amused by that expression as if your very life was a big test, only this was a test everybody failed.

It had been difficult for her, watching her mom get thinner and thinner. Terri's pain was eased by spending a lot of time in bars. Drinking had turned down the noise in her head since she was fifteen. During her mother's long illness, Terri relied on alcohol even more. Drinking kept her from thinking about this very moment, but now it was here. Terri rolled over in bed, confused, frightened.

At twenty-five, her life should have been open to all kinds of possibilities but it wasn't. The year was 1974. It was a liberal self-indulgent time. Terri didn't enjoy it much and often wondered whether she was hindered more by her strict Catholic upbringing or by living in the confines of this basement room with her parents above her. A lot of her high school friends had taken the famous doctor's advice to turn on, tune in, and drop out. Some of them had difficulty tuning back in to anything as they became mired in their addictions. Some had relocated to California—a dream she could never realize while her mother was alive.

Terri figured she was having a long run of bad luck.

After her failed marriage, she'd ended up in her parents' basement, unable to stretch her paycheck from week to week. Theresa Micelli had aspired to nothing and just watched as her mother slowly slipped away.

Her father didn't call down for her and she didn't go up. Cowardice was one of her biggest defects.

She decided to lie in bed until the ambulance pulled away. She would wait about ten minutes and then go to the hospital. Her body was shaking the way it did years ago, when she woke from a nightmare. The reality of what was now happening brought on unwholesome thoughts.

Jesus Christ! I thought the men were supposed to go first. Shit!

She pulled on her jeans and headed for the local emergency room. She was hoping to find her mother sitting up on the gurney complaining about the pizza that had got stuck in her throat.

* * *

As she drove, Terri tried to conjure up some memories of her mother, but her mind was flooded with thoughts of her father, Chick Micelli. It wasn't that she didn't have any love for the guy. She had to love him. He was her father, although Terri sometimes felt that the hand of fate had been somewhat unkind in this regard.

The fact was, she just didn't like him. He had an explosive temper and a despicable habit of throwing people out. Her mom and dad lost their little luncheonette in town years ago because he threw out so many customers.

There was the time when she was eight-years-old. She'd just made herself an ice cream cone. She had to hoist herself over the edge of the freezer to reach the ice cream tubs below. After digging in with all her might, she finally slipped back down to the floor with her well-deserved treat held firmly between both hands. As she strolled along the row of pink and silver counter stools, Terri noticed a thin gaunt man in a wrinkled brown suit lean across the counter and whisper something in her dad's ear. She stopped short as her father's face grew red and his eyes bulged wide.

"What?" he hollered. "Open the door, Sonny!" he yelled to his nephew, who was sitting at the counter quietly enjoying his coffee. Sonny quickly obeyed.

Terri's eyes widened as she licked at her cone. Chick had snatched the man off the stool. With one hand on the man's pants and the other on the collar of his wrinkled suit, he tossed him out onto Main Street. She took a few steps forward and stared in amazement at the man lying helplessly in the gutter.

"And don't come back, you dirty bastard," Chick bellowed.

Terri watched, confused, wondering what had upset her father so.

Later, when she was a teenager, she learned the man's grave error. He had complimented her mother's behind.

Terri realized now that she still liked her father when she was eight.

Growing up in a luncheonette did hold some warm memories though, like her love for Fogarty, the drunk who worked part time cleaning the place.

Fogarty was unreliable and he'd often disappear. When Terri would ask for him, her mother would tell her he was "on a bender." Terri didn't know what a bender was and figured he was was away at the beach on vacation. Fogarty once caught Terri in his arms as she slipped and tumbled down the store's basement stairs. From the moment she looked into his steely gray eyes and smelled the pungent scent of alcohol on his breath, she fell in love with him. (She often wondered if this was the moment she fell in love with alcohol, too.) Terri promptly asked her mother if she could marry Fogarty when she got big. "No doll. You can't marry him. He'll be an old man when you grow up, and besides he's a drunkard."

There were the frequent visits to the store by the juke box man, who always gave Terri all the forty-fives he took out of the brightly lit machine that week. She'd take them home and play them over and over again on her tiny record player, singing along to Screamin' Jay Hawkins or Jerry Lee Lewis. The loud music seemed to calm her somehow.

The allure of jukebox music and Genevieve Micelli's home cooking was far overshadowed by Chick's uncontrollable outbursts and their business suffered.

There were the regular customers though, the ones who kept coming back like gawkers at the scene of an accident, just to see what he'd do next.

Although Chick said horrible things to people and his temper always got the better of him, he had a sense of humor, and that's what got him through.

As Terri walked into the small emergency room, she could hear her father's shrill cries. Between sobs, he was telling the doctor how much his wife had suffered. Terri stood in the doorway and stared at him.

Chick Micelli was a first-generation Italian, a living testament to the American Dream. He was a small man who stood only five foot four. With a full head of curly dyed-black hair, a prominent nose, and black-rimmed glasses, he had the look of an old-time gangster. He was usually bedecked in polyester, patent leather, and gold. He still considered himself a handsome man.

Terri thought of her father as the original Dead End Kid, and didn't have to ask herself why Jimmy Cagney was her favorite actor. She often wondered if Chick ever pushed a grapefruit into a woman's face. His demeanor was tough, but he had an extremely sensitive side. The remorse he would feel after lashing out at loved ones would always end up with a long crying jag. As a child,

Terri hated the sound of his crying, but she had now grown accustomed to it. He'd say apologetically, "Don't mind Daddy now. Men have to cry too, ya' know."

Terri listened as he sobbed to the doctor.

"She was so sick, Doc, we couldn't go to Florida in February. She couldn't even make a flight of stairs anymore. She was so weak."

Terri stepped into the room and the doctor looked over at her. It was Dr. Mond, the same doctor who had delivered her.

"I'm sorry, Terri. Your mother must have died instantly. It was a massive heart attack."

Terri swallowed hard, trying to hold back her tears and said to Chick, "C'mon, Dad. Let's go home and call Sarah."

Chick looked over and greeted her with a long wail.

When they left the hospital, he was still crying.

As Terri drove home, she tried to comfort him. "We'll call Sarah, and then we'll take a little ride. Okay, Dad?" Terri started to cry with him.

Chick suddenly snapped, "Tell her she better be here tomorrow!" Then he resumed his bawling.

Terri rolled her eyes and blew her nose. "Of course she'll be here, Dad."

"Ya' never know with her."

Chick was silent during the rest of the short ride while Terri cried quietly.

When they got home, Terri called her sister in Manhattan. It was around eleven o'clock.

"Hi, Sarah. It's me."

Sarah seemed to know something was wrong.

"What's the matter, Terri?"

"Mommy died."

"Oh, shit. When?"

"Just now…I mean, like an hour ago. I guess she had a heart attack on the couch."

Chick sat in the kitchen sobbing.

"Oh my god," Sarah gasped.

"You wanna talk to Daddy?"

"No. Just tell him I'll be there tomorrow."

"What train?"

"Just a minute," Sarah's voice cracked. "I can make the 12:35."

"Okay, I'll pick you up at the station."

Before Terri had time to say goodbye, Chick started flinging open prescription bottles all over the kitchen.

"Shit. I gotta go. He's goin' nuts." Terri slammed down the phone.

"Those dirty fuckin' bastards! They killed her with all these damn pills."

Jeez. I can't fuckin believe he said fuck in front of me already. She's only been dead an hour.

Fuck was rarely heard in this house. Terri often said it in her head, but not out loud.

Multicolored pills bounced all over the kitchen floor. Chick's dachshund, Peppy, jumped off the couch and lunged for the little treats.

"Dad! The dog's gonna eat the pills. Oh shit!"

As Terri crawled around the kitchen floor and tried to gather them all up, Chick whacked the little dog on the rump.

The dog let out a painful yelp.

"Get outta here, ya' little bastard."

"Dad. Stop *hittin'* him!"

"Shut up. If I wanna hit the dog, I will." Chick shoved the dog into the bathroom.

Terri finished cleaning up as her father sat and sobbed. She didn't want to go anywhere with him now but figured getting out of the house was a good idea.

"C'mon, Dad. Let's go." Terri grabbed a six-pack from the fridge. It was going to be a long ride.

As Terri drove around she felt numb, but not numb enough. She opened a can of Budweiser and took a long swig.

"Where do ya' wanna go, Dad?"

"Just drive around," Chick instructed.

Terri had lived in this little river city all her life. It was small enough so that everyone knew everyone else's business. Terri remembered what it was like when she was little—all the stores were filled with shoppers then. In those days, the city's most renowned landmark was an incline railway with two trolleys that took passengers up the steep mountain overlooking the town. For fifty cents, you'd get a long, slow ride to the top and a panoramic view of the valley and river below.

Now the city was dying. Most of the stores were boarded up and the trolleys were no longer running. They stood frozen to the tracks watching over the small city like two ghostly sentries. The only work available was at the local prison, the sanitarium, or the Veteran's Hospital.

Terri was content with her job as secretary to the chief psychologist at the sanitarium. It was called Willow House. The pay wasn't great but the convenient location, pleasant atmosphere, and minimal workload appealed to her.

There were plenty of bars in town, and that's where Terri sought her solace.

"You wanna go get a drink, Dad?"

"What are ya' kiddin'?" Chick raised his voice. "I'm not goin' in a bar now. Your mother just died. You crazy?"

"Okay, Dad, okay."

Chick needed to talk. Terri just drove around and listened. There was no other choice. As she drank her beer, Chick began with the familiar stories.

"Boy, your mother and I had a good time when we were goin' together. Your mother was a lotta fun in those days. We used to go up the mountain, ya' know, up to the casino. They used to have dances up there with big bands. I think Benny Goodman played up there once. Your mother would go up there with her sisters from across the river. She was the best lookin' one in the bunch. Your Aunt Vi was good lookin' too, but I liked your mother. I liked her as soon as I saw her. Hey, did I tell ya' the story about the time your mother broke up with me when we were engaged?"

"Yeah, Dad. You told me that story."

Terri hated riding in a car with no music. She flicked on the radio. Robert Plant was singing *"Black Dog"* to the echoes of Jimmy Page's sweet guitar. She felt a bit of relief.

"What the hell is that? Turn that shit off!" Chick yelled.

"Dad. That's…"

"I don't give a shit what it is. That guy's screamin'. He can't sing."

She turned the dial aggressively and took another gulp of beer. The absence of music left a hollow feeling deep inside her. Chick continued with his story.

"It was a coupla months after we got engaged. We had a big fight. I called her to go up to the casino and she says 'I got a date with a cop.' Real fresh, she said it. So I went up there and your mother was all dressed up. She was with the cop, see. She wasn't talkin' to me 'cause she was mad."

Chick continued in his thick Brooklyn accent. Chick had been brought up in Bay Ridge where a girl was a *"goil."*

"So your mother was dancin' with him, see, and havin' a real good time. So I says to myself, 'I'll fix her', and I slid a big chunk of ice right across the dance floor. It hit her in the ankle and knocked her right on her ass. And you know what? Your mother went back with me after that. Then we got married and had you kids."

"That's really romantic, Dad." Terri rolled her eyes and popped open another beer. She knew he wasn't finished yet.

"Ya' know, your mother was crazy about yous kids, even though she didn't show it. Your mother wasn't like that. She didn't show affection much, but she was really crazy about her kids."

"I know, Dad, I know." Terri's face grew hot and tears started to fill her eyes again.

"Hey, don't cry, baby, or I'll start again. Did I ever tell

ya' about the last time I saw my father?" Chick asked.

Terri didn't answer.

"I was thirteen. I was out in front of our house in Brooklyn shovelin' snow. My father was on his way out, so I said, 'Where ya' goin', Dad?' He says, 'I'm goin' to pay the gas bill. Just keep shovelin'.' That was the last time I saw him. Dirty bastard. Your grandmother had to bring up six kids all by herself, but she was a tough woman, your grandmother. Remember Grandma? She was tough but she had a heart too. Ya' know, your grandmother loved Enrico Caruso."

Chick changed topics so fast Terri became confused. She didn't know why he had started talking about Caruso.

"When I was a kid, I'd come home and she'd be at the table makin' macaroni. Remember how she'd make the macaroni, Terri?"

"Yeah, Dad, I remember."

"She'd be cuttin' the macaroni and she'd have the Victrola on, listenin' to Caruso. She'd be cryin' right along with him. Ya' know, Caruso used to cry when he sang. Then Grandma would say to me, 'C'mon, Giovanni. Sit with me and listen, and you cry too.' And damned if I didn't. Then we'd both be sittin' there cryin', Grandma and me. She'd say 'See, Giovan'. It's good to cry. It makes you live a long life. Even men should cry.'"

Terri became fatigued now as Chick rambled on and on. It was difficult for her to hold on to her own thoughts. She changed the subject.

"Why do you think Mommy was so cold, Dad?"

"Ahhh. That's the way her people were. The whole family was that way. Her father was a mean son of a bitch. Anyway, ya' know how your aunts are. Those bitches better not start anything at the wake."

"They won't, Dad."

"Your mother's sisters are nuts. Your Aunt Nilda wanted to smack her husband while he was laid out."

Terri gave Chick an astonished look.

21

"That's right. Your aunt said, 'Look at him layin' there. I feel like beatin' the shit outta him.' They're crazy, your aunts. They turn on you. They're like Dr. Hyde and Mr. Jeekle."

"Jekyll and Hyde, Dad."

Sarah had told Terri that they had it on both sides of the family. Terri didn't like to think about what "it" was.

"The only nice one is your Aunt Vi. She's a lot like your mother. The rest of them are a buncha bigmouths."

"*They're* bigmouths?" Terri mumbled under her breath, overcome with a weariness even the alcohol couldn't remedy.

"What did you say?"

"Nothin', Dad."

Chick had been talking for nearly two hours.

"We better go back, Dad. Tomorrow's gonna be a busy day."

Terri turned the car toward home and hoped her father would quiet down. His constant droning was interfering with the pleasant anesthetic effect of the five beers she'd finished. Chick had been so busy reminiscing, he didn't notice that only one can of Budweiser sat between them.

Chapter 2

He looked up at her as she tied the knots. She tried not to hurt him as she secured each wrist to the bedposts at the head of the narrow bed and each ankle to the bedposts at the foot of it. His limbs were thin and fragile. He studied her beautiful crystalline blue eyes. Now they showed a certain sadness. Her face looked weary. The past few years had been hell for both of them and his love for her was sometimes the only thing he was sure of.

"That's not tight enough. Make sure they're tight, Ma."

"Jesse, are you sure this is the right thing to do?"

Annie McLaughlin still spoke with an Irish brogue, even though she had come to this country at sixteen.

"Ma, this is the only way," he said as he looked into her eyes again. "And listen. No matter what I say or do, don't untie the ropes. You hear me, Ma? I don't know why you wanna stick around. You should leave the house, like Mark said."

"I don't know what I'll do. I guess your brother knows best."

"If you stay, you gotta promise me you won't come in here. Now go ahead. Promise."

"I swear to God, son. I won't come in."

Jesse knew what it meant when Annie swore to God. He felt confident she'd keep her promise.

"Go on. Get outta here. I'll get through this. And after this, I'm goin' out to Colorado to be with Mark. He'll get me to the right place."

"Okay, Jesse." Annie bent down, brushed away his hair and kissed his forehead. Glancing back at him one more time before leaving the room, she said, "I'll say a prayer for ya', son."

He knew her prayers wouldn't help him through this. As she headed for the door, he cried out, "Wait, Ma. Put the radio on for me."

John Lennon's voice filled the room with *"Mind*

Games."

"Thanks, Ma."

The pain started late in the evening, and he began to cry. The cries turned to screams soon after that. He didn't hear the front door close as his mother left the house.

His screams echoed throughout the sparsely furnished home. He was desperate now and he wanted out. The sharp pains in his stomach and thighs were becoming difficult to bear. The music coming from the radio was drowned out by his cries.

"Ma. It hurts, Ma. Get me outta here. Get in here and untie me, Ma." He sobbed and yelled between each vain attempt to reach her. He hollered louder. "You there, Ma? If you're there, you better untie these fuckin' ropes. If you untie me, I won't do it again. Ma, please. I won't do it again." His pitiful cries remained unheard. "I promise. I wasn't bad, Ma. I really wasn't bad. This is a mistake. We all make mistakes. I wasn't really hooked, Ma."

More loud screams pierced the darkness. As he writhed in the bed and pulled at the ropes, his words flew from him like caged demons set free by the incessant pain.

"You bitch! It's your fault anyway. You hear me? It's your fault your sons turned out to be junkies. You gotta untie me 'cause it's your fuckin' fault. Why'd ya' do it, Ma? Why'd ya' stay with that fuckin' bastard, huh? You hear me, you bitch? You did this to us, Ma."

He sobbed violently but then tried to calm himself.

"I'm sorry, Ma. Please let me out. I'm sorry I said that. I'm okay now. Pleeease, Ma." His verbal barrage waned but he cried long into the night until he fell into a dreamless sleep.

* * *

When it was all over, he woke up with a start. His mother was standing over him.

"Ma. How long you been standin' there?"

"Not long, Jesse. I was just watchin' you sleep. And ya'

know…you looked just like ya' did when you were little."
Annie brushed the wet hair from his face and freed his
hands. She started to untie the ropes to his feet but he
stopped her.

"Wait, Ma. Before you do that, will you go downstairs
and get me a couple of cold beers?"

Annie did as her son asked.

* * *

Terri woke up the next day fully expecting to be totally
devastated at her mother's passing. But her mind was filled
only with trivial details, none of which had anything to do
with her mother. This brought on a sense of shame.

She could hear her father in the kitchen talking on the
phone. He was calling all the relatives. With each call, he'd
tell the story, cry, hang up, and compose himself. He'd talk
to the dog for a while and then make the next phone call,
repeating his pitiable tale. Terri sensed Chick relished the
attention. She rolled over in bed and tried to reckon with
the day ahead. She would have liked to linger there but her
bladder couldn't hold all that liquid much longer. Her
mouth was dry from the beer and she needed water, but
she wasn't ready to deal with Chick yet. Terri hated the
inconvenience of living in the basement. She had had
resentment toward her parents since they split their house
into a duplex. Sure the rent money helped them, but Terri
and Sarah had always felt put out.

Terri had to call her boss, Harvey Katz. She knew he'd
allow her the time off from work she needed. She hoped
for a couple of weeks, enough time to drink as much as
she needed as well.

"Hey, you up? You goin' to get your sister?" Chick
called down.

Terri groaned and glanced at the clock. It was eleven
thirty.

"Yeah, Dad. I'm gettin' up. Yeah, yeah, yeah." She

pulled herself to her feet and ran straight up to the bathroom.

Chick had taken the dog out and the phone was free. She called Mr. Katz. As she expected, he readily agreed to the two weeks off. Terri was at the kitchen table reading the paper when Chick came back in.

"Hey, don't you have to pick up your sister?" he demanded.

"Dad, I know what train to meet. I'm going in a little while."

Chick was always anxious to see Sarah. Terri knew he loved her a lot, and the fact that she lived in Manhattan made her that much more appealing. Sarah's visits were few and far between. She disliked being around her father just as much as Terri did.

Terri planned to pick her sister up and drive around for a while. If they came straight back to the house, Chick would monopolize the conversation.

When Chick Micelli was in a room, nobody else got a chance to talk. Chick was a bitter man, but had a keen sense of humor. He'd talk about every injustice he'd suffered at the hands of friends, relatives, and the U.S. Government. Just when the listener felt he had had enough, Chick would begin to pepper the conversation with clichés and malapropisms. Terri and Sarah never knew whether he did this purposely or not. After spending time with him, people usually felt drained.

Chick was in the bathroom when Terri was ready to leave. She called to him.

"I'm going to the train station now, Dad."

"And hurry up. I wanna see your sister."

"We might take a little ride first, Dad," Terri said as softly as she could, hoping he wouldn't hear.

Chick was always suspicious. She knew if she got caught putting one over on him, there'd be hell to pay. As she left the suffocating atmosphere, Terri felt a sense of freedom. It was getting smaller in there by the minute. She was anxious to see her sister. On the way to the station, *"Beck's Bolero"* was playing and Beck's effortless guitar playing soothed her agitation. Terri thought about her sister and the differences they'd had in the past. They did have one strong bond though: They were the only two people on earth who knew what it was like to be Chick Micelli's daughters.

* * *

Sarah's train pulled in right on time. Terri scanned the passengers one by one as they came up the stairs from the exit tunnel.

There she was. Sarah always looked beautiful—blond, blue eyed, tall and thin. Terri envied her coloring and stature. Even though Sarah was six years older, they both looked the same age.

When Sarah got in the car, the sisters hugged but neither of them cried. Terri was all cried out, and guessed Sarah was too.

"You look great, Terri."

"You too."

Sarah rested her head back against the car seat. "So how is he, bad? What the hell happened last night when you hung up on me?"

"Oh, he was throwin' Mommy's pills all around the kitchen. He's crying a lot. Ya' know…and he's *real* crabby."

"So what else is new? Let's take a ride. I don't want to go to that shitty house yet."

"That's what I was thinkin'."

"So what was it like when Mommy died? You weren't right there, were you?"

"No, but it was kind of nice the way she went. She was in such a good mood…nothing like the usual. We had pizza and I was drinkin' wine with her. We were havin' a real nice time. Then I kissed her goodnight and went down to bed and she died." Terri snapped her fingers in Sarah's face. "Just like that!"

"Yeah," Sarah said. "I heard people get real happy right before they die. Guess you're really gonna miss her, huh?"

"Well, I don't know." Terri was surprised at her own reply.

"What? What do you mean? I thought you were so close to Mommy. You were always hanging on her when you were little."

"I quit that a long time ago. I tried to get close to her but it just didn't work. She wasn't there much. I mean, when you were a teenager, and you guys stopped all that fightin', they started to go out a lot and left me home alone. The funny thing is, I got to like it. It was so peaceful when everybody was gone…and it just seemed, like, after that, she was always sleepin' all the time. It was her high blood pressure."

"Yeah, why do you think I moved to New York?"

"Uh…'cause Daddy threw all your clothes out on the lawn?"

"Yeah, that too," Sarah laughed. "But I know how Mommy was. You never felt like you were getting through, right? Hey, how about all those hot breakfasts, Terri?"

Terri giggled. "Yeah, right. Hot breakfasts nothing. The woman was always tired. She must have been sick a long time. Some people never feel good a day in their life. And livin' with Daddy. That must have really put her over the edge. I didn't tell you this story but a couple of months ago, Aunt Vi, Aunt Nilda, and Esther were over. They were having a nice visit with Mommy. So then Aunt Jo turns up with a pot of pasta fagioli. Daddy answers the door, and what do you think he does?"

Sarah's eyes widened. "No. Don't tell me he…"

Terri took both hands off the steering wheel and shook them emphatically. "Yeah, he threw her right off the porch with the pot of pasta fagioli. Imagine how Mommy felt— her sisters *and* her best friend, Esther, are there. She started cryin'. It was awful, just awful. All the ladies ran out and went home. Ya' know why he threw Aunt Jo out?"

"Why?"

"Because she didn't come over soon enough."

"What? Shit! His brain just doesn't work like a normal person." Sarah shook her head.

"You said it! Why do ya' think I spent the last ten years of my life over at the Shea's house. Ya' know…my good friends, Patty and Bridget?"

"Oh yeah. You took me over there a few times. They're a real nice family. They seem so normal, even with all those kids."

"Yeah, that's what I mean. I even spend holidays over there, and go on vacation with them. It's just so much nicer. Their mother and father are so easygoing. I mean, all these kids are fightin' and making a commotion, and the parents just sit there. They never get mad, Sarah—never."

"Wow! That's amazing," Sarah responded.

"I hate to say it, but sometimes I liked Mrs. Shea better than Mommy. That's really an awful thing. I shouldn't have said that."

"Nah. It's not so bad. I know what you mean."

Terri always felt better when her sister gave her absolution.

"So Daddy's crying, is he?" Sarah asked.

"Yeah. He's kinda like the boy who cried wolf though. He's been crying for so long, you get desensitized to it. But in a funny way, he also seems to be taking the loss pretty well. Know what he said last night?"

"What?" Sarah wanted to know.

"He said, 'Don't think I'm gonna lay down and die. Not me. I'm gonna live.' Do you believe that guy? I don't know what the hell he's made of."

Sarah sighed at the sight of the decaying buildings as they drove along Main Street. "Look at this place. How can you stand it here? What else is going on in your life besides living in that disgusting basement? Why the hell are you living down there anyway?"

Terri shrugged and made an attempt to justify her present living conditions. "Well, I kinda ran out of money."

"What do you do with all your money? You have a good job. You buying drugs or something?"

"No, I quit smoking pot. I don't know where the money goes."

Sarah began to dig around in her purse. "Gee, you had money when you were singing. Why'd you quit the band? Everybody wants to sing in a rock band. Shit. Where's that joint?"

"Well, I went right from that awful marriage to singin' in the band. Then that got to be like a marriage too...rehearsing four nights a week and then every Friday and Saturday night doin' gigs. It was just too much."

Sarah was still looking around in her purse. "Hey, you still seeing that bass player?" She finally found the joint.

"No. I'm not seein' him anymore. But there is somebody. I haven't told anyone."

"What do you mean? A married guy?" Sarah's eyes widened.

"No, not that. It's Romeo. Romeo Fabiano. A guy in town. He's older than me. He used to hang out with the Clipper gang, in front of the diner. You remember him?"

"Damn right I do! He's drop dead gorgeous."

Terri was pleased at her sister's response. "That's him! He's the one. I've been sleeping with him, and I'm a little worried about it. Nobody knows, not even Patty or Bridget...or Sharon, and ya' know, she's my best friend. We gotta stop it, but you know how that goes."

Sarah was becoming amused at the story. "Oh yeah. I know how that goes. So, that's it? That's the thing that's been bothering you? You're a riot. You love to feel guilty, don't you?"

Terri wondered why her sister's Catholic upbringing had no impact on her at all.

"Jeez, Terri. It's 1974! Don't you know we're in the middle of a sexual revolution? You can sleep with whoever you want."

Sarah had something there. There were no consequences except maybe the occasional social disease and Terri never knew anyone who had one.

"But don't you get it? This guy is trouble. You remember he got shot in the foot by a cop in the phone booth on Main Street? And Sarah, I think maybe he's a junkie. He's always noddin' out when he's with me."

"Oh, you're such a worrywart. Yeah, I remember when he got shot. The cop shot him 'cause he wouldn't come out of the phone booth. But the guy is really hot, so just enjoy yourself."

"Yeah, sure. Enjoy myself. Everybody's enjoyin' themselves every chance they get."

Terri pulled over. "I have to stop for some beer. You want anything?"

"Yeah, get me some matches."

Terri came out of the deli with a six-pack of Beck's and the matches. "Here."

As Terri pulled away, Sarah lit the joint.

"Gee, I feel kinda funny talking about this kind of stuff. After all, Mommy just died. She wouldn't like it."

"What stuff?"

Terri threw her hands up. "Me and Romeo. *Remember?*"

"Oh, Jesus Christ!" Sarah inhaled deeply and held her breath for a few seconds. "Loosen up, will you? Here smoke some. You need it." Sarah offered her sister the joint.

"No. I hate pot. Makes me feel paranoid." Terri wanted to add that it ruins a really good drunk, but figured Sarah wouldn't understand.

"So, you gonna tell me how you started up with this junkie?"

"Well, it wasn't my fault." Terri touched her hand to her chest and shook her head. "I didn't start it."

"Oh, no. It's never our fault."

"We were partying at the bar. It was last summer, a while after I moved back home and I was feeling pretty down. I'd been drinkin' a lot that night. So Romeo says, 'You wanna go party down by the river? Just me and you?' And I said, 'Sure.' So we go down by the river at Sandy Beach and we start makin' out. Then he says, 'Let go for a swim, darlin', and he takes off his clothes. So I took my clothes off and followed him into the river. I never would have done such a thing if I wasn't a little loaded. You know how filthy that river is. But that water felt so good, warm and soft like velvet. When I think about it now, I cringe."

"Get to the good part!"

"Okay. To make a long story short...I was standin' in the water and feelin' real good lookin' up at the moon. It was just about full. And Romeo swims up to me...remember Sarah, he's naked too!"

"How could I forget?"

"So, he swims up to me and stands in front of me and wraps his big arms around me. Muscles the size of eggplants! You can imagine what that felt like, right? He's a big, big man."

"Ohhh, yeaaah."

"Then he kisses me, a real long one. You know the kind I mean. So how's that for a move?"

"That's a good move, Terri."

Terri glanced at Sarah, and waited until her lungs were full of smoke.

"I guess you can see how I was caught between a rock and a hard place."

Sarah choked on smoke and laughter. "Jeez, you trying to kill me?"

"And what's really terrible is we had sex on the beach."

"So what?"

"*So what?* That sand is real rough and I skinned both of my knees really bad. They were a mess for weeks."

Sarah burst out laughing again.

Terri glanced at the clock. "Oh shit! Look at the time. Daddy's gonna be pissed." She turned the car toward home.

Sarah desperately drew in on the joint as if it were the last one she'd ever smoke.

"So, how the hell are ya' gonna handle living with Daddy now that Mommy's gone?"

"Here's how." Terri held up her bottle of Beck's and took several long gulps.

* * *

Terri pulled into the driveway and hurried toward the door. Sarah grabbed her bag and followed.

As soon as the screen door opened, Chick bellowed, "Where the hell were ya'? I been waitin' here for two goddamn hours."

He pointed to Sarah. "You don't care if yer mother just died. You were never any damn good anyway."

Then he looked at Terri. "And you, ya' little snot. You got no respect for nobody. You run around all the time with your friends drinkin' beer. You kids are no damn good."

Sarah dropped her bag and shot back, "Thanks for the pleasant welcome, Dad."

Terri tried to appease him. "I *told* you we were goin' for a ride."

He turned to Terri, his thin lips drawn taut, and screamed, "You did not! You're nothin' but a little liar."

"I can't stand this shit anymore," Terri screamed back. She took another Beck's from the six-pack and put the remaining beers in the fridge.

"See why I hate to come here? It's always the same old shit," Sarah said to Terri. She turned to Chick, "Gee, Dad, you didn't even say hello."

Then he started—long shrill sobs. The girls looked at each other, disgusted. Terri sighed.

Chick sat on the couch and sobbed. He finally composed himself and spoke.

"Ya' know yer daddy loves his daughters. I can't help it. She died, Sarah. She died."

"I know, Daddy." Sarah sat next to him, wrapped an arm around his shoulder and pulled him close.

Then he started again, pointing toward Terri. "She knows we have to go to the funeral parlor and pick out a casket at four. Why didn't ya' come back?"

"Dad, it's only three-thirty. Terri knows what time we have to be there. We just wanted to take a little ride, that's all."

Chick took off his glasses and wiped his eyes with the back of his hand. "Well, let's go. I wanna take a ride too, ya' know."

The girls went downstairs to get ready. Sarah looked around the dismal room. It contained only a twin bed, a dresser with a mirror, a stereo, and a TV. The rug Chick had chosen for his daughter's homecoming was brown and the walls were brown plywood. Little light entered through the tiny basement windows.

Terri brushed her hair briskly as Sarah relit the joint.

"Ugh. How can you live down here? Why don't you hang up some artwork or something?"

"Why bother? I'm not stayin' here anyway. I just have no other choice right now."

"Where're you going?"

"Far away. Maybe to California. I only stayed here for *her*. Not *him* and his bullshit."

"C'mon. He's over it already. He wants to go to the funeral parlor now, so let's just go. You got an ashtray down here?"

"Yeah, here," Terri shoved the ashtray toward Sarah. "He might be over it, Sarah, but he didn't apologize. I'm sick of jumping for this guy all the time. He's like the cowboy in the westerns who's always makin' people dance with his guns."

"I know, I know. C'mon, let's go."

Terri pointed to the joint. "Yeah, *let's go*! Easy for you. You're all mellowed out. You better put that out or he's gonna smell it."

"Terri," Chick called down. She recognized the syrupy quality of his voice right away. "Daddy's sorry. You know Daddy loves his little goil."

Sarah motioned upstairs. "There you are. There's your apology."

Chick continued, "You know Daddy doesn't mean anything when he hollers."

The girls went upstairs. Terri didn't hug her father, fearful of bringing on another crying jag. But she tried to make peace as well.

"It's okay, Dad. We'll go now."

She grabbed another Beck's from the refrigerator. Terri was *not* looking forward to being in a room full of coffins with Chick.

During the five-minute ride to the undertaker's, Chick was unusually quiet except for confirming his earlier instructions. "We're going to Walcott's Funeral Parlor, right? Everybody gets laid out at Walcott's. He makes everybody look good."

The girls rolled their eyes and held back giggles. Sarah was feeling the pleasant effects of the pot. Terri was enjoying the after-buzz of her Beck's.

They were greeted at the door by Martin Walcott, the owner, and he made sure to extend his condolences to each of them.

Terri thought he was extremely polite and acted the way an undertaker should: smooth, real smooth.

No wonder he gets everybody's business.

Terri studied Mr. Walcott. He was a tall thin man with glasses. His hair was dark and seemed to be plastered to his head. He was extremely plain with pasty grayish skin. She thought he'd look quite at home in one of the boxes. Terri wondered: If he made the stiffs look so good, why couldn't he do something with himself? A little rouge he had lying around or something?

He led them into a room lined with caskets and began talking to Chick. "This one is our steel model and these are the wooden caskets over here. The steel model is our biggest seller."

Chick piped up. "What's less expensive? The wood or the steel?"

"Cheap bastard," Terri whispered to Sarah and gave her a nudge in the ribs.

"Would you like the casket sealed or unsealed, Mr. Micelli?"

"What's the difference?" Chick looked suspicious.

"Well, the seal encases the casket in concrete. With the unsealed coffin, over a long period of time, there could be some shifting of the casket itself…and since the cemetery is on a steep hill…"

Walcott paused for effect.

"You wouldn't want your loved one *sliding* down the hill, now would you?"

Terri pictured her mother's coffin shooting out of the ground at the bottom of the cemetery and landing on the street.

"How much is the seal?" Chick asked.

"A seal will run you about four hundred dollars, Mr. Micelli."

"I'll take the unsealed. I don't need no seal."

Terri leaned over and whispered in Sarah's ear again.

"Do you believe this shit? Get a load of this mortician, will ya'?"

"Shut up, Terri. Don't start!"

The grim atmosphere in the casket room was starting to get to Terri. Chick and Mr. Walcott were still discussing money. She breathed on the inside of her hand to check her breath for alcohol.

She likened the scenario to the many pious and solemn occasions in Catholic school that could only be remedied by irreverent humor. Terri leaned over to Sarah again.

"Pssst. Hey."

"I said, don't start," Sarah whispered.

"Did you hear the one about the gravedigger with the big dick?"

Sarah gasped and ran out of the room to the bathroom. Terri followed. They locked themselves in and both doubled over.

When Sarah finally spoke, tears filled her eyes. "What the hell is wrong with you? Are you nuts?"

Terri inhaled deeply before she could speak again. "Remember the time I made you pee your pants in the car? How old were you, seventeen? What the hell was that about anyway?" Terri loved making people laugh. It gave her such a sense of control and power.

"I don't remember. Shit! I can't straighten up now. Damn you! What the hell was the punch line anyway?"

"Punch line? I don't need a punch line in this place!"

They both started laughing hysterically again.

Sarah placed her finger over her lips. "Shhh...shit! Here comes Daddy. He's gonna get mad again. Let's go back out."

Terri tried to compose herself. "I can't go out there and look at that undertaker anymore. You'd think *his* mother died."

They waited a few more minutes trying their best to act straight.

"Hey!" Chick shouted as he knocked on the bathroom door. "C'mon. What the hell ya' doin' in there? I wanna get somethin' to eat."

The door opened and they came out smiling.

"What the hell is so funny?" he snapped.

"You, Dad," Terri said. "You're funny."

Chick lowered his brows and turned to leave.

"I don't see what's so goddamn funny about a funeral parlor. C'mon, let's go home. I'm hungry."

When they got home, Chick headed for the bathroom

and Sarah fell onto the couch in the living room. She threw her head back.

"That was fun. Shit, I'm exhausted!"

Terri walked into the kitchen and reached into the fridge for another Beck's.

"Man, that undertaker was really freakin' me out. Thought *I* was gonna die if we didn't get outta that place."

The phone rang and Terri grabbed it.

"Oh hi, Uncle Jimmy. Sure. Yeah. Come on over. We're gonna order pizza. You want pizza? Okay. See you in a while." Terri was glad her uncle was coming over and was already planning her escape. She hoped her dad and his brother would become closer in the months to come since they were both widowers now.

As Terri hung up, Sarah ran into the kitchen and put her hand to her mouth.

"Oh shit! Oh no!"

Terri gave her a puzzled glance. "What? What now?"

"I think I put the joint down in the bathroom before we left for the funeral parlor. You think he'll notice it? He's gonna yell again."

"So what! Who cares?"

Terri was feeling the beers now and wasn't worried about a thing.

Sarah looked down the hall toward the bathroom door.

"He's been in there a long time. What do you think he's doing?"

"Maybe he's just goin' to the bathroom, Sarah. You know how old people are. It's probably takin' a while."

Just then, Chick came out and headed for the living room. He flicked on the TV and sat down on the couch. He was unusually quiet and a faint smile fell over his face as he stared at the TV.

"Look, Terri. Look at Daddy."

"What? What about him?"

"Look at his face."

"So?"

"I think he smoked my pot."

"Get out! He did not!"

"Watch this! Hey, Daddy."

Chick looked over at the girls, eyelids drooping, still with the tiniest hint of a smile.

"Yeah? What?"

"Did you see a cigarette in the bathroom? I think I left one in there."

Chick furrowed his brows. "Yeah. I saw it. I saw it and I smoked it! And don't think I don't know what that stuff is. You can't fool yer daddy, ya' know."

Chapter 3

Uncle Jimmy came over for pizza and Terri took the opportunity to slip out and meet the Shea's at Howie's Tavern, her favorite bar. Sarah was tired and stayed home. Smoking pot all day had caught up with her.

On her way there, Terri's stomach churned with anticipation. The feeling was familiar, like the one she used to get waiting on line for her favorite carnival ride. She remembered that twinge of excitement as the ride ticket turned to mush in her hot sweaty hand. She always felt this way before going into a bar.

Howie's wasn't far from the house and Terri was grateful everything was close by—one advantage to living in a small town.

Terri had lost any trepidation about walking into bars alone years ago. This bar was even easier because she knew Sharon Saunders would be there.

Sharon was Terri's best friend; her oldest friend. Howie's was owned by two burly brothers, Howie and Dave Farley. Howie was the one who really ran the place. Sharon lived with him and worked at the bar most nights.

When she walked in, the people she longed to see all day were there. Bridget and Patty Shea were at the bar and Romeo was playing pool. Peter Frampton's *"Do You Feel Like We Do"* was playing on the jukebox. Terri breathed in the musty stale scent of the place and felt as if she were home.

"What took ya' so long?" Patty asked. "C'mon, sit down. Howie, get Terri a drink."

"Vodka, club, and lemon," she ordered.

"So?" Bridget asked. "How's your dad doing?

"Oh, he's okay. Where's Sharon, Howie?"

"I dunno. In the bathroom, I think," he said as he placed Terri's drink in front of her. "Here. It's on the house. Sorry about your mom."

"Thanks, Howie." She turned to the Shea's. "Be right

back, guys."

Terri headed toward the bathroom and gave Romeo a flirtatious smile as she passed the pool table. When she walked in, Sharon was applying lipstick. She turned to Terri and they hugged.

"How are ya' doin', honey? I can't believe your mom's gone. God, I'm gonna miss her. I loved your mom."

"I know. I know how much you loved her."

Sharon looked Terri up and down and handed her the lipstick.

"Do I look that bad?" Terri asked. "I've been drinkin' since noon. Does it show?"

Sharon turned to her as she fluffed her long honey colored hair. "Well if you're gonna drink, remember what I always told ya'. Don't stagger. Don't slur your words. And make sure you always look good, 'cause if you look good, you can do whatever you want."

Sharon looked more than good. The gangly freckled tomboy Terri remembered had turned into a tall willowy beauty with a flat stomach and hip bones set wide apart. She just couldn't help but sway when she walked. With light green eyes and dimples that showed with even the smallest smile, men loved her.

Terri had to contort her face until it hurt to make her own dimples show. But theirs was a friendship free of envy. She had loved Sharon since they were kids. Terri remembered the tall tales Sharon would weave for the sheer joy of traumatizing her, even if just for a few minutes. And then the ultimate shock, the story of what their parents did to bring them into the world. Sharon told her that one when they were about nine. Now grown women, Sharon could still get Terri to plug her ears to shut out her latest shocking story.

The one thing that brought Terri closer and closer to Sharon was their common bond. They were usually the only women still left in the bar in the early morning hours. Sharon did follow her own advice. She never staggered, never slurred her words, and always looked good—but she did have her flaws.

She was sometimes contrary when she'd had too much to drink and tended to have a dirty mouth. Then Terri would drive her home, usually at Howie's suggestion.

"C'mon. Bridget and Patty are waiting. My drink is getting warm."

As they sat down, Howie was in the middle of a story. Sharon leaned toward him.

"Honey, give us all a shot of Cuervo."

"Ran out of Cuervo. This stuff okay?" He showed them the bottle.

Terri eyed the cheap tequila. "Maybe we shouldn't."

Howie poured the shots.

Sharon raised her glass, as did Bridget and Patty.

"To Terri's mom. We all loved her."

They downed the tequila.

"Jeez, Howie. This stuff hurts. Give me one more," Terri said as she shoved her shot glass toward him.

Terri laughed at Howie's stories. She loved to hear about the crazy things people did at the bar. In this town, it was an inexhaustible topic.

Terri had avoided looking at the clock all evening. Bridget and Patty had left by now. Sharon and Romeo were playing pool. The barstool glue had her immobilized again.

Sharon was flirting wickedly with Romeo. Terri didn't blame her. He was so good-looking. Terri had one more shot of tequila in front of her. Howie glanced over at the pool table and scowled.

"Sharon. C'mere. I wanna talk to ya' in the kitchen."

Sharon dropped her pool stick on the table and dutifully followed Howie into the kitchen but not before giving Romeo's ass a soft squeeze.

Romeo came over and joined Terri at the bar. She needed to talk to him, to tell him the thing between them was freaking her out. He looked in her eyes briefly and then down at his drink.

"Sorry to hear about your mom. How are ya' doin?"

"Oh, pretty good."

The clear shot of tequila sat waiting. She picked it up and took a small sip. He looked through her with his sea green eyes.

"Listen, I gotta talk to ya' about somethin'. I really don't think we can keep doin' what we been doin'. Know what I mean?"

He beat me to it. Damn.

She downed the rest of the tequila in one gulp. The innocent looking liquid stung almost as much as his words.

She swallowed a few times before speaking.

"Well, I feel the same way."

He placed his hand on her face and kissed her cheek. The musty scent of him made her want him again.

"You're too nice a girl for me."

Too nice? Bullshit! Her thoughts were interrupted by Howie's booming voice.

"Terri! Give Sharon a ride home. I gotta close soon and she needs to go home!"

Sharon came out of the kitchen and grabbed Terri's arm.

"C'mon, honey. Take me home. Asshole!" she shouted to Howie.

Terri looked back at Romeo one more time.

"You stayin'?"

"Yeah. Howie will give me a ride. Take it easy."

As Terri drove, her head was filled with thoughts of a naked Romeo standing before her in the soft black river. Sharon's words startled her.

"That Romeo is so fuckin' fine. Did you ever feel his ass? Wouldn't you love to fuck his brains out? He makes my cunt quiver!"

Terri smacked her hard on the thigh. "Shut up. What a thing to say! Why do ya' have to talk so dirty all the time?"

"Jeez. Sorry. You're so touchy. Well I guess you're

allowed. I know you're upset about your mom."

"It's not that. You just should watch your mouth sometimes."

Sharon smiled at Terri and patted her thigh. "Ya' know, Terri. You should say fuck more. You never say fuck. Women can do that now."

"Shit. I don't wanna say fuck. Damn. See that. You made me say fuck. Shit. I said it again, damn you."

They both laughed. A few seconds later, flashing red lights invaded the car.

"Oh shit. Not again! Damn it! Sharon, keep your mouth shut."

Terri pulled over. A tall state trooper approached the car, bent down and looked inside.

"Out of the car please, miss."

Terri hoped she could walk a straight line. Six times this year she walked that line and not one ticket, even though she was wasted every time.

"Been drinking, miss?"

"Well. Just a little. My mother died and my friend...I really need to get her home. She's kinda sick."

Sharon couldn't keep quiet.

"Why don't you go arrest the drug dealers on Main Street and leave my friend alone?"

Terri looked back into the car and glared at her.

"I need you to walk a straight line for me, miss."

"Yes. Certainly, sir."

She prided herself on the great job she was doing as Sharon shouted out again.

"My friend's not drunk. She never gets drunk even when she drinks all night."

"Okay, miss. Get back in the car and give me your license and registration."

Terri did as the trooper instructed. He walked back to his car. The lights were still flashing.

"Shit. Now what the hell is he doing? He's gonna sit there now, ya' know. He's gonna make us wait here like a coupla' jerks. I'm convinced this is some form of psychological torture. Ya' know, this is the seventh time this year I've been stopped."

"How do you know? Do you count?"

"Sure I count. Ya' know I like to count."

"Oh that's right. I remember you always would count the cracks on the sidewalk when we were little and I had to shut up until you were finished. Why do you do that, Terri?"

"It gives me a sense of order. Shit, what's takin' so long?"

When the trooper returned, he handed her the license and registration.

"Okay, miss. Get your friend home, but don't try this again. Next time you won't be so lucky."

"Oh thank you, sir. Thank you so much."

Terri pulled away slowly—she'd dodged another bullet.

"Those bastards," Sharon said. "Why don't they leave people alone?"

Terri drove her friend home. Sharon and Howie lived in a huge white apartment house that overlooked the river. Terri referred to it as the *House of Excess* because every time she went in, she came out wasted. It was as if the house was possessed by some sort of demon spirit that made people overindulge in their favorite vice, whatever it might be. She pulled into the parking lot.

"C'mon up. I just bought a bottle of Smirnoff. There's wine in the fridge. Don't go. I'm still wide awake."

Terri looked up at Sharon's balcony. "No, I gotta go. You comin' to the wake tomorrow?"

"I can't. I can't see her dead," said Sharon and hugged Terri again. "But I promise I'll see you at the funeral, okay?"

"Okay. Bye."

Terri drove home, parked in the driveway, and went inside. Chick was in bed and Sarah was asleep on the couch. She quickly threw off her jeans and jumped into bed in her T-shirt.

The ceiling started spinning. Terri leaned over and threw up in her wastebasket.

Damn you, Howie. Damn cheap tequila!

Terri Micelli needed to pray. She did it because it was drilled into her during her eight years at St. Paul's School, a habit that was impossible to break.

However, she had an aversion to the kneeling position. The last time she was made to kneel in the schoolyard during the May procession as a child, Terri vowed never to get down on her knees again. She recalled the girls in their white communion dresses with beet-red knees after a long session of adoration of the Blessed Mother. Once, as a small girl, she explained her painful knees to one of the nuns, but the sister told her to offer it up to Mary. Terri didn't understand why Mary would want to see kids picking gravel out of their knees.

Praying in the horizontal position in such an inebriated state made for stingy prayers.

God. It's me, Terri Micelli. I'm drunk again. Sorry. I have to make this short 'cause I was just sick. Mom...I hope everything's okay...I...I gotta...

Terri passed out.

* * *

Terri stood close to Sarah as she watched her mother's casket slowly descend into the soft earth. Chick stood on the other side of the grave, flanked by the Shea sisters, his brother Jimmy, and Sharon. Terri felt a heaviness in her chest, a kind of longing. She glanced at her father and was startled by her own thoughts.

Why did she have to go first? She imagined how it would be, alone with her mother—shopping, eating out, finally together. Her mother, attentive, relaxed, loving, without him around. *Now that would have been a life!* Terri tried to put the image out of her head but the seeds of resentment and self-pity that lay dormant for so long began to grow.

Just then, Sarah leaned over and whispered, "Listen, take me to the station after this. I gotta go back to Manhattan."

Terri's mouth dropped open. "What? You're kidding, right?"

"No. Why would I kid about a thing like that?"

"Sarah. Everybody's comin' to the house—Aunt Nilda and Aunt Vi. You can't leave now."

"Yeah? And how long do you think they're gonna stay? They don't wanna see *him*," Sarah said, motioning toward Chick. "They can't stand him. They only came over to see Mommy. After today, they'll never come back to the house again."

The daughters looked over at Chick. His head down, his shoulders shook with each sob.

"Okay. Go if you have to," Terri said as she took Sarah's arm. "C'mon. We gotta say a prayer." She motioned toward the open grave.

"You go say a prayer. I'll be in the car."

Terri stared as her sister walked away. Then she walked up to the grave and bowed her head. Her face contorted with sadness now and swallowing hard didn't help. She covered her face with her hand.

Bye, Mom. A distant memory flashed across her mind. *I...uh...I wanted to sit on the porch with you one more time and eat cherries. Remember, Mommy? Remember we'd spit the seeds off the porch? You and me? I was hoping we could do that just once this summer...*

Terri looked at Chick and continued her prayer.

So, God. I was just wondering. Is this some kind of joke, or maybe a test? If it's a joke, it's not funny, and if it's a test, I'm gonna fail. Anyway, take care of her, okay?

Terri walked over and took Chick by the elbow.

"C'mon, Dad. Let's go."

"Okay," he said. He sobbed a few more times. Then with miraculous composure, he turned to Terri's friends and called back. "Hey, you goils comin' to the house?"

"Oh sure, Chick. We'll be there," Patty replied.

"Good. We have a lotta food. And I know you Irish goils like Italian food. Ain't that right?"

"Sure, Chick," Bridget chimed in. "See you there."

Terri helped Chick into the back seat. Sarah was already in the passenger seat. As she drove out of the cemetery, Terri was afraid to mention Sarah was leaving. Sarah turned to Chick.

"Dad, I have to get back to New York. I can't stay for the party—for the food I mean."

"WHAT? Whaddya' mean yer not stayin'? All your aunts and uncles are comin' over. You got some noive."

Sarah raised her voice. "Listen, I gotta go! I can't stand it here. You people are nuts!"

Terri figured the past two days had been too much for Sarah. *She probably ran out of pot.*

"Who the hell ya' think yer talkin' to?" Chick screamed at Sarah. "You were never any damn good."

Terri threw both hands up. "Shit. Again with the 'no damn good.' Shut up! Shut up, both of you! I can't even drive."

"Who ya' tellin' to shut up, ya' little shit?"

Terri's head jerked forward before she'd even realized she'd been slapped. She shouted:

"That's right! That's real smart. Smack a person while they're driving. You wanna kill us all?"

Chick started crying again.

"Oh, Christ!" Sarah said. She shifted in her seat and stared out the passenger window.

"Nuts! Don't start cryin' again, Daddy. You're right, Sarah. You're right to go back. It's too crazy here."

Terri pulled into the driveway and dropped Chick off at the house before heading for the station. She turned to look at him. He'd collected himself enough to get angry all over again. She watched him stomp up the three cement steps to the house. When he turned to look at them, she could see his thin lips drawn taut over his false teeth.

"Daddy, go wait for everybody," Terri said. "I'll be right back."

Before she could pull away, he turned and pointed a crooked finger at Sarah.

"And don't come back here no more."

"Don't worry. I won't." Sarah waited for him to go in the house before she added, "You crazy fuckin' bastard."

"Coward," Terri said.

As Terri drove to the train station, a sense of dread came over her. She gripped the steering wheel tightly, holding on to *what*, she didn't know.

"Shit, Sarah. I knew a fight would break out. The wake went too smooth."

Sarah studied her sister's face.

"Are you gonna be all right? I mean with him? I hate the thought of you stuck in that basement with him. When you gonna get yourself together?"

"Don't worry about me. There are a lot of people I know out in California. I think I just might go out there soon."

"Good. Do it. Better than staying in this shitty town."

Terri pulled into the station.

"Bye, Sarah. Call me."

Sarah patted Terri's thigh gently. "Okay. Next week. I promise."

Terri watched her sister disappear down the station tunnel.

Don't go Sarah. Please stay a little longer.

Terri wondered what the world would be like if people blurted out what they were really thinking.

Chapter 4

It had been about two weeks since the funeral and Terri was scared. Each morning as she woke up, she felt as if she were an actor in a play who hadn't memorized the script. There was a tightness in her chest and she found reality a cruel invasion of her peaceful dream state.

Terri needed to talk to Mr. Katz. He'd been so good to give her two weeks off from work. She waited until Chick left for the diner and dialed his number.

"Hi, Mr. Katz. It's Terri."

"Hi, Terri. How are you doing, dear? I've been thinking about you."

"Thanks for the flowers you sent to the funeral parlor. They were really beautiful."

"Think nothing of it. Everything okay at home?"

"Well...uh...there's something I need to talk to you about. You have some free time, Mr. Katz?"

"Sure, Terri. It's slow here right now. Why don't you come on over?"

"Thanks. I'll be there shortly. Thanks so much."

Willow House was only ten minutes away on the outskirts of town. The sanitarium's main building was a large Victorian gothic-style mansion. It stood in the midst of about twenty acres of lush, well-manicured property. Terri had always wondered how such a beautiful place could exist in this otherwise dreary town. There was something about it though, that said *looney bin,* and Terri had expected to see a group of lobotomized zombies milling about the vestibule the first time she walked through the towering doors.

She'd worked at Willow House since she'd graduated high school. The pay wasn't much, but the atmosphere and convenient location made her job tolerable.

She rushed to Mr. Katz' office at the back of the building, trying to avoid small talk with the nurses. She knocked anxiously at his door, relieved there was no replacement sitting at her desk to ask questions.

"Come in," he said.

Mr. Katz was a small man in his late fifties. He wore wire-rimmed glasses and had patches of gray on each side of his balding head. He came around his desk quickly and gave Terri a hug.

"Hi, Mr. Katz. I'm really sorry to bother you, but..."

"Sit down, dear. You've been through a lot, so let's talk." He returned to his seat, folded his hands in front of him, and stared at her calmly. "What's on your mind?"

Terri appreciated the way he was always there for her, having listened to the smallest, grimmest details of her life for the past couple of years.

"Well, it's been a few days now...well, maybe it started just after my sister left for New York. I...I get this really bad feeling when I wake up."

Mr. Katz nodded his head and said, "Go on."

"Well, I just don't like it, waking up I mean. It's kind of a shock. There I am dreamin' these really nice dreams and then I wake up, and it's like *Oh shit! Not this again.*"

"I see, Terri. It sounds like depression. That's quite understandable after a loss like this."

She sat up straight. "No. No. I don't feel like I'm sad or anything. I just hate waking up. I feel like I don't know what's gonna happen to me next...a little nervous, ya' know. But then at night I go out and have a few drinks, hang out with people, and then I'm okay. Maybe 'cause I'm with people. Then the next day, the same thing happens."

"Hmmm. Depression and anxiety. That's to be expected, considering all that's happened in the past few years. Think about it, Terri. You were married to a man who physically abused you. You came home to a very sick mother, and your father is verbally abusive."

She moved to the edge of her seat. "Wait a minute. I never said my dad was verbally abusive."

"But, Terri. Some of the things you tell me he says to

you and your sister!" He paused for a moment. "Whenever you've talked to me, I notice you drink a lot over your problems."

Yeah? So? Doesn't everybody?

He continued. "That's not good. Alcohol is a depressant, you know."

"That's funny, Mr. Katz. It seems to have the opposite effect on me."

"That could be the problem, Terri," he said glumly.

Terri knew immediately she'd said the wrong thing.

He reached into his desk and started rummaging through papers.

"Here. I have some brochures you might want to take a look at."

Terri grabbed the pamphlets and read them. Her throat tightened. She swallowed hard, afraid she'd be unable to utter another word. Big blue letters stared back at her— Alcoholics Anonymous. Her thoughts raced wildly. *This is what he thinks of me? Holy shit!* She'd rather he told her she had bad breath.

Suddenly Mr. Katz seemed like a very presumptuous man. Terri shuffled the papers in her sweaty hands.

"I'll take a look at these. Thanks." She got up to leave.

"Oh, by the way, Terri. How are things going with Romeo?"

Nosy, interfering bastard, she thought.

"Oh...uh...okay, I guess. See you when I get back to work next week. Bye."

Terri ran out to her car and drove away. *"Superstition"* was blasting over the radio. She took the back roads home, and when she got to her favorite spot near the river, Terri flung the pamphlets out the window. She watched in the rearview mirror as they scattered all over the road.

* * *

Chick found the perfect remedy for his loneliness at the

local interstate diner, sometimes going there several times a day. He had been in and out of the apartment three times already and it was only eight-thirty. The screen door constantly slamming woke her up.

Terri hated Sundays. It meant she only had one day to get straight and didn't want to call in sick on a Monday so soon after returning to her job.

It had been close to three weeks since Terri talked to Mr. Katz about her depression and decided to handle it her way. Sleep and alcohol seemed to be the best medicine.

Now she lay in bed afraid to move. Her head pounded at even the slightest turn. She was sick and the proximity of her wastebasket was a troublesome sight. Terri leaned over slowly and took a look inside.

"Ugh. Damn those Kamikazes." She felt it was beneath her to throw up into her wastebasket, but the layout of the house afforded her no privacy, the one bathroom being right outside her father's bedroom door.

Terri sat up carefully. She pulled on a pair of shorts, grabbed the wastebasket, and headed outside to the trash cans behind the house. She removed a full black trash bag from the can and pushed her wastebasket with its putrid contents deep down inside. Then she covered the wastebasket with the black bag.

Shit! That was the second one this month. Terri was replacing the cover as Chick pulled back into the driveway.

"Hey, what are ya' doin'?" he yelled. His voice always seemed louder when Terri was hung over.

"Just puttin' out the garbage, Daddy."

"I already put the garbage out."

"Well, this is my garbage. That okay with you?"

Terri felt herself getting irritated. She went back into the house and poured herself a cup of coffee. Chick came into the kitchen, carrying a brown bag and a great big canvas.

"What's that, Dad? You gonna start paintin' again?"

"Damn right I am. You think I wanna just exist?"

She had to admit, just existing sounded awful.

"Where ya' gonna paint, Dad?"

"Right where I always painted, in the cellar."

"You mean right behind the wall next to my bed?"

"Yeah, that's right. Don't worry. Daddy won't bother ya'. I can paint quiet."

Terri knew damn well Chick couldn't do anything quietly. She recalled listening as he painted when she was a kid. He never got through a painting session without swearing, whistling, or dropping something.

She sipped her coffee and hoped for a reprieve from the crushing hangover. Chick began to whistle loudly, as he unpacked his paint supplies. Then he turned to Terri, fists clenched. He gently smacked her temples.

"C'mon, baby. Let's go a few rounds."

"Cut it out, Dad. I have a headache."

"Ah, c'mon. Try to give yer daddy a right hook. Watch how I block ya'."

"Daaaad," she whined. "I don't wanna give you a right hook. I don't feel good."

"Aaaah…" Chick lowered his fists and his brows. "Ya' used to like it when you were a kid. Whaddya crabby today? Did ya' eat yet?"

"No, Daddy. Not yet."

"C'mon, let's go to the diner for breakfast. You wanna eat breakfast with yer daddy?"

God, no! Anything but that! "Uh…I don't think so, Dad. I didn't even take a shower yet, and I…"

"C'mon. C'mon out with yer daddy. I made a lotta nice friends at the diner and they wanna meet ya'."

There was no way out. Terri sighed.

"Okay, okay, Dad. I'll be with you in a few minutes."

As usual, Chick talked continuously on the ride to the diner.

"Where were ya'? Out with yer friends again last night? Well, forget yer friends. They'll never help ya' out. Yer family, that's what counts."

What family?

"Ya' know Van Gogh, the painter?"

"Yeah. What about him?" Terri was aggravated already and they'd only been in the car five minutes.

"His friends never helped him out. His brother, that's who helped him out. His brother was in real estate. He got him a big break. Then Van Gogh went crazy, ya' know. He cut off his ear and sent it to a woman. After that, he died in a nut house, and whaddya think? Nobody bought any of his paintings 'til he was dead."

"You're full of really interesting information."

By the time they got to the diner, Chick was droning on about Rudolph Valentino.

"That Rudolph Valentino. He was somethin'. When he died, his funeral was mobbed. There'll never be another Valentino. He was the best. *The Sheik*. Now that was what I call a movie, *The Sheik*."

Terri figured Chick must have felt like *The Sheik* when he walked into the Interstate Diner because the Greek owner rushed over to him with a huge smile and quickly summoned a waitress to get them a table.

"How dooooo ya' dooooo?" Chick sang out. "Hey Georgie boy. This is my daughter, Terri. Remember her? She's my baby…the one that sings."

Terri shook George's hand, thinking it was hard to smile when you were trying not to roll your eyes. Her head pounded and she was beginning to feel faint. She desperately needed more coffee and something to eat.

After they sat down, a waitress with high hair approached them.

"Hey, Marcy, did ya' miss me?" Chick sat up straight in the booth and smiled.

"Sure I did, Chick, even though you just left half an hour ago." The slim waitress patted him on his polyester clad back and handed them menus. She winked at Chick flirtatiously.

When the waitress left, Chick continued.

"And I'll tell you who was the best painter—Michelangelo. Ya' know he was so poor, he used to paint for bread. That's right! Bread. The Italians were the best, ya' know. Ya' know how long it took him to paint that Sistine Chapel? It almost killed him."

Terri could see the people in the booth behind Chick were giggling. She let out a sigh and motioned toward them.

"You're talkin' so loud. Can you talk a little quieter? Those people can hear every word you say."

"What the hell do I care?" Chick blustered as he tossed his menu on the table.

Terri hid behind her menu and stuck her tongue out at him. She glanced around to see if anyone was looking.

"Anyway, it was the Pope's fault!"

"What Pope? What are you talkin' about, Dad?"

"The Pope who made Michelangelo paint that ceiling. Ain't you listenin' to me? That Pope was a real mean bastard. He forced him to paint that ceiling and he almost killed him."

The people behind Chick laughed harder.

After Terri and Chick ordered, Terri tried to talk.

"Hey, listen, Dad. I was thinking. Maybe I should go to college or something. Do you think—"

Chick cut her off as he slammed his coffee cup down on the saucer.

"Well, I can't help ya' out. Don't ask me for any money. If you wanted to go to college, you should've never married that jerk right outta high school. I couldn't stand that guy. Your mother and your sister told you not to marry him. He was a little bastard, and he walked like Charlie Chaplin. I'm not payin' for anything else. I paid for your damn wedding! What the hell is the matter with you anyway?"

"What's the matter? What's the matter? I'll tell you what's the matter. I talked to my boss the other day. You know, Mr. Katz, the one who came to the funeral, and he says I'm depressed."

"What the hell does he know?" Chick yelled.

Terri threw her hands up. "He's a psychologist!"

"So what. They're all fulla shit anyway."

"Well I talked to him a few weeks ago. I haven't been feeling good mentally, ya' know, since Mommy died...and Mr. Katz says I'm a little depressed, and..."

"Depressed?" Chick shouted.

"Shhh. Dad, will you please lower your voice?"

Chick pointed at her.

"I never get depressed. I never get depressed, and I never get bored. When I was thirty-one, they drafted me, those dirty bastards. You think I got depressed 'cause I had to start my life all over again after the war? When I was a kid I had to live with my uncles and my grandfather 'cause your grandmother couldn't take care of us. They used to kick the shit outta me. Whaddya' think I did? I took it. That's what."

"Yeah, Dad, but..."

"Why don't ya' get a hobby like me? See, I'm gonna paint. All you do is run around with your friends and drink beer. Nobody in my family ever got depressed, not me, not your grandmother, not uncle Jimmy. Nobody! Ya' know what your grandmother used to say?"

"No, what?" Terri rested her head on her hand in defeat.

Chick imitated his mother in his best Italian accent. "She used to say, 'Ya' know, Giovanni, sometimes at night I have lotsa worries, but then I say *va fangul* and in the morning my worries, they gone.' Why don't you be like your grandmother?"

Terri felt her ears grow hot.

"Wait a minute. Let me get this straight. When I wake up tomorrow morning so depressed I don't even want to open my eyes, I should just say *va fangul!* Is that what you're saying?"

"Yeah, that's right. You kids have it too soft. That's

what's wrong with you."

After they left the diner, Terri drove Chick home and went back to bed. She tried her hardest to nap as Chick painted and whistled on the other side of the wall.

Chapter 5

Terri stood doubled over outside the bathroom door, legs crossed. The bright morning sun stung her eyes as it streamed in through the hall window. She banged on the door.

"Whaddya' want?" Chick yelled, obviously irritated.

"I gotta get in there, Dad. Pleeease, I gotta go."

"Oh, Jesus Christ!"

Genevieve Micelli had been gone for more than two months now. Lately, Terri had been hearing the smooth, throaty sound of her mother's voice and it seemed to take gallons of alcohol to quiet it. Terri squeezed her legs together tightly as she waited, thinking about what she drank last night—beer, vodka and club soda, tequila.

Finally, the door swung open and Chick appeared, red faced.

"Son of a bitch," he said, as he stomped away down the hall. Terri noticed him wobbling a bit, his anger throwing him off balance as it often did. She saw there were patches of hair missing from the back of his head.

She rushed into the bathroom and was about to sit down when she saw large yellow drops all over the toilet seat. Chick never lifted it.

"Oh shit! Damn slob!" she cried, as she reached for the washcloth to clean off the seat. Terri hated the way Chick's presence invaded even her most private moments. Then she saw Chick's black curls strewn over the vanity and in the sink.

"Jeez, what a mess!" she mumbled. When she was through, she brushed her teeth and splashed some water on her face.

As she left the bathroom, Chick was on his way back in. She stared at his head as he passed her.

"You givin' yourself a haircut, Dad?"

"Mind your own goddamn business," he said as he slammed the bathroom door.

A short time later, as Terri was having breakfast, Chick walked into the kitchen. She dropped her spoon in shock when she looked up at him. "Oh my god...oh shit! Dad, what did you do?"

Chick was bald. Not only was he bald, but he also had several red nicks all over his smooth, shiny scalp. Terri's mouth dropped open as she wondered at the evenness of his small round head.

"Shut up. Don't talk to me," he snapped. His head was hidden for a moment as he looked into the refrigerator.

"Dad, why didn't you ask me for help? I would've given you a haircut."

He spun and faced her.

"Yeah? You're fulla shit! You wouldn't do anything for me. You wouldn't even wash your mother's hair when she was sick. Yer no damn good!"

She got up and flung her bowl into the sink, milk splashing over the countertop and floor.

"That's right. Blame me 'cause you made a mistake. You always have to blame people."

"Go on. Get the hell outta here. Get out. I ain't listenin' to your shit."

Nice start to the day so far.

As he took a few steps toward her, she grabbed her purse and ran out. Pulling out of the driveway, she glanced back and saw him standing on the small cement porch, crying.

By the time she pulled up to the Shea's, she'd lost her anger and giggled as she envisioned Chick's bald, bleeding head.

"Crazy, nutty bastard," she said out loud. She ran into Shea's kitchen where Kevin sat reading the paper at the table. He was shirtless and his long blond hair was draped over his shoulders. He had one hand wrapped firmly around a quart of Budweiser. Terri was still laughing.

"Kevin. You won't believe what my father did now," she said as she joined him at the table.

His hazel eyes widened as he lowered the paper to greet her. "He's not smoking your sister's pot again is he?"

"No. This is better. He's bald!"

"Bald? No shit. How did that happen?"

She threw her hands up. "He was giving himself a haircut and I guess he slipped up."

Kevin laughed. "That's far out. He's a riot. I love that guy. Wanna beer?"

"Kind of early, isn't it?"

"Nah. It's never too early." He got up and reached into the cabinet for a glass. "Ya' know, Dugan's deli sells the coldest beer in town. Feel that quart. It's like ice. You'll never get beer colder than that."

Kevin was the closest thing to a brother she had. They had a genuine admiration for each other and they had a lot in common.

"Here," Kevin said as he poured the golden liquid into her glass.

She took a long sip. "Yeah. Yeah. It is cold. Where're the girls anyway?"

"I don't know. I just got up," he said picking up his beer.

Just then, Marge Shea came into the kitchen with her usual load of laundry and threw it into the washer. Marge had a beautiful face with red, shiny cheeks from overwork. Terri wondered how she maintained her youthfulness in the face of all this drudgery. The only telltale sign of aging was her round belly, a reminder of her six pregnancies. Terri thought she'd always remember Marge this way, doing laundry in her shorts and oversized tank top.

"What are you two gonna do now? Sit here on this beautiful Saturday and drink beer all day?"

Kevin looked at her. "No, Ma. After this beer's gone, we're going to Howie's and drink some more. Hey, tell my mother what your father did."

"Oh, he shaved his head bald by mistake…and then got mad at *me*."

Marge shook her head. "Oh, Jesus, Mary, and Joseph. Your poor father. Sounds like he's having a rough time of it."

Terri gave Kevin a puzzled look and shrugged her shoulders.

They finished the last of the quart and headed for Howie's. As they left, Marge shouted down the hall.

"You kids are just like hamsters on a wheel. Ya' know that? You go round and round but you never get anywhere. Stay out of trouble now!"

Terri felt a twinge of guilt at Marge's last remark, and glanced at Kevin. "Did you hear that? What does she mean?"

"Ahh, just ignore her. C'mon."

"But what do you think she means by *trouble*?" He didn't answer. She followed Kevin out of the house, worrying over Marge's comment.

* * *

Later that evening, Terri was sitting next to Sharon at the bar. Joni was pleading *"Help Me"* from the jukebox.

"Shit, Sharon. Did I eat anything? I'm starting to feel a lil' woozy."

"I didn't see you eat anything."

"Where's Kevin? When did he leave?"

"He left a while ago. Said he had to meet some guy named Jesse. Don't you remember?"

"What time is it? I can't see that damn clock."

"It's seven-thirty."

"Oh god! I gotta go. I don't think I'm gonna make it. Shit, I can't believe I forgot to eat. I always eat. Damn."

"I've got an idea. Let's go out dancing. You go home and eat and meet me back here. We'll go to New Paltz."

"Are you kiddin'? I'll never make it."

As Terri drove, she had trouble keeping the car on the road. She closed one eye and forged ahead. She was grateful again that Howie's was so close to home.

When she walked in the house, Chick was standing at the sink. She spotted a box of baking soda on the kitchen counter and watched as he downed a glass of murky fluid. The car ride hadn't lessened her drunken state and she needed to brace herself on the door frame for balance.

She wasn't ready for the sight of him. His hairless head seemed to be glowing under the fluorescent kitchen light. She was glad she wasn't doing acid. He looked over at her and let out a loud sickening belch.

"Where the hell were you?"

"Out. I was out...and now I'm in."

"Oh yeah? Well you look drunk to me."

She pointed a weak finger at him. "Oh yeah? Well, I'd rather be drunk than bald." At times, when she was this drunk, her thoughts fell from her mouth and she couldn't stop them. She watched as his lips stiffened. He grabbed the first thing he could get his hands on. It was a Carmen Miranda planter sitting on the window sill, the last of a set.

No, not that. Shit! Her mother had treasured those planters. Terri loved the way the philodendrons grew out of Carmen's fruited hat and cascaded over her bare alabaster shoulders.

Chick started toward Terri. She ran out the door for the second time that day. As she raced to her car, she felt it whiz by her head. She jumped in the car and took off. She took one last look at Carmen Miranda as she lay face down in pieces on the driveway, but got a shot of adrenaline that would probably enable her to drink for a couple more hours. For that, she was thankful. She headed to Sharon's apartment.

Pounding loudly on Sharon's door, she yelled, "Sharon...Shaaaaaaron! Open the door. It's me."

Sharon opened the door. "What's the matter? What the hell happened?"

Terri threw her head back and laughed before she spoke. "A bald guy threw a Carmen Miranda planter at me.

That's what!"

Sharon grabbed her arm. "C'mon in. Let's go sit on the balcony. I got some wine. Tell me what happened."

They never went out dancing that night, but talked until the wine was gone.

"I don't like it here, Sharon. I wanna get out of this town. Maybe go out West."

"Oh, my sister loves it in California. I'll give you her number. Maybe you can stay with her until you get on your feet. Maybe I'll go too."

"That would be great. It's this town, Sharon. It's gonna kill me. There's bad joo joos here."

"What?"

Terri patted Sharon's hand as they sat on the floor of the small balcony.

"You know. Bad joo joos...Karma. That stuff John Lennon sings about."

Sharon nodded. "Yeah, you said it."

"I gotta get out. I'm scared, Sharon."

"Remember when we were little?" Sharon asked. "You were afraid of every little thing."

"Yeah, I was a real nervous kid."

"Well, I never told you this, 'cause I felt I had to look out for you all the time, but I was scared of all those same things."

Terri's eyes widened. "Really?"

"Yeah," Sharon nodded. "You know when I stopped being scared?"

Terri already knew the answer, but asked anyway. "When?"

Sharon lifted her glass high. "When I started drinkin', that's when."

"I know what ya' mean. Thanks. Thanks for tellin' me that. Listen, I gotta lie down right away. You think Howie will mind if I sleep here tonight?"

"Nah. He probably won't even come home. Go on. Get some sleep. You need a rest."

Terri went into the spare bedroom and passed out on the mattress on the floor.

* * *

Terri placed her martini on Howie's juke box and made her selections in the usual methodical fashion. This machine made it easy because Howie made sure it was stocked with a diverse collection. She chose a rock song, "*Excitable Boy*" by a new guy, Warren Zevon and "*Hey, Good Lookin'*" by Hank Williams, solely to irritate the hard rockers at the bar. She selected "*I Feel Good*" by James Brown for Bridget and Patty, who would depart for the dance clubs at exactly ten o'clock. Terri took a long gulp of her drink and as the vodka and the music warmed her, she knew she wouldn't be leaving with them.

She reached into her pocket for more quarters when she saw Kevin in the back room playing pool with a guy she'd never seen before. Forgetting about the quarters, she paused and stared at him.

He was thin and muscular, and not too tall. His dark brown wavy hair grew past his shoulders. Moving around the pool table with a self-assured bounce, he proceeded to clear the table. There was a cockiness about him she found appealing. His long thin fingers caressed the pool stick smoothly and precisely. Terri wished she were the cue. As he leaned forward and aimed, the smoke from his cigarette curled in front of his face. Even behind the smoke, Terri could see the blueness of his large eyes.

She went over to the bar to get some quarters. Patty and Bridget were ready to leave. "Hey, Patty. Who's the guy playin' pool with Kevin?"

Patty leaned over and glanced into the back room. "I have no idea, but if he's with Kevin, he's probably an asshole."

Bridget chimed in. "C'mon. Come with us. You never go dancin' anymore. Don't sit around this place all night."

Terri shook her head. "Nah. No thanks. I'll stay here with Sharon. Have a great time, guys."

Terri sidled up next to Sharon at the bar and ordered a Beck's. "Look back there at the guy playing pool with Kevin."

Sharon leaned back and took a look. "Yeah. He's kinda cute. Wonder where *he* came from!"

"Look at his eyes, and watch him. Watch the way he moves and handles that stick. Boy, can he play!" Terri said as she poured the Beck's into a glass.

"So, go talk to Kevin and move in. Don't you know how to flirt?"

"Yeah," Terri lied. "I know how to flirt, but it's too much of a commitment."

Sharon shot her a glance. "What? Why's flirting a commitment?"

Terri shrugged. "If you flirt, eventually, you're gonna have to deliver something."

"That's stupid!" Sharon leaned back and took another look at the guys playing pool. "Well, with a guy like that, you might wanna deliver."

Terri took several gulps of her beer. "You're right. Give me a few more minutes."

Sharon sipped her martini. "Hey, where's your martini?"

"I switched to beer for a while. The vodka was too much."

After she'd drunk enough courage, she decided to look at him just one more time before heading for the back room. But the guy with the blue eyes was following Kevin out the door. She felt a familiar, inexplicable pang of loneliness and turned back to her drink.

* * *

Staring at the stars from Sharon's balcony, Terri wondered how another night had slipped away from her.

She watched her friend drink the last few drops of her beer and appreciated the fact that no matter how late it was, she was always there for Terri.

She patted Sharon's hand and asked, "Do you ever feel really alone, even when there are people all around you?"

Sharon shook a lock of honey blond hair from her face and leaned back against the apartment building. Then nudging Terri in the ribs, she said, "You're startin' to bum me out now. First, you're sad over the guy at the bar, and now this. C'mon, let's go next door to Angel's place. Laura will be there. They're always up and they have a lotta fun over there. Angel has cocaine, ya' know."

Terri shook her head. "Nah. I don't think I can get up. I'm starting to fade. Besides, I've seen that Angel guy. He makes me nervous."

Sharon stood up and grabbed Terri's hands. "C'mon girl. You'll like Angel. Why would he make you nervous? 'Cause he's in a great band and has a beautiful voice?"

Terri looked up at her, astonished at how well Sharon knew her.

"C'mon. He's really nice. Besides, maybe a little cocaine will perk you up." Sharon yanked her up, but fell against the wrought iron railing and both of them tumbled to the ground laughing.

Terri sat up and straightened her clothes. "Okay, okay. I'll go. But I'm not snorting anything up my nose. That's gross."

"No, it's really great. And you can drink a lot longer when you do coke!"

They walked down the dark hall and Sharon knocked on the door. Terri had become more curious about Angel. "What's with him and this girl Laura? What goin' on with his band? How well do you know these people? Aren't they a little weird?"

Sharon turned around. "Shhh. You're asking too many questions. Jeez, what're you so nervous about?"

She knocked harder. Terri hid behind her.

"Who is it?" a man's voice called out.

"It's Sharon."

Angel opened the door and embraced Sharon. "Hey, Sharon, come on in. Who's your friend?"

"Oh, this is Terri," said Sharon putting an arm around Terri's shoulders.

As they entered the apartment, Terri felt as if she'd stepped back into the sixties. The place was gaudily decorated with black lights, beaded curtains, and a beat up oriental rug.

"Where's the lava lamp?" Terri whispered to Sharon.

Sharon shot her a glance to quiet her.

Angel Quinteira sat in front of the glass top coffee table where he had been cutting and arranging perfect lines of white powder. Terri sat across from him and studied him as he resumed his chore. He was a small man, almost delicate, probably in his early thirties. There was something extremely sensuous about the way he moved. He was wearing a tank top and jeans. Terri thought he was the palest Puerto Rican she'd ever seen, his white skin almost transparent next to the thick black hair that reached the middle of his back. It was tied loosely with a bandana. His eyes were large and dark—so dark you couldn't make out his pupils. As she watched him, she remembered listening to him sing at a local club. His voice was high, smooth, clear, and soulful. His energy on stage was infectious. She glanced over at the guitar that stood in the corner, and rested back in her chair.

Then Laura strolled in from the bedroom, her baggy paisley dress flowing with her movements. She was a plain looking hippie type with long frizzy colorless hair. She had features that seemed too large for her face. Immediately, Terri thought of her as a "horse face" and was annoyed that Chick's vernacular was strong enough to invade her thoughts at any given moment.

"Hey," Laura said as she sat next to Sharon.

These people are definitely from another planet.

As the girls sat talking, Angel proceeded to dump more cocaine onto the table and cut it up. Terri knew she was drunk but it didn't matter because everyone else seemed so wasted. The girls snorted some of the coke and Angel turned to Terri with the straw.

She waved him off. "No thanks." She just wanted another drink.

"You have any beer?"

Angel put the straw down on the table and got up.

"Sure. Anything you want. C'mon, follow me."

She followed him down a narrow hall into the kitchen. Terri glanced at the erotic charcoal drawings hanging on the wall as they went by. Angel turned to her.

"You like those?"

"Yeah. Yeah, I do. They're really great drawings. My father paints naked people too."

"Wow, far out." Angel handed her a beer. "Here you go."

Back in the living room, Angel sat next to the girls on the floor and Terri moved as far back in her seat as possible. The trio snorted some more coke and Terri took several gulps of beer, realizing she might fade at any time. The Doors *"Riders on the Storm"* was blasting over the stereo. It was too loud for conversation, but she knew there was no chance of that anyway given the condition everyone was in.

Then Angel began making out with Laura and Terri wondered why they couldn't wait until everyone left. Rather than watch them, she dropped her head back on the soft chair and listened to the music. As she listened to Ray Manzarek's piano break, she began to see colorful snowflakes dancing down on her face. *Don't,* she thought, grasping at the last bit of consciousness she had. *Lift your head up now.* She had to pick her head up or risk passing out in her chair and waking up embarrassed, sick or worse.

She opened her eyes and the snow dream vanished. What she saw caused her to hold her breath for what seemed like an hour. Sharon and Laura were wrapped in each other's arms, kissing. Angel sat staring at them, glassy-eyed. Sharon proceeded to remove Laura's baggy dress. Terri sat rooted to the chair, it was like she was invisible. Now Laura removed Sharon's shirt and they continued to make out. Terri had the feeling Sharon had done this before. Terri noticed Laura's large breasts which had been concealed under the baggy clothes. Terri became fascinated, only because large breasts were an oddity to her. Angel was still in a trance. Terri swallowed and the sound of what little saliva she had left burst loudly in her ears.

Angel looked over at Terri now, smiled, and slid the bandana from his hair. She sensed he wanted some kind of reaction, but she had none to give. He strutted over to her chair, placed both of his hands on her knees and kissed her gently. A long slow kiss. She felt his soft hair fall around her face. As his tongue moved around inside her mouth, she thought about the first sloppy French kisses she received as a teenager. This one was different. This was a kiss she wanted to lean into, and she shocked herself by kissing him back.

Then he walked back over to the girls, who by this time were lying down, still embracing. Angel held his hand out to Terri.

"C'mere, Terri."

Overcome and confused, the taste of Angel's sweet velvet tongue still in her mouth, she held up her finger to hold him off.

"I...uh...I'll be right back, okay?"

Holy shit! I gotta go.

She ran out the apartment and down the stairs so fast, she missed several steps on the way. With the Doors still blaring from the stereo, she ran out the front door and drove home.

She threw off her clothes and jumped into bed, angry at Sharon for inviting her over to Angel's place. She wondered if Sharon would even remember what had happened the next morning.

That night she had a dream she was in bed with Laura but by the time the dream was over, Laura was transformed into the blue-eyed guy at the pool table.

* * *

Terri pulled up in front of the big white apartment house, feeling less hung over than usual. Taking a big gulp of coffee, she contemplated what she'd say to her best friend about the previous night.

As she ran up the stairs to Sharon's place, Angel was on his way down. *Oh shit! How embarrassing. Wait a minute! I didn't do anything wrong. Why should I be embarrassed?* He looked happy to see her.

"Hey, Terri. What're you doin' up so early?"

"Goin' to see Sharon." She tried to squeeze by him but he reached out and cupped her chin.

"Hey, I hope we didn't freak you out last night. Maybe that's not your thing."

"Hey, no problem. I wasn't freaked out," she lied.

There was something about this guy. He was smooth.

"Good. Glad to hear that. I'll see you around, okay?" He kissed her cheek and she caught his masculine scent.

"Yeah, sure."

Terri knocked loudly on Sharon's door.

"Sharon, you awake?"

Sharon opened the door looking sleepy and beautiful, even with morning hair and no make-up.

"Hey, come on in. I just made coffee."

"I just met Angel on the stairs."

"Don't you just love Angel? He's so great. Such a great guitarist. And whatta voice!"

"Yeah! He's good at a lotta things, right? Tell me, *how* good is he?"

"What do you mean?"

"Last night, Share, ya' know—you, Angel, that girl Laura. I almost got an eyeful. Ran out of there so fast I almost broke my ass."

"Oh, yeah. Hope you weren't freaked out, Terri."

Terri threw her hands up.

"Jesus Christ, not again! Everybody's real worried about that. No, I *wasn't* freaked out. I almost killed myself runnin' down the stairs last night but...noooo. What, me? Freaked out? What's the matter with you anyway? You can't warn me about something like that? You can't give me a little hint. Like, 'if I start makin' out with Laura, don't worry. We do it all the time!' Jeez, Share. You been doin' this to me since we were little. How long has this been goin' on?"

Terri stared at the spray of freckles on Sharon's nose that gave her dimpled face a look of innocence.

"It just started a little while ago. Doesn't Laura have a beautiful body?"

"I don't give a shit about Laura's body. You worry me, girl."

"Don't worry about me. I just want to experience life to the fullest and try new things."

"Does Howie know about this?"

"You know we have an open relationship, Terri. And we haven't been gettin' along anyway. I think we're gonna break up."

"Really? Gee, I didn't know that. So what about this guy Angel? Did you know he invited me to join in? How many women can he handle anyway? You think he could've handled the three of us?"

"Oh, definitely. Want to hear how he does it?"

Terri put her hands over her ears. "No I don't. Save it for another time you wanna shock the shit outta me."

"Hey, how are things going with your dad?"

"Well let's just say I'm staying out of his way. You know how he is. I told you he threw that planter at me."

"That was awful. I remember how he threw the

customers out of your store when we were kids. He's got some temper. I was scared of him when we were little. Did he ever hit you?"

"No, but he hit Sarah once and gave her a bloody nose and cried for an hour after he did it. He can never catch me. I'm way too fast."

"Aww. Don't let him catch you, Terri. Hey, maybe you should move in with me. I really think Howie's leaving. Think about it."

"Thanks. I definitely *will* think about it. Remember that blue-eyed guy from the other night? The cute one playing pool with Kevin. I'd like to run into him again."

"A lotta good it'll do you. You probably won't even talk to him if you do."

"Well, I'll talk to him if he talks to me."

"You spend your whole life waiting for everything, Terri. Why don't you get some guts and live it up? I can give you some lessons on how to flirt. How 'bout that?"

But Terri wasn't listening. She pictured herself wrapped in his arms, high on a bluff overlooking the river. Terri knew this reverie would repeat itself over and over and be the highlight of the dreary week ahead.

Chapter 6

Jesse James McLaughlin walked into the plain two-story house and kicked off his construction boots.

"Hey, Ma. You home yet?"

He grabbed a beer from the fridge, climbed the stairs to his old room, and flicked on the stereo. *"Marrakesh Express."* Taking a long swig of beer, he stretched out on the twin bed he'd slept in as a child.

He thought about how the people in rehab told him to stay away from alcohol, but what the hell could a few beers hurt? After all, in the last few months he'd kicked heroin and the beer really took the edge off. Jesse felt he was entitled to a few drinks after *that* lousy experience. He never wanted to have to kick again.

He was glad to be back home with Annie. She'd done so much for him and he wanted to do the right thing by her. He owed her a lot more than the money he'd stolen from her. He owed her his life. As he began to wonder how safe he'd be back in this crazy little town, he heard his mom come home from work. He lay there awhile thinking about what she'd cook tonight. She had cooked every night since he'd been back and he liked that. He knew she was trying to fatten him up and he loved to watch her smug look as he took seconds. He got up, washed his face, and ran downstairs to meet her.

"Hey, how's my best girl?" He gave her a quick peck on the cheek and helped her unpack the groceries.

Annie McLaughlin was a solidly built woman with gray hair streaked with reddish brown strands. She looked older than her sixty-four years, but her blue eyes still sparkled despite her haggard appearance. Jesse opened the fridge and got himself another beer.

"Oh, Jesse, can't you wait until supper to have a beer? I thought they told you in that school not to drink at all. Ya' know your brother hasn't had a drink in five years."

"Ma, it wasn't a school. It was detox. Ya' know, rehab."

"Well, whatever it was, please watch yourself. You know your father had that curse…and your brother. Please be careful." Her Irish brogue was more noticeable when she spoke sternly.

"Ma, I'm okay. So how was my favorite lady's day?"

"You are full of it but I love ya' anyway." She smiled and pinched his cheek. She looked at all the groceries they had unpacked and realized something was missing.

"I forgot to pick up milk. Can you go out to the corner store and get some? Here."

She gave him the keys and some money, something she wouldn't dream of doing a year ago.

"Take my car and come right back. I'll have supper on."

"Anything you say, Ma." Jesse bounced out the front door and hopped into the car. He found Neil Young's *"Heart of Gold"* on the car radio and thought about how good it felt to be trusted again. He drove downtown and scanned the main drag. He was told in rehab to stay away from people, places and things. He figured he could handle at least one of those suggestions. He knew the people to stay away from.

There was a tight group of young junkies in town and these were the ones he'd taken up with shortly after his marriage broke up. The marriage ended when he crashed through a sliding glass door after she had locked him out. He'd been out all that night shooting dope and drinking, and could hardly remember the incident. He remembered being thrown into the police car and that was it.

He never blamed Amanda for leaving him and wasn't bitter at all. It didn't even matter that he still cared for her. He knew she was gone forever. He just wanted to start over now, sick of the scams and the lies. Jesse was twenty-four now and was certain the worst part of his life was over. He felt lucky, really lucky.

As he drove down Main Street, he thought about some of his friends who didn't make it—like "Chicken" Eddie who overdosed in the decaying casino on top of the mountain. Eddie got his nickname because he was always playing the game. He could hold a burning cigarette to the inside of his arm longer than anyone else. Eddie loved to shoot dope on that mountaintop.

Jessie thought of Lil' Big Man who was shot in the back of the head as he ran from the cops. They thought he had a gun but it turned out to be just a big wad of tin foil. *Stupid fuckin' cops.* Then he thought of Flynn, his best friend. He hurt when he thought of Flynn. They'd known each other since they were ten. *Nobody shoulda died the way Flynn died.*

As his thoughts drifted away from lost friends, he turned up the radio. Jesse danced in his seat and now drummed the steering wheel to Van Morrison's *"Domino."* He'd always had a hard time sitting still and music exacerbated the problem.

He stopped for the milk at the corner deli on Main and as he strolled out, Romeo was on his way in. Jesse wasn't ready for this.

Romeo had been shooting heroin since he was fourteen. He supported his habit by dealing drugs and driving an old taxi around town. It was a good cover and a good way to do business.

He was nicknamed "Romeo" because he was so damned handsome. His half Irish, half Sicilian heritage gave him a face any woman would envy. With thick black wavy hair, dark olive skin, and eyes the color of tropical waters, he stood about six-foot-four with broad shoulders and a muscular physique. A lot of women wanted him, but none could get too close because his first and only love was heroin. He was a heartbreaker, a liar, and a cheat. He'd do anything for dope.

Romeo grabbed hold of Jesse's shoulders.

"Hey, man, JJ. When did you get back in town?"

Jesse tried to act enthusiastic.

"Hey, Romeo. How ya' doin'?"

They gave each other a high five.

"You still drivin' that beat up cab?"

"Yeah, man. It gets me where I wanna go. You know what I mean? How was Colorado? How's your bro' doin'?"

"He's doin' great. Colorado was good. Hey listen, I gotta get goin'."

Jesse knew what was coming.

"Hey, JJ. You wanna take a ride with me? I got some really sweet stuff. You wanna taste?"

"Oh, yeah? Is it anything like that shit you sold me the night Flynn died?"

"Man, I didn't know what that stuff was cut with. You were with him, not me."

Jesse looked up at Romeo and poked him hard in the chest.

"Listen you fucker. I'm clean. You fuckin' got that?"

Romeo backed off, hands raised. "Okay, man. That's all you gotta say. No harm done. I'll be seein' ya' around."

Romeo got in his cab and took off.

* * *

Terri was getting ready to go to the bar. Friday was the biggest night at Howie's and Terri never missed it. As she came up the stairs, Chick was waiting for her.

"Hey, you goin' to the place with the pool table tonight?"

She'd been ignoring Chick since the Carmen Miranda incident and she sensed he was looking for absolution.

"Yeah. Why?"

"I feel like playin' pool."

The thought of running into that beautiful pool player had crossed her mind more than once. Having Chick with her would ruin it, but she relented.

"Okay. Let's go then. I'm leavin' now."

They walked into Howie's and were greeted by Pink

Floyd's *"Money"* blaring from the jukebox. Sharon was there with a group of young girls she and Terri sometimes hung out with. Chick knew them and waved hello.

"Hey, goils. How are the goils?"

They all giggled, probably at the sight of his now peach-fuzzed head. Terri knew they all found him amusing as hell. She was already getting irritated.

"What do you want to drink, Dad?"

"Just get me a ginger ale."

She ordered a vodka and club for herself and the soda for Chick. She began talking to her friends but was interrupted immediately.

"C'mon, if we're gonna play pool, let's play for cryin' out loud."

The back room was empty. She was glad because she knew he'd shout and curse throughout the game. Chick was a great pool player and could run the whole table. He'd taught Terri to play when she was eight, so she wasn't half bad. She figured he'd only run off a few and then give her a chance, but she was wrong. He ran the whole table.

"Put another quarter in, baby, and see if you can beat yer daddy." He was smiling, having a good time. Terri was thinking about the waitress with the big hair from the diner. Maybe she had something to do with his joy. He let her break and she sunk four balls but missed the next one. Chick was up again and she knew he'd finish it off.

As she stood leaning against the pool cue, the blue-eyed guy walked in the room and put a quarter up. He sauntered over to Terri.

"Hey, how ya' doin'?"

She had a hard time looking into his ocean blue eyes. His irises were flecked with amber. She felt a quiver of excitement but soon lost it when she looked over at her father. Chick glared at the newcomer as he bent over to make the next shot.

"I'm fine."

"Yeah...you *are*. I've seen you with Kevin. I'm a good friend of his. What's yer name?"

"I'm Terri."

"Hey, I'm Jesse."

"Nice to meet you, Jesse. I'm..." She wanted to flirt in the worst way, but didn't know how. She tried to act relaxed but she knew Chick was watching and could see right through her. Everyone could.

"Okay, who's playin' over here?" Chick hollered as he sank the eight ball. "You next?"

He glared at Jesse again.

"Yeah, I'm up." Jesse racked the balls as he smiled enticingly at Terri. She noticed the smile created a long deep dimple on either side of his face. He racked with such proficiency he hardly looked down, keeping his eyes only on her.

"Hey, kid, are you watchin' what yer' doin'?" Chick's happy mood was gone.

"Yeah, I got this. Don't worry." Jesse walked over and stood very close to Terri. Chick broke and sunk three balls.

"You'll never beat him," she told Jesse. "And now he's mad, so he'll probably run the whole table."

"Why's he so mad?"

"He doesn't seem to like you."

"I don't even know him! We'll see about this game," Jesse said confidently. "You're not such a bad pool player yourself. I was watchin' you."

"Thanks."

"Who is that guy anyway?" Jesse asked.

Terri was hesitant to admit it. "He's my dad."

"Son of a bitch," Chick hollered.

Jesse put his beer down, picked up the stick and chalked it. Terri watched his every movement, so slow and smooth. Graceful, yet brash. Chick came over and stood next to Terri. Her eyes remained on Jesse as he sank ball after ball, calling out each shot. *Go on Jesse. Beat him!* Her thoughts were interrupted by Chick's harsh voice.

"Who's that Mick?"

"Dad, shhh. How do you know he's Irish anyway?"

"He's drinkin' beer, ain't he?"

"Quiet. He's a friend of mine."

Jesse looked over at Chick. "Eight ball in the side." He sunk it. Chick had been holding his stick in anticipation of winning. He angrily threw the stick against the wall.

"C'mon, let's get the hell outta here."

Terri rolled her eyes.

"I gotta go. See ya' around."

Her father was already out the front door and down the street. He walked fast for a guy his age.

Jesse grabbed her arm gently.

"Wait. Listen. You gonna be around tomorrow? Wanna do somethin'?"

She tried to look aloof all the while staring into those blue eyes.

"Sure."

She felt something she hadn't felt in a long time; a joy she somehow wasn't comfortable with. It was fleeting as Chick popped his head back in the door.

"What the hell are ya' doin'? You comin' or not?"

She gave Jesse her number and took Chick home. She was feeling so good on the ride, she was able to tune out his tirade about the Irish.

She had a strong wave of contentment that night and didn't feel the need to drink anything else. Instead of immediately passing out in her usual drunken haze she fell asleep naturally, just like when she was little, and it felt so good.

Chapter 7

Terri hung up the phone. Jesse was on the way to get her and they were going to hike the mountain. This was the best she'd felt since her mother died. No crushing hangover. Chick's loud voice intruded on her new found tranquility.

"Who was that?"

"A guy. I'm goin' on a date. We're hikin' up the mountain."

"Who you goin' with? That Mick from last night?"

"Yeah, that's the one."

She sneered at her father and stared out the picture window. A few minutes later, a large white car pulled in the driveway.

"Gotta go, Dad. See ya' later." She ran out the door before he could say anything else.

* * *

The mountain stood before them in its lush leafy splendor. From a distance it always looked pale blue and luminous, but when you were right at its foot, it was deep dark green. It didn't look like a challenging hike, but within the first twenty minutes of brisk walking, you'd break a sweat.

Terri thought this was a wonderful idea for a first date, just the two of them in the forest. She wondered what part of herself she'd let him see and what he'd reveal to her. The newness of this beautiful stranger exhilarated her. The past months had been an empty and dangerous time for her. She'd been drinking way too much and knew she needed to take better care of herself.

Jesse was dressed in jeans and a red and white checked button-down shirt. He carried a back pack. His blue eyes looked teal green under the trees. Each time she looked at him, he looked better and better. She remembered a few things Kevin had told her about his shadowy past.

"Which way?" he asked. "The old road or the path straight up to the pines?"

She loved the pines and didn't mind the steeper hike. She wanted to be right in the heart of the mountain and always felt you missed the beauty of the woods by taking the road.

"I'd like to take the path to the pines but you've got that backpack, so do you mind?"

"No, it's not that heavy. Let's go straight up."

The small path up the mountain was lined with thick foliage and bright green ferns. Alongside the path there was a brook that splashed down over the rocks and broke the silence of the hike.

"What's in the backpack?"

"Oh, a couple of bottles of wine and some glasses. Hope you like wine." Jesse gave her a wide grin and the vertical dimples she first noticed looked even deeper now.

"Sure, I like wine." *And beer and vodka and...* She was thrilled he brought something as she was feeling a little shy and self-conscious.

"Have you ever been blind on tequila?" he asked out of the blue.

"No, but I heard of people who have. I think I'll leave it alone for a while." She thought about the severe stomach pains she'd been getting each morning after drinking it.

"Good idea. You don't want to go blind on tequila. Believe me. I don't touch it anymore."

Jesse stood on a rock and gently reached his hand down to pull her up. Terri noticed how warm his hand was.

They talked all the way and the walk went quickly.

"Here we are," he said as they came to the clearing in the pines.

It was a place she'd been to many times before. The wide open space made it a favorite camping spot. She remembered camping there as a girl scout. The opening was surrounded by tall dark pine trees but you could still see the stars peeking through them when you camped out at night. Terri couldn't stop thinking about the wine.

Jesse patted the small blanket he'd pulled out of his backpack.

"C'mon. Sit down."

She felt a twinge of anticipation as he poured the wine and handed it to her.

"So, I hear you can sing."

She looked down and felt herself blushing.

"Yeah. I sang in a band for a while and maybe I'll do it again. The time hasn't been right lately." She wondered about what Jesse had been doing when she was singing in the local clubs. "How did you know?"

"Kevin told me. He also told me not to bother asking you out, 'cause you wouldn't be interested."

"Well, I guess Kevin was wrong." She looked straight into his eyes and saw the depths of the sea. She felt lost in time for a few seconds and shifted uncomfortably on the blanket.

"So...uh. You said you've been out of town for a while?"

He smiled. "Yeah. I've been out to Colorado with my brother. He lives out there but I came back home to help my mom out. It's kind of hard for her to get by with my dad gone and all."

"He died?"

"When I was about twelve. You have any brothers or sisters?"

"One sister. She lives in the city, and ya' know, I have my dad. My mom died not too long ago."

"Sorry to hear that."

"That's okay. Thanks. Hey, I'm sorry my dad was so rude last night. He's like that. Your dad must've been young when he died right?"

Jesse looked down and a shock of brown hair fell over

his face. He rested his arm on his raised knee with the wine glass in hand. "Yeah pretty young, about forty-nine. But my daddy, see…he liked to drink a lot. Guess you could say he just drank himself to death. Wasn't a pretty sight either, especially for my mom."

Her eyes were fixed on Jesse. His honesty shocked her. Her attraction to him was strong and it was becoming stronger.

"Hey, let's keep goin' up to the old casino." He pulled her up.

"Sure. My parents used to dance there when they were young. It was a real hot spot with those old big bands."

As they came upon the deteriorating building, she could see how much it had changed since the last time she'd been there.

The large white stucco structure was surrounded in its entirety by a deck. The deck had a four foot wall around it. You could walk all around the building and get a different view of the valley and river below. Inside, the old wood dance floor was warped and covered with plaster and broken glass. The mirrored ball on the ceiling had been shot out by vandals with bee bee guns. The old bar was in one piece but it was also covered with debris.

She looked at the old bandstand and pictured a Glen Miller type orchestra playing and people dressed in their best forties garb, drinking and having a good time. Seeing the place as it was now gave her an eerie feeling. There was no life, no music, no color, just emptiness and decay.

He stepped onto the deck and reached out his hand. "C'mon. Here's a safe spot."

"I'm kind of scared of heights."

"Take my hand. When we get to the wall, I'll hold you. Don't worry. Just look at the view."

He took her hand and led her to the wall. He stood behind her and gently placed his arms around her waist. She could feel his breath in her hair. Being up on the mountain made everything below look so clean and perfect.

"Man, they say the Rockies are beautiful but they're not half as pretty as this valley. Hard to believe that dirty little city is down there, ain't it?"

He seemed to read her thoughts. "Everything does look better from far away."

"Let's go in." He led her back into the dance hall.

Terri followed him over to the old bar. He pulled out the blanket and started cleaning off the debris.

"Have a seat." He lifted her up gently and sat her on the spot he'd cleaned. "More wine?"

"Sure." She was feeling giddy now and wanted to intensify the warm feeling. He poured the wine and she downed hers in an instant.

"Never met a woman who drank faster than me."

"Well, now you have." She gave him a sly smile.

He filled her glass again and took a few steps toward her. He placed his hands each side of her. His face was very close.

Terri's heart started to flutter. She wanted to avoid his eyes but couldn't. He stared right at her and she fidgeted. He leaned forward and kissed her. He used his lips more than his tongue and she liked that. His lips were full and soft. He kissed her for a long time and she saw little bursts of light behind her closed lids. As she held on to him she could feel his leanness. The kiss was slow and long and when he stopped, he held her in a tight embrace. He took her hand.

"Wanna dance?"

She felt she was in some sort of trance and was worried she wouldn't be able to speak.

"Uh…there's no music," she said, her voice breaking.

"You always got music." Jesse tapped his index finger to his temple. "Right here. C'mon."

He took her onto the ancient dance floor and held her close. Swaying to the music in their heads, she glanced up to look for falling plaster. Then she rested her head on his chest. As she breathed in the damp sweet scent of him, she could feel his whole body against hers. She realized falling plaster was the least of her worries. She felt herself a fool but couldn't shake the feeling she was falling crazy in love with Jesse.

* * *

It was Sunday morning and the smell of bacon frying wafted up to Jesse's room. He got up, washed his face, and raced downstairs. Singing as he entered the kitchen, he grabbed his mom and danced her around the floor.

"Jesse, stop it now. I have a fork in my hand. What's gotten into you anyway?"

"I feel good, Ma. It's a beautiful day and I feel good." With that he broke into the James Brown song and started sliding and side stepping across the kitchen floor.

"I'm glad to hear that, dear. Since you're feelin' so good, why don't you come to church with your dear old mother and thank the Lord for your good fortune. You know, Jesse, I've always relied on the Lord in times of trouble and he's always seen me through. I hope you'll learn to do that someday."

Jesse frowned. "I don't think God wants to hear from me, Ma. I think he'd rather hear from you. You just keep sayin' those novenas for me and Mark. Ya' know, on days like this, I almost think all those prayers you been sayin' are payin' off."

Jesse picked up the phone and his voice became softer now.

"Hi, Terri, it's me, Jesse. I just wanted to tell you I had a real nice time yesterday. Uh huh. Good. Good. Listen, we're havin' a little campout on the mountain this Friday. Okay. I'll call you about it during the week. Okay. Bye."

Annie turned toward him and smiled. "Oh, so that's what put a spring in your step, ay? A girl."

"That's right, Ma. A girl. And she's a nice one too. I

like her, Ma."

"Good, Jesse," she said as she sat down. She became more serious. "Maybe that's what you need. It's been rough on you the last few years, I know."

"Ma, it's been rough longer than that. You forget about Dad? Now that was rough."

He looked over at his mom. She dropped her eyes sadly. He didn't want to upset her more than he already had.

"Hey, Ma, I wanna say, I'm sorry for all the rotten things I said the night I kicked. Ya' know, that night you had to tie me up. It wasn't me talkin', Ma. Ya' know what I mean. It wasn't me."

She smiled at him. "Oh, love, don't worry about it. I understand completely."

Jesse was ashamed of the things he'd said that night and was determined never to hurt Annie again.

* * *

Terri took special care getting ready to meet Jesse at the campout. He'd called during the week to let her know exactly where they'd be setting up the beer kegs. She felt a fluttering in her stomach as she thought of the way he kissed her up in the casino. She thought of how his long wavy hair tickled her cheeks as he leaned toward her face. It had been such a long time since she felt anything like this.

Her little daydream was interrupted by Chick's voice.

"I'm comin' down there. I gotta paint."

"Okay, okay." *Oh, that fucking stupid painting.*

As Chick walked through her dreary room, he asked, "Where ya' goin'? Out with that Mick?"

"Do you have to call him that?"

"That's what he is, ain't he? What's his last name?"

"McLaughlin."

"See. I told you he was a Mick."

She rolled her eyes and made a growling sound under her breath as he went into the back room to paint.

"Bye, Dad."

Terri picked up Sharon and they headed for the campsite.

"Look what I brought." Sharon pulled a bottle of vodka out of a paper bag with two glasses and some lemon wedges. "We can drink on the way."

"You think of everything."

After they parked, they had to walk about two hundred yards to the campsite. Sharon waved her flashlight around.

"Look! I see the campfire," Terri said. She could feel butterflies in her stomach again at the thought of seeing Jesse.

The campsite was in a small clearing with just enough room for the few tents that were set up.

"Oh boy, two kegs," Sharon said as she approached Kevin sitting by the fire.

"C'mon, have a beer," he said. There were about ten people there. Terri sat down next to him. She glanced around the campsite. "Hey, have you seen Jesse?"

Kevin pointed up the mountain path. "There's your boyfriend. Up against that tree. See him?" She caught a hint of sarcasm in his voice. He shone a flashlight on Jesse and handed it to Terri. "Here you're gonna need this."

She started up the path. As she got closer, she saw Jesse's head was hanging down and his long shiny hair covered his face. He used his arm to steady himself against the tree and his legs were planted apart. She thought he might have passed out. She brought her face very close to his.

"Jesse."

He raised his head slowly until she could see the blue of his eyes.

"Hi...Hey, Terri." He smiled and ran his fingers gently down her cheek.

She took a deep breath as his full lips opened. The

strong smell of alcohol was intoxicating and reminded her of being cradled in Fogarty's arms as a child, after he'd caught her at the bottom of the stairs. She closed her eyes and breathed in deeply. That smell, Jesse's wavy hair, his eyes. At that moment, she was drawn to him in a way she didn't understand.

"Hi," he repeated.

"You already said that."

"Oh yeah. I did, didn't I?"

She knew he was a wretched drunken mess and she couldn't rationalize her intense attraction to him. She figured she could solve the whole problem if she drank a lot more and he sobered up a bit.

"Jesse, I'll be right back—I need to get my drink."

He sat down and looked up at her with a childlike grin.

"Okay. I'll be right here." He patted the ground. "See right here." He smiled sheepishly. "Terri, bring me a beer, okay? I'll be right here."

He was still patting the ground and grinning as she looked back.

Back at the campsite, she poured herself a large glass of vodka, squeezed a lemon wedge in it, and threw the wedge in the glass. She grabbed a beer and burger for Jesse, and got a blanket.

When she returned, he was still sitting there with a drunken smile.

"Hey, you got lots of stuff. Let me take some."

He started to get up but lost his balance and fell back into a sitting position. "Oops."

She spread out the blanket. "Here, sit here and eat this burger." He ate the burger in about three bites and they drank their drinks. As they sat, Jesse stared at her with a loving but distant gaze. She noticed a slight drooping of his right eyelid and it seemed he was having trouble focusing. She wondered if he could see her at all.

"Are you okay?" she asked.

"Oh yeah. I'm fine. Got here kind of early after work

and we tapped the kegs and…here I am! I'm glad you brought me that burger cause sometimes I forget to eat, especially on Fridays."

"C'mon, you wanna go down to the campfire?" she asked.

"No!" he said as he lay down on the blanket and pulled her down with him. His embrace was tight and warm. He kissed her the way he did in the casino but this time he used his tongue more. She could feel his whole firm body against hers and she delighted in the taste of him.

After the best kiss she'd had in a very long time, he stared into her eyes and stroked her hair. His intense blue gaze was almost unbearable.

"I want you to stay here with me tonight. I got a lot to tell you, Terri."

She knew then and there she'd let him have her tonight. She also wondered how a guy in his condition could get over like this.

"So, are we gonna sleep right here under the stars?"

"One of those tents down there is mine. I was gonna share it with my friend, Taylor, but I'd rather sleep with you."

"That's not a very nice thing to do to Taylor."

He stroked her hair. "Well, Taylor's not as pretty as you." He kissed her again, longer, and with more passion, pulling her closer. She felt all of him.

"Let's go back down," she breathed into his ear.

They joined the others at the campfire and sat down. Terri leaned over to Sharon and whispered.

"Pour me some more, Sharon. I'm staying here with Jesse tonight and I'm getting nervous."

"He's so cute, Terri, but jeez, he's so loaded."

"I know. I have to catch up to him." She held up her cup. "Give me some vodka."

As they sat by the fire, Jesse placed his hand on the inside of Terri's thigh pulling her a little closer. Her awareness of his hand made socializing difficult. At some point, Sharon got up and left, but Terri was oblivious. It seemed that Jesse was the only one there. Her thigh burned. She put her head on his shoulder and breathed in his musky scent.

He leaned over and whispered in her ear, "It's getting late. Let's go to the tent."

"Okay," she whispered back. It had worked. Jesse seemed to have sobered up a bit and she'd drunk enough vodka to lose her inhibitions. She was ready for him now. They walked up the path into the darkness.

"Here we go." He opened the flap of the tent, crawled inside, and sat down on a sleeping bag. She followed him in. "Terri, sit by me and listen to me for a minute. I gotta tell you some things."

She sat down next to him and listened intently.

"First of all, I gotta tell you that I was married before and you should know why my marriage broke up. I got married real young—eighteen."

Terri felt they had a lot in common and was excited to hear the rest of his story.

"A little while after I got married, I started hangin' out with some people in town. I'm sure you know them, Romeo, Flynn, and some of those other guys. Ya' know who I mean?"

"Yeah, I heard of them," she said, thinking: *I know Romeo all right!*

"Well, what I'm tryin' to say is I used to shoot heroin and I got hooked real bad. I didn't expect to. I thought I could handle it. Shortly after that I lost Flynn. He was my best friend."

She stayed silent. She could tell Jesse wasn't done yet.

"Well, after he died, I got into the dope even more. That's what broke up my marriage. I really don't blame her. But you're gonna hear bad things about me. You probably already have. I'm through with the dope now. I just wanted you to know all this stuff 'cause it could be hard on you goin' out with me and all."

"Why?"

"Why? 'Cause ya' know what they say, 'Once a junkie, always a junkie' and I wanna prove myself to you. I know it takes a long time to lose the label. I need ya' to trust me."

"Okay, Jesse." She brushed his hair from his face. "Was it hard to get off the heroin?"

"Was it hard? Just think of the worst pain you ever had and magnify it like a hundred times for hours and hours."

"How did you do it?"

"You really wanna know?"

"Yeah." She was fascinated with his story and her breathing became shallow in the silence of the woods.

"I had my mom tie me to the bed. It was the hardest thing I ever had to do and I don't wanna do it again."

She was holding her breath. "Well your mom must be somethin'."

"She is. She's all right." He pushed up and knelt on the sleeping bag. "C'mere, Terri." She knelt in front of him and he pulled her close. She felt recklessly in love.

He pulled off his shirt revealing his thin muscular chest, and began to undress her. "Right now I feel real good, and I just wanna make you feel real good too."

Terri didn't expect much in the way of lovemaking because he was still quite wasted, but as he began to touch her, she realized she was mistaken.

He kissed her again and pressed his chest to hers as he ran his fingers slowly down her bare arms, and over her stomach. He lowered her bra straps while still kissing her and gently ran his fingers over her shoulders. They felt like burning feathers. A warmth emanated from deep inside her and spread throughout her body down to her toes. He unsnapped her bra and looked at her naked chest.

"Just beautiful." He kissed her neck softly and moved his lips slowly down to her breasts. He ran his soft tongue around one nipple, at the same time unsnapping her jeans. She was ready for him now.

He put his hand into her pants and reached down.

"Ooooh. You're so wet, Terri."

She could barely speak. "I...I..."

He began caressing her most sensitive area and used his fingers to stimulate her in the gentlest way. He inserted a finger inside her. "Wow...so wet."

She pulled him closer and they rolled down onto the sleeping bag. She felt as if she'd come immediately. Jesse pulled his pants off and then hers. He put his nimble fingers back to work. He flicked his tongue over the other nipple.

Oh. No. No. Stop, I can't. Not yet.

She came in waves. There was *no* stopping it. It had been a while. "Oh my god. Fuuccck." She had no control.

"Oh, yeah, that's right." he murmured in her ear.

She looked down at his naked body and thought it was pretty amazing that his excitement was obvious despite his drunken state. She closed her eyes and arched her back. She really wanted him inside her. She was about to tell him but didn't have to.

He slid into her as she came again and again. They moved together in perfect rhythm. She could hear music she'd never heard before in her head.

He held her hands over her head and threw his head back, his long wavy hair dangling over his shoulders. As he came, he let out several deep loud growls that seemed to vibrate throughout the forest. She didn't care if anyone heard him. She didn't care about anything but him.

Chapter 8

Almost a year had passed and Terri had been seeing Jesse nearly every day. She'd either go to his house or he'd come over. They'd stay in her dark basement room late into the night, until Chick yelled down to Jesse to go home. It was difficult to find a place to have sex and Terri felt foolish. She was, after all, an adult! They wanted each other all the time. They'd gratify each other as quietly as they could down in her room. Other days, they'd make love at Jesse's house while his mother was out. When they made love there, she'd think about him tied to that bed kicking heroin. She fantasized about tying him to the same bed and pleasuring him all over, to make up for the past hurt. Someday she would. But now their lovemaking was always rushed.

They still both drank as much as before, but now it was pure joy. With the drug addiction so far behind him, Jesse didn't feel he had to take the edge off anymore. Terri's depression and loneliness were things of the past. Now they just drank for fun.

It was Friday night. She waited in her room for Jesse, but he didn't show. Hours had passed, so she decided to go to the bar looking for him.

As she walked in, he was there, looking exactly the way he did leaning against the tree on the mountain. She walked up to him and patted his shoulder.

He turned to her but it was as if he was looking right through her.

"Hey, baby. What's goin' on?"

"You didn't come over at seven. We were going to a movie, remember?"

"Yeah, I remember, babe, but I cashed my check, and I came here, and lost track of the time."

She knew exactly what he was talking about. She'd done it herself. She was angry anyway.

"There's a clock right there, Jesse."

"I know, babycakes, but I forgot to look at it."

She ordered a vodka and club.

He slapped a wad of cash on the bar.

"Let me get that, babe. I cashed my check."

"Yeah, you already said that." She downed the drink and ordered another one.

"That's my girl." He squeezed the inside of her thigh.

The warmth in her throat and the burning on her thigh made her feel better.

They continued to drink through the night. She realized that when Jesse drank, he seemed to enter a world where no one else was allowed.

* * *

"Is the Mick comin' over tonight?"

Terri was having dinner at home with Chick.

"Yeah he is, Dad. His name is Jesse."

"Why the hell does he have to put beer in my refrigerator every time he comes here?"

"To keep it *cold*, Dad." She was losing her patience.

Chick was rude to Jesse every time he came over and Jesse was good-natured enough to just shrug it off.

"Why's he gotta drink beer all the time anyway? Can't he come over here one night without beer? I'm gonna start callin' him *Beer Can*."

"Great. The Mick is bad enough. Anyway, we like beer, Dad. I drink it too."

"Ya' think I don't know that? Jeez!"

Terri thought it best not to mention the bottle of vodka she had hidden downstairs.

There was a knock at the door.

"Shhh now, Dad," she admonished. "C'mon in, Jesse."

Jesse walked in and bounced over to the fridge with a six-pack of Budweiser.

"Hey, Chick. How ya' doin'?"

Chick scowled at him. "I'm gonna watch TV." Chick

never left the house when Jesse was over.

Terri and Jesse grabbed a couple of beers and went downstairs.

Jesse turned on the stereo. Jackson Browne's crystal clear voice sang *"The Pretender"* as they fell onto the bed.

"How was your day, babe?" Jesse asked as he ran his warm hands up the back of her T-shirt.

"It was good. How was yours?"

"It's a lot better now," he said as he began kissing her and moving his hands over her ass and breasts.

They began making out. She was already aroused. But he stopped and looked in her eyes. "I can't do this with *him* up there."

"I know, Jesse. He'd kill us. He really would. He's got a temper like nobody else. He breaks down doors."

"Really?" Jesse asked. "He's just a little guy. Now you got me scared." Jesse had chugged the first beer. "Will you go get some more beers? I'm too scared," he laughed.

Terri was feeling the alcohol and started giggling. She ran up, got two more beers, and ran down quickly before Chick could make eye contact with her.

She handed one to Jesse. "Hey, you wanna see what my dad is paintin'? C'mon." She led him to the back of the basement and pulled on the light.

He stared at the painting.

"You gotta be kidding. Your dad is paintin' this?"

It was a life-size nude woman reclining on a couch. It wasn't quite finished and the couch was only partially painted a pale pink.

Jesse burst out laughing. "A naked lady?"

They both exploded with laughter. Jesse pulled a joint out of his pocket and lit it. He looked at the painting again.

"I can't fuckin' believe this. Hey want some?"

He motioned the joint toward Teri.

"No, I can't smoke and drink at the same time," she said laughing. Terri turned off the light and they went back to the bed.

Jesse was naturally funny and always had a new joke from the construction site. He really knew how to entertain her. After he smoked some of the joint, he began telling her a succession of jokes until they were both laughing loudly.

"Hey," Chick yelled down, "what's goin' on down there?"

Terri put her finger over Jesse's lips.

"Nothin', Daddy, nothin'. We're just tellin' jokes," she answered, her voice cracking with laughter.

A little later, Chick yelled down again.

"It's gettin' late. It's time for him to go."

Terri heard the stern tone of Chick's voice.

Terri and Jesse both made sad faces, which got them laughing uncontrollably again.

"That's it," Jesse said. "I know when I'm not wanted."

She put her arms around him and whispered, "Oh, but you are."

He gave her a long kiss. She felt his warm tongue exploring her mouth.

"It's ten-thirty," Chick hollered, his angry voice interrupting the kiss.

Jesse looked directly into her eyes. Those eyes. She was swimming in them and her heart beat faster.

"Terri, I want you so bad right now. C'mon let's get outta here." They grabbed their beers and slipped out of the house.

* * *

The sleazy motel was on the outskirts of a neighboring town. They'd been there three times already in the past month or so. She had him drive her car and on the way there, she held on to him, kissing his neck and rubbing the inside of his thigh.

When they entered the room they fell onto the bed immediately. He undressed her gently despite his urgency. No matter how wasted he was, he was good, real good.

There was nothing he wouldn't do to please her and she wanted to do the same for him.

She took him by the hands and pulled him off the bed leading him over to the wall. She pushed him gently against it and unbuckled his pants, sticking her hand inside and massaging him gently up and down. His groaning was deep, almost musical.

She pulled his pants down to the floor and fell to her knees, taking him in her mouth. With her hands on his hips, she sucked and flicked her tongue around the tip of his cock. It didn't take long for him to climax. She tried to hold his hips firmly to the wall, but she couldn't stop his writhing as he cried out with pleasure. When he was finished, he took her face in his hands and they tumbled back onto the bed.

"My god, Terri. What're you tryin' to do to me, girl?"

She snuggled closer to him but didn't answer.

After a short silence, Jesse began.

"I don't think yer daddy likes me much."

"It's not you, Jesse. He doesn't like anybody. He's got a temper and used to throw everyone out of our store. He used to embarrass my mother. Your mom probably remembers our store."

"You think *your* dad was bad? You should have met mine."

"Why? What was he like?" She couldn't fathom anyone being worse than Chick.

"I told you how he drank himself to death, right? Well, he was a downright mean drunk. Sometimes he'd spit on us or mom. We'd just stay outta his way. Sometimes my mom would speak up for us, and he was real mean to her. The worst thing I ever remember was when he shot our dog."

Terri was appalled. "Wait. What? He shot your pet? How horrible. Why would he do such a thing?"

"He shot him 'cause he wouldn't stop barkin'. It was awful. I loved that dog. Shot him right out in the yard."

Her heart felt like it was breaking in two for the dog *and* for Jesse.

"Oh please, don't talk about it anymore."

She began kissing his neck. He took her face in his hands and looked right into her eyes.

"Listen," he said. "I want to be with you more. I think about you all day long. We can't keep comin' here. I thought maybe we could get a place together in town. I make pretty good money at work. Maybe we can swing it."

She threw her arms around him, feeling his body against hers.

"I'd like that, Jesse."

He kissed her and it felt as good as the first time. He sat up and lit a cigarette.

"Oh shit, look at the time!" he said. He thought for a second. "Tell you what, let's not go to work tomorrow. Let's take off. I know a swimming hole in the woods where you don't need clothes."

At this point anything Jesse McLaughlin suggested sounded good to her. They made love one more time and fell asleep.

* * *

The swimming hole was at the bottom of a steep cliff. It was a difficult walk down but well worth it. At the bottom of the hike, there was a large deep pool of clear water fed by a twenty-foot waterfall that splashed into the pool with a thunderous din. The pool was surrounded by lush greenery. You could feel the spray of the falls as you sat on the rocks surrounding the water.

"Wow, I've never seen a place so beautiful," Terri said as she looked up at all the pine trees.

They were sitting on a rock beside the deep pool. Jesse pulled two small tabs out of his pocket and swallowed one. "Here you go. It's mescaline."

She took one of the tiny pills and bit it in half. She handed the other half to Jesse and he popped that in his mouth too.

Jesse took his clothes off, walked into the pool, and swam over to the falls. He stood up. "C'mon, the water's nice." He motioned for her to come in.

It was a hot sticky morning but she was reluctant to take off her clothes.

"Do you think anyone will come?"

"No. Come under the falls with me."

His lean naked body looked blurry under the falling water as he began climbing up the rocks. She undressed and waded in quickly. She swam to the falls. He was climbing higher.

"What are you doin', Jesse?"

"I'm gonna jump. Just stay there." He went almost to the top, stood on a small rock jutting out of the cliff, and jumped into the water right beside her. His head popped up and he grabbed her. They kissed under the waterfall.

"Are you nuts? How can you do that? I'm so scared of heights."

He pulled her close. Their bodies meshed and he kissed her again. "Ya' know, when we get out, we have no towels and we're just gonna have to stand real close, just like this to dry off. We might have to do this for a long time."

She could feel every inch of his body against hers.

"Do you think you'll have trouble doing this for a long time?" she asked him.

"Well, I think I might just have a hard time with that." They both laughed and kissed some more.

They got out of the water and sat on a rock. They talked for a long while about their future. He confided that he'd always wanted to be a nurse.

"Yeah, my mom works at the VA Hospital. I always thought about it, helping those poor guys out, especially those young guys who got stuck over there in 'nam. I'd be good with them."

"That sounds wonderful, Jesse." She told him she'd always wanted to live in California. She thought it'd be a happy place to live.

He took her chin in his hand. "Hey, we'll go together. But are you happy now?"

"I'm happier than I've been in a long time." She rested her head on his shoulder until they were both dry.

They got dressed and hiked back up the cliff. Things looked beautiful before but now more so. The waterfall below had taken on a pinkish hue and she stared a little longer. The drug had taken effect and she felt a joy that could have pierced her heart.

"C'mon," he called from the car.

As she got in, *"Pinball Wizard"* blared over the radio. Jesse turned it up and they sang together.

"Hey, you ever been to Paddy Dunne's Tavern?"

"No, where is it?"

"It's just a few minutes from here. You're in for a treat."

They pulled into the parking lot. The tavern was a low clapboard structure, paint peeling from its walls.

"Wow, I've passed this place a million times. I didn't know it was a bar. It always looks so dark." She was getting excited at the prospect of a new place to drink.

"Oh, Paddy doesn't like to turn on the lights, even at night. He likes candles."

They walked in and she was impressed with the seedy atmosphere.

"Hey, Paddy, how ya' doin'?"

The old white-haired gentleman shuffled over as they sat down, candlelight glowing on his ruddy face.

"That you, Jesse? Well I haven't seen you around here in a while. What'll it be?" His Irish brogue was thick.

"I'll have a Guinness."

Paddy placed a candle down in front of them. He scrutinized Terri over his black-rimmed reading glasses, but she didn't mind at all. "Ahh, she's a pretty one, Jesse. What'll it be little lady?"

"I'll have the same."

"Ahh. A gal who likes Guinness!"

Terri felt honored she'd gained his approval. She immediately loved Paddy Dunne and his old run down place. The quaintness of the room was enhanced by the huge amount of dust and the smell of stale alcohol. Paddy's famous pickled eggs floated behind the bar in a murky liquid. A small brown and white mutt was curled up in the corner. Terri knew she wanted to come here again and again. The mescaline was having an increasing effect on her now and she was happy that time would stand still, even if just for this afternoon.

* * *

It was around seven that night when Terri walked into the kitchen. Chick was standing there and started in on her immediately.

"Where the hell were you, with that alkie?"

She stood in the doorway staring at him. His face was becoming distorted as he continued yelling.

"I don't like that guy. I don't like his looks, or that long dirty looking hair. I seen plenty of guys like him. He's a punk. I can tell the way he walks that he's no damn good. You and your sister. You really know how to pick 'em. A bunch of bums you go out with."

Terri just stood there staring. The whole scene turned surreal and comical—his face, his glasses, his nearly bald head with the tiniest hairs sprouting through, and his nose. Especially his nose.

She ran downstairs and started to laugh hysterically, secure in the fact that she'd soon be out of this house.

* * *

A few days later Jesse sat cross legged on Terri's bed looking through the paper for apartments. "Here's one. It's right up the street, at the foot of the mountain. This sounds great. Furnished and carpeted. Let's call tomorrow." She was thrilled at the thought of getting out of this basement room and moving in with Jesse.

On this particular evening, he'd brought her a couple of bottles of wine. They both loved wine and were having a great time listening to Chick and his brother Jimmy who had come to visit.

"Listen to these guys," Jesse said as he motioned up the stairs. "They're a fuckin' riot."

"I know. They're both mad at my other uncle. Listen."

They could hear Chick:

"You said it, Jimmy. He's a no good bastard. That fuckin' guy told me he uses four sticks for his tomato plants. He's crazy. You can't use four sticks. I told him he was fulla shit."

Jesse had just taken a toke of a joint and he fell back on the bed, laughing uncontrollably.

"Holy shit," he said. "These guys are killin' me."

Terri poured herself another cup of wine. Then Chick piped up again.

"He got mad at mama cause she gave us each a house and he had nothin' but he didn't do a damn thing for her. He was never any good."

Uncle Jimmy started a new story, "Hey, Chick. Remember that woman at the Wonderbar? What was her name, Fanny? She used to chase Tony Carlucci. Remember her? She was a tramp. I never saw a woman grab a guy's dick in public the way she did."

With that, Terri and Jesse almost rolled off the bed, laughing hysterically.

"Oh, I love these guys," Jesse said.

The evening went on and they finished the wine. Chick had such a good time with his brother, he forgot to throw Jesse out.

The wine and pot had taken over and Terri and Jesse passed out. When Terri woke up to daylight with Jesse next to her, she panicked. "Jesse, Jesse. Wake up. We fell asleep. It's morning."

She was having a hard time waking him. She could hear Chick walking around upstairs. She put her mouth right to Jesse's ear. "Jesse. Wake up."

He opened his eyes. "What's wrong, babe?"

"It's morning. You're not supposed to be here. My father will kill you."

"Is he up there?" He sat up and looked up the stairs, stunned.

"Yeah, and if he wants to work on his painting, we're screwed."

There was no room for Jesse under the bed. His only exit was the front door which was directly up the stairs.

"Jesse, when I say go, you run up the stairs and get outta here. I'm waiting for him to go to the bathroom."

She went to the bottom of the stairs and listened. "Okay. C'mon. There he goes. Go, go!"

Jesse ran up the stairs as quietly as possible. On his way out he had no time to think and the screen door slammed loudly.

Terri was in the kitchen now. Chick walked in.

"Who was at the door?"

"Oh, nobody," she said innocently and walked toward the bathroom.

"Wait a minute." She heard Chick's voice change. She saw him looking out the picture window.

"What the hell are you tryin' to pull?" As Chick stepped toward her, she ran into the bathroom and locked herself in. She knew what was coming next. He started to holler.

"Open this fuckin' door. If I ever see that son of a bitch here again, I'm gonna kill him. I said open the goddamn door or I'm gonna break it down."

Thoughts of the night he broke down the door to get at Sarah flooded her mind.

Nah. He won't do that.

Still, she glanced at the bathroom window to be sure it

was unlocked. Chick started pounding and the door seemed to bulge in its frame.

"Son of a bitch," he screamed.

It sounded like he was ramming his whole body against the door. She opened the window and was halfway out just as the door came down with a thundering bang hitting the tub. He grabbed her by the back of her pants in an instant. She was more than halfway out the window and she flung herself with all her might and rolled face first into the chain link fence behind their house. There was nothing else to do but get up and run like hell. By the time she was on the street in front of the house, he was screeching even louder.

"You little bastard."

She was just far enough away to say her piece, something that had been on her mind for months.

"Hey, ya' crazy old man. Where's mommy's diamond ring? I bet ya' gave it to that waitress with the big stupid hair! Ya' hear me? I know what you did, ya' son of a bitch."

She ran a few more steps but could still hear him.

"So what the hell do you care? That woman is good to me. You snotty kids don't deserve that ring."

Terri gave Chick an obscene Italian gesture and ran up the street to find Jesse.

She saw him about three blocks away and ran even faster to catch up with him.

"Jesse, wait." She was out of breath and crying. Her face was scraped and red from hitting the fence.

"Babe, what the hell happened?"

"I guess he saw you. He kinda threw me out."

"Did he do that to you? I'm gonna go back there and kick his fuckin' ass."

"No, he didn't. I fell. Don't do anything."

"But look at your face, baby. He didn't hit you, did he?"

"No. Really. I fell climbing out the bathroom window.

He could never catch me."

"C'mon. Let's go to my house so you can clean up. We need to get a place real soon. You can't put up with this shit anymore."

He pulled her close as they walked on.

Chapter 9

The apartment Jesse had seen in the paper was even nicer than it sounded in the ad. They scraped together the security deposit and first month's rent and moved right in. But Terri's joy of getting the hell away from Chick and living with Jesse was short-lived.

Within a few months, there were problems.

The stability she was looking for was nowhere to be found. Cooking for Jesse didn't keep him around and he always looked anxious when they shared a meal together. He was like a caged animal backed into a corner, fidgeting in his chair and hurrying through the meal.

She began to realize it was difficult for him to stay in one place for any length of time, unless it was a bar stool. She'd anticipated they wouldn't drink as much when they moved in together, but she was wrong.

She began to feel bothered by her own drinking, not that it interfered with her daily routine so much as it was a minor nuisance, like a mosquito buzzing around her ear when she was trying to sleep.

She had dinner prepared one Saturday evening. Jesse said he'd be coming home to eat and she was expecting him around six-thirty. But six-thirty came and went. She was getting used to eating alone now. She knew once he started drinking, he'd lose track of time. She opened a bottle of wine and sat down. The longer she waited, the more she drank. She refused to look for him in the bars. It was ironic the way she used to walk into Howie's as if she were born in the place, but now she stayed away. She didn't want to feel like she was following him around. It was like it was a contest. Whoever got to Howie's first could stay there and the other one lost. Jesse always won.

She poured herself another glass of wine, went into the living room, and put on an Aretha Franklin album. She started to sing along. Her voice was something she could always depend on. As she sang, the wine took over and she dozed off on the couch. She woke when she heard Jesse come in. She sat up.

"What time is it?"

"I don't know." He was wasted.

"I had supper ready, ya' know. You can't even call?"

"Oh, now I gotta call? I didn't know I'd be on a time schedule when we moved here. I just came home to take a shower and I'm goin' back out."

"What is this? A pit stop for you?"

"I don't have time to listen to your shit. I gotta take a shower."

There was a loud knock on the door and Terri opened it. It was one of the local cops, Officer Reilly. He looked straight past her and addressed Jesse.

"Well, well. If it isn't Mr. McLaughlin. I knew it wouldn't be long before we'd meet again. So, you recall taking out a fence on Union?"

Jesse stood there with his mouth open. "No, sir. I didn't hit any fence. I think you got the wrong car. Right, Terri?"

Before she could answer, the officer interrupted, "Mr. McLaughlin, step outside with me, please."

Jesse and Terri followed him out to the driveway.

"Take a look." The officer pointed to the front of the car where pieces of a picket fence were attached with divots of dirt on the bumper.

"McLaughlin, face the car and spread your legs." The officer handcuffed Jesse and slammed his face on the hood. The cop bent down and spoke firmly in Jesse's ear.

"Listen, you punk. You skated once already and I'm gettin' sick of your shit. This is the last time I want to run into the likes of you. Get it, McLaughlin?"

Terri ran over to the cop.

"Wait, officer. He wasn't driving the car, I was. It was me. The bartender called 'cause there was a big scene at the bar. I had to go get him. I was in a rush and we were fightin' in the car comin' back."

"That true, miss?"

"Yeah. Like I said, I was in a rush gettin' him home."

The cop released Jesse's head. "Well, I guess that explains why you're dressed like that." The cop pointed to her bare legs.

She was dressed only in her sleep shirt.

He released the handcuffs and Jesse turned around and glared at him.

"Well, it looks like you get to skate again. But like I said, you're a punk and it won't be long." He looked at Terri. "You're gonna have to pay to have that fence repaired."

"Oh, I will, Officer Reilly. I'll take care of it. I'll go over there first thing."

The cop tipped his hat to her. "Good luck, miss. You're gonna need it."

She felt bad enough already without cop humor. She went inside with Jesse, her anger mounting.

"What the hell is wrong with you? You have no self-control. You get wasted and wreck a damn fence? You want me to trust you but—"

He raised his hands calmly and stumbled toward the bedroom.

"Terri, I don't wanna fuckin' hear it."

The calmness he exuded only incited her rage.

"You don't? Well you're gonna hear it, 'cause you're an asshole. I can never trust you. I can't depend on you. You don't even know what you're doin' half the time."

He threw his clothes off and got into bed. He'd forgotten about going back out.

"Get up. Get up and listen to me, ya' jerk. Hey! Don't go to sleep. Ya' hear me?" She was shouting now but it made no difference at all.

"Shut the fuck up. I'm gonna sleep."

"Get up, Jesse. Get up. I hate you, ya' fucking asshole. You hear me?"

With that, he looked up at her. "I really don't give a

flyin' fuck, Terri." Then he rolled over and passed out.

The fury she felt welling up deep inside was unstoppable. She'd been angry before but this was intense. She wanted to hurt him and she had to muster an enormous amount of self-control herself to stave off the urge to start pounding him with her small fists. She ran into the living room. There was nowhere to hide from her anger. She ran into the kitchen. One by one, she grabbed every glass from the dark wooden cabinet and smashed them against the wall. When she had destroyed the last one, she sat down and cried. After a few moments, she felt relieved. Reaching for the dustpan, she swept up all the shards of glass. First, she began to smile a bit, and then laughed at the absurdity of the situation. Then she started singing the song she had listened to earlier, *"I Love Every Little Thing About You."*

Jesse never heard a thing.

* * *

The next morning she sat at the kitchen table reading the Sunday paper. She had snuck out of bed very early before Jesse woke up. She couldn't be near him and wanted to keep a safe distance, knowing what would happen the minute he touched her. The things he'd said to her, the whole contemptible incident, would be forgotten by the mere touch or scent of him. She was ashamed of her lack of resistance. Now she heard him moving in bed and knew he'd be awake soon. She wished she'd left the house.

A deep guttural growl came from the bedroom. Then another.

"Hey, baby. You out there?"

She didn't answer and tried to keep reading.

"Baby! C'mon back to bed and bring your ol' man a beer, will ya'?"

Still she didn't answer. She looked up. He was standing

in the doorway of the bedroom in just his boxer shorts, his hair long and wild. He looked good to her even though he was obviously hung over. He sauntered over to the fridge and got a beer. Popping it open, he took several long swallows. She looked at him and scowled. He held up the beer can.

"Nothin' like a little hair of the dog to take the edge off."

She tried to remain calm. "I wouldn't know, Jesse."

He came up behind her and started to rub her shoulders and back.

"You're not mad about anything are ya', baby?"

He knelt down in front of her and she felt herself softening.

"Look, Terri. I'm down on my knees. Don't be mad."

He stood up and pulled her to her feet. Then he kissed her, his tongue moving quickly and softly in her mouth. She reciprocated without hesitation. When he pulled away, he looked in her eyes. *Those fucking blue eyes.* Now any fight she'd had left was gone. She shoved his shoulders weakly.

"Go on. Get outta here, ya' bum. I've got a hangover. Listen, I'm sorry I said I hated you."

He opened the fridge and grabbed a bottle of orange juice.

"Ya' did? I didn't even hear that one. See, you shouldn'ta told me that. Last thing I heard was 'fuckin' asshole.'"

When he reached into the cabinet, there were no glasses to be found. "Hey can't a guy get a glass around here? Where the hell are the fuckin' glasses?"

She looked up from the paper. "I broke them."

"What the fuck?"

"I said, I broke them last night. Didn't you hear all the glass breaking?"

"You mean to tell me you broke every fuckin' glass in the house?"

"Yeah. That's right."

He smiled at her, his dimples creasing both cheeks. "You're one crazy woman. Ya' know that, baby? One crazy woman. Let's go back to bed, babe." He took her by the hand and she followed him into the bedroom.

* * *

When she woke up late Sunday afternoon, her arms and legs were wrapped around Jesse and the warmth of his body was tantalizing. She started kissing his neck, inhaling deeply. The unique aroma of his skin combined with the scent of the alcohol peaked her desire. She moved her lips down his chest and then further down over his lean lower belly. She knew he was difficult to wake up but this usually worked. He moaned as she continued and then he gently placed his hands on both sides of her head.

"Hey, babycakes. C'mere." He guided her face up to his lips and kissed her. "How ya' feelin'? Still hungover?"

"A little...Jesse, we should talk about last night."

"Yeah, we'll talk, but first let me get your mind off your hangover."

Then he kissed her again, deeply, as his hands moved over her body. He did the same with his lips and tongue. She rolled on top of him and he was inside her. Holding his arms over his head, she thrust her body wildly toward his and whispered in his ear.

"You're the only one, ya' fucker. The only one."

She wanted to hold him there forever. She came. After he let out a deep groan she buried her face into his hair, exhausted. He was breathing heavily as he embraced her tightly.

"Whoa! What got you goin'?"

"You. You got me goin'. I meant what I said. You're the only one who ever made me feel this way and I...I don't know if it's good or bad."

"Hey. Don't get crazy on me now. Hold on. I'll be right back." He got up and went into the kitchen to get another beer. Naked, he stood next to the bed and chugged down most of the can. Then he hopped back under the covers.

"It's Sunday. Let's stay in bed the rest of the day." He knocked the phone off the night table. "We don't need that fuckin' thing."

He made her laugh. "You're gonna break the phone."

"Who fuckin' cares?"

He lit a cigarette and laid his head back on the pillow. She stroked his hair off his face.

"I'm sorry about last night, Jesse. I'm sorry I called you a 'fuckin' asshole' and I'm sorry I broke all the glasses."

"Ahhh. Ya' already apologized. Anway, shit like that happens to people all the time."

"But not to me, Jesse. Not to me."

He finished his cigarette, put both arms around her, and drew her face close to his.

"Hey, after we spend the day in bed, let's go get somethin' to eat and then maybe drive down to Paddy's Tavern. You liked his place, right? He'll have those candles goin' again. Whaddya think?"

What did she think? Spending a whole day and night alone with Jesse, without his drinking friends around, seemed like a gift. She loved being with him and matching him drink for drink even though the outcomes of their drinking bouts together were becoming more and more unpredictable. She was a bit worried about work.

"Let's do it. But don't forget, tomorrow's Monday. We both have work tomorrow."

"Not necessarily." He reached into the night table drawer and pulled out two large white tablets.

"Look what I got last night."

"Quaaludes?"

"Yeah. Here." He handed her the large white tablet and his beer. She'd never done them before but she'd try anything once.

"It'll make ya' feel real relaxed. And after we spend a few more hours in bed, you're gonna feel really *good.*"

She downed the pill with a large swig of beer.

"Okay, but I really can't miss work."

He began kissing her and they made love again.

She had no idea how long they'd been at it, but the drug intensified the touch of his lips, fingers, and tongue. It felt as if he were reaching into her soul. Helped along by the sweet intoxication of the quaalude combined with the alcohol, she came over and over. Finally she fell back on the pillow and sighed.

Jesse sat up and lit another cigarette. It was now about eight o'clock.

"Oh my god, Jesse, aren't you exhausted? I feel a little woozy."

"Nah. C'mon. Let's go out."

Terri got out of bed but when she tried to stand, she fell to the floor.

"Hey, baby. What's wrong?"

She began laughing hysterically. "I can't stand up. You think it was that pill or too much sex? I can't go out like this."

He pulled her up gently. She was still giggling. "My legs are like rubber. They don't work."

"You need somethin' to eat. C'mon, we'll go get some pizza and then go to Paddy's." He held her tight. "Hang on to me and walk around till you feel better. Too much sex! You're funny."

The walking seemed to help and she made it to the bathroom. When she returned, he was ready to go.

"Where's the keys? I'll drive."

"They're on the dresser." She had to admit, he was in a lot better shape than she was. She wondered how he could keep going after the feats he'd just performed.

* * *

When they walked into Paddy's, the candles were lit and the hard boiled eggs floated in the large jar behind the bar. Paddy shuffled over to them and laughed.

"Well, Jesse, long time no see." He held a candle to Terri's face. "And your lady friend again. What'll it be?"

"Two stouts, Paddy."

Paddy poured them slowly and placed them down.

Jesse held his glass up to her. "Did you ever see a more beautiful sight? Watch this stout settle."

She stared at the glass. The frothy liquid created patterns as it settled in the glass.

"Now, that's a real work of art," Jesse said.

As they drank, Terri began to think about what Officer Reilly had said. She'd been wanting to ask him, but they'd been too busy this afternoon. Now Jesse was in a mellow mood.

"Jesse. Remember when the cop said, 'You skated once before?' What did he mean?"

"Officer Reilly? Well, if you wanna know…"

He picked up his beer and took a long swig. Then he looked her straight in the eye.

"When I was on dope, I had a lot of run-ins with the cops, but he was talkin' about the night Flynn died. You said ya' knew him, right?"

"I knew of him."

"Well, he was my age. We knew each other since we were ten. We did everything together when we were kids. We got into a little mischief, ya' know? Anyway, Flynn was real gutsy. He was always the guy to jump from the highest place. Ya' know the crik' behind the dye factory?"

She nodded.

"Well, there were three places to jump in—Gorilla Rock, Aces, and Diamonds. Only a few guys in town ever jumped from Diamonds, but he did. He'd *only* jump from there. He was a crazy kid. And we did other crazy shit, like playin' chicken on the train trestle. I once saw him put a cigarette out on his tongue. He was some tough dude. You ever see a guy chew glass?"

She giggled. "No. Never. I can't say I've ever seen such

a thing."

"Well, Flynn...he could chew glass. He'd take a bite right outta a bar glass and chew it. It was something to see. So anyway, we were kind of crazy, so it was no surprise that we started shootin' dope together. I guess we were a bad influence on each other. Kinda' like you and me."

He gave her a wink. Terri didn't laugh. She felt there was too much truth in it.

"Anyway, we'd been shootin' dope for a while. We used to go down by the river. Ya' know, over by the train trestle. Know where I mean?"

"Sure I know. I was afraid to go there. Thought I'd get stuck on it. I'm such a coward."

He gave her a smile but she saw his eyes go dark.

"Anyway, we went down there to shoot some dope, just me and Flynn. But we got some bad shit from Romeo. I don't know what it was cut with, but ya' know how your legs felt a while ago, real rubbery? Well, this stuff we shot, it was like you couldn't move.

"A few minutes after shootin' up, I was frozen on the ground. I was sittin' down, but after I shot that dope, I just fell back and I couldn't move. And I had a real sick feelin' that I never had before with heroin, kind of like the sky was spinnin' around. Or I was spinnin'. So I was just layin' there and I asked Flynn after he shot the dope how he felt. He said he felt okay. He got up and said he had to take a piss. But somehow, that shit must have hit him as he crossed the trestle and he got stuck there.

"I was startin' to black out. At one point, I really thought I was dyin'. There was nothin' but the dark sky, the stars, and that feelin' of bein' paralyzed. I was goin' in and out of consciousness. At one point, I heard the train whistle blowin' and the next thing I knew, the cops were draggin' me into the police car. It was just startin' to get light out. They took me to the station and that's when the bad part started. That's when I found out what happened to Flynn, that he was hit by a train. The cops tried to get me to tell them who sold us the dope. They started tellin' me awful things about Flynn's body, the way it looked. They thought they'd get me to talk. But they had nothin' on me, and I knew it.

"So I didn't tell them anything. But they kept it up for a while. They were so fuckin' worried about where that dope came from. They didn't care if my best friend was just hit by a train. That's the part that got me. So that's what Reilly was talkin' about."

He shook his head sadly.

"Ya' know, Flynn tempted those trains so many times when we were kids and got away with it. The train finally won."

Terri was frozen to the bar stool, mesmerized by his story.

"I really miss Flynn," Jesse said. "He was a great guy."

"That's horrible. I'm so sorry." She leaned over, ran her fingers through his hair, and kissed him.

"Thanks, baby. Paddy, two more stouts over here."

At that moment, she felt an intense wave of love. She felt like she was being sucked deeper and deeper into some kind of vortex, but it felt so good, she didn't want to escape.

Chapter 10

It was Christmas Eve day and everyone at Howie's bar was filled with the spirit of the season. Christmas was a good excuse to drink as much as they could possibly tolerate. Terri had been living with Jesse in the small apartment for well over a year now.

Jesse's thigh felt warm against hers as she swallowed her vodka and club. It made no difference to her that the cheap decorations were hastily thrown about, the multicolored garland falling down in some places over the shiny liquor bottles. John Lennon was singing *"Happy Christmas (War Is Over)"* on the jukebox.

Jesse squeezed her thigh as he often did before he spoke. "Hey, babe. Don't you have to get to the store? You gotta cook dinner for your dad, remember?"

Terri was lost in Lennon's voice and moaned at the thought of what she had to do. She'd invited Chick for Christmas Eve Dinner. It was their second Christmas without her mother. He'd become accustomed to the traditional Italian fish meal and she was trying to be nice. Now she wondered if she could make it to the market and the liquor store and still maintain the perfect alcohol buzz she'd spent the past few hours cultivating. She had to make this quick. Downing her drink, she kissed Jesse's cheek and got up. "Yeah, I better hurry. Will you try to make it to dinner, please?"

"Sure, sure, babe. I'll be there, but I ain't eatin' that squid stuff. I'll just have spaghetti."

"Okay, see you later."

She made it back to the apartment still feeling great. She switched on the stereo and poured herself a glass of white wine, downing her first glass before attacking the chore of squid cleaning.

She rinsed each piece of fish under cool running water. She giggled at the sight of the water-filled bodies, dancing the squid around as Elton John sang *"Honky Cat."* Then, realizing the water-filled squid looked just like a condom, she doubled over with laughter.

As she reached into the squid's long cold body to remove the transparent membrane, she longed to be back at the bar with Jesse's thigh touching hers while they drank. Agitated that she'd offered to cook tonight, she wiped her hands dry and poured herself more wine. Her dad would be here in an hour. She wondered if Jesse would show up at all.

By the time Chick arrived promptly at seven, she felt pretty well-lit, but she knew she could pull this dinner off. Terri recalled the days she'd sang in clubs drunk as hell and no one seemed to notice. Maybe it was a gift, she thought, that her small body could handle so much booze. She had quickly rinsed with mouthwash before Chick knocked on the door.

"Hi, Daddy. Merry Christmas." She hugged him.

"Hey, how's my little goil?"

He was dressed in his polyester best, complete with a tie and shiny patent leather shoes with gold accents.

"Dad, you didn't have to dress up. It's just us."

He squeezed her cheek hard. "I like to dress up for my baby." He glanced around the apartment. "So who's here? Just you?"

"Yeah. Just me for now."

Chick sneered, "Where's the Mick?"

Terri shook her finger at him. "That's not nice, Daddy." Then she caught herself. Her words were slightly slurred. Very carefully she said, "C'mon in the kitchen. I'm cooking."

He sat at the table and watched her. "So, ya' been drinkin'? You can't fool yer daddy ya' know."

"Just trying to have a Merry Christmas, Dad. Doesn't everybody? Mommy used to love a few drinks at Christmastime. Remember? Remember the eggnog she used to make in the store? It was so strong." Terri remembered sticking her finger in her mother's shot glass full of gold whiskey as a kid. She loved how it burned the back of her throat as she swallowed.

Chick nodded. "Yeah, I remember. Your mother loved the holidays and she loved to have a good time." Then his tone changed and he pointed at her. "Your mother was a good woman and don't ya' forget it. Hey I got something for ya'."

He reached into his suit pocket. She knew it was a hundred-dollar bill in a bank holiday envelope.

"Here, open it." He waved the envelope in the air. "And don't forget. This is the real thing."

She took it. Inside the card was Ben Franklin's face beaming through an oval window. On the card, Chick had written. "This is it! Merry Christmas, Love, Daddy." He had drawn arrows pointing to Ben's face.

"Thanks, Dad." She bent down and kissed his cheek. "We can really...I mean *I* can really use it."

"Hey, whaddya' cookin'? Ya' makin' squibs?"

"It's squid, Dad. Yeah, sauce with squid. I made an antipasto, too."

"Good, 'cause I'm hungry. Let's eat."

"Let's wait a bit. Jesse's supposed to be here."

"You said we'd eat at seven-thirty and I wanna eat! I can't eat late. You know I get heartburn."

"Okay, okay. We'll eat."

Terri banged the platter of antipasto down on the table. "Here, start with this." She felt herself getting irritated at both men and poured herself more wine.

"So, what are ya' gettin' to be, a wino? Yer always drinkin' wine."

"No, you're wrong. I drink beer and vodka too."

"Hey don't get wise wit' me, little goil." Chick looked around the small apartment. "This ain't a bad place. Your mother wouldn't like it though."

"Why? You just said it was nice."

"She wouldn't like you livin' with that guy. Ya' know what I mean?"

Terri refused to feel guilty. "But it doesn't bother you?"

"Nah, what the hell do I care? Yer old enough to do what you want. So when's the Mick comin'?"

"Don't call him that! How would you like it if somebody called you a wop all the time?"

Chick looked up from his plate. "I been called that plenty of times. Wop, guinea, dago. You think I give a shit?"

Terri took a small amount of pasta from the pot and threw a little sauce over it. She offered it to her dad for tasting just as her mom had always done.

"Here, Dad. Taste the pasta."

She watched as he slurped the mouthful.

"It's good. C'mon. Let's eat some macaroni."

Terri placed a large bowl of pasta and squid on the table. Chick's eyes widened behind his glasses as he served himself, spilling sauce all over the tablecloth.

"Now, that's what I call a dish of macaroni."

Terri helped herself and watched him eat. Chick was a messy, noisy eater and her mother wasn't there to tell him to wipe his chin.

"Dad, wipe your chin. There's sauce all over it."

He followed her order and continued slurping and gulping down the pasta. She looked down into her dish. Her appetite was dwindling.

"Hey, Dad. Why didn't you want me to invite Uncle Jimmy? I have enough food. He's alone too."

Chick waved her off.

"Nah. Let him eat with his own daughter. He's gettin' on my noives anyway. Ya' know what he said to me the other night?"

"No, what?" She forced herself to swallow another bite of pasta.

"I says to him, 'Hey, Jimmy, you wanna come over and watch the fight tonight?' And ya' know what he says to me? He says, 'No, Chick, not tonight. I feel like bein' by myself tonight.' The noive of that bastard. So I said, 'Go ahead. See what the fuck I care. And don't bother callin' me for breakfast tomorrow either.' Then I hung up on him."

Terri sighed and pushed her plate away.

"Well, that's a nice holiday story."

Chick scowled. "Don't get fresh with me. I don't have to listen to your crap either."

As she cleared the table, she realized this evening would probably be filed in her memory as one of the worst holidays ever. It was beginning to rival the Christmas Eve her mother didn't come home from work. Terri was ten then and recalled asking Chick repeatedly, "When is Mommy coming home?"

That Christmas morning, as Terri and her sister eagerly opened their gifts, Genevieve Micelli watched them through two black eyes as she sipped her morning coffee. The girls were told it was just a little car accident and nothing more was ever said.

"You gonna make coffee? Got any cookies?" Chick's voice broke her quiet reflection.

"Yeah, here." Terri dropped a plate of festively decorated cookies on the table.

"Where's the coffee?"

"Just a minute. Jeez, I can't do two things at once."

She was anxious for him to leave now and she knew he'd leave immediately after dessert. The more he talked, the more she drank. She poured herself more wine and placed a cup of coffee in front of Chick.

"Be careful. It's hot."

As she began to wash the dishes, she thought of Jesse and wondered how late he'd be. Then she looked over at Chick just as he took his first sip of coffee.

Suddenly, he slammed the mug down, the hot liquid splashing on his hand and the tablecloth. With his other hand, he placed his index finger into his mouth and flipped his upper denture onto the table.

"Jesus Christ! Cocksucker. Sonofabitch! This coffee's

too fuckin' hot. What are ya' tryin' to do to me for Christ's sake?"

Terri stared in disbelief at the spilled coffee and the false teeth.

"Dad, get those teeth off the table. I told you the coffee was hot. It's supposed to be hot. Couldn't ya' wait?"

He pointed at her. "Don't talk to me like that. I don't have to take your shit."

He snatched his teeth off the table and headed for the bathroom.

"I gotta rinse my teeth and then I'm goin' home."

He stormed into the bathroom and slammed the door.

The front door opened and Jesse lurched in, carrying two full shopping bags of presents. As drunk as she was, she took one look at his deadened eyes and knew he'd drunk himself into oblivion.

"Oh shit, Jesse. Where the hell were you?"

He dropped the packages and strutted over to her. Pushing her gently against the wall, he leaned in for a kiss.

She pushed him away. "Cut it out. My father's in the bathroom. What's all this stuff?"

He gave her a sly grin. "I was just out shopping and gettin' myself some of that Christmas cheer, baby. Got you a lotta nice presents, too."

"Oh yeah? With what money?"

"I took the money out of your dresser."

"You stupid asshole. You spent the rent money? Oh shit."

"Ahhhh. Don't worry about it, baby."

Just then the bathroom door swung open and Chick stomped out. He shot Jesse a disapproving look.

"Oh, Jesus Christ! Look at this!"

Jesse staggered over to Chick and stuck out his hand.

"Hey, Chick, my man. Merry Christmas. How ya' doin'? You wanna beer?"

Chick pushed by without shaking his hand. "Nah, I don't want nothin'. I'm gettin' the hell outta here."

"Are you really leavin', Dad?"

"Damn right I am." Chick grabbed his overcoat and hat as he raced toward the door, slamming it so hard that a small picture fell to the floor. Terri sat down at the table and sighed.

Jesse started laughing.

"What the hell is so funny?"

He pointed to the picture on the floor. He looked so innocent and happy, standing there laughing.

"Why's everybody so mad? It's fuckin' Christmas, ain't it?"

Terri stood up and slammed her hands on the table.

"Why's everybody so mad? You really wanna know?"

Jesse shook his head no.

"Well, you're gonna hear it. First of all, I had to eat with that guy which is an ordeal so disgusting you can't imagine. Then after dinner, he slams his false teeth on the table which makes my stomach do flips. And now *you* come home so fuckin' drunk you can hardly stand. And you spent the goddamn rent money!"

Jesse began laughing hysterically.

"False teeth on the table? Shit. That's fuckin' funny!"

"You think it's funny? Between you and him, I can't stand it anymore. You're a couple of fuckin' assholes."

Her anger made her stomach churn. Or was it the wine? Tears welled up.

With that, Jesse stood up laughing. He wiggled his fingers by his ears.

"Well, all I have to say to that is...booga, booga."

"You fucking bastard."

Terri picked a mug up off the table and threw it at him, hitting him in the chest.

"Ow! Ya' crazy bitch. Ya' fuckin' nut. I come home in a good mood and I gotta hear this crap and get hit with shit. You're just like your dad."

She composed herself enough to pour another glass of wine. She downed half of it in a quick gulp.

That did it.

The buzz she'd had all night was gone. She'd crossed into that other realm of drunkenness. Her pleasant anesthetic state had given way to intense nausea. She had more fight in her but was rendered speechless by an onslaught of sickness.

"Oh...Oh shit." She ran into the bathroom and locked the door. Falling to her knees, she thought it funny that this poison she was about to spew forth was like the anger she was feeling. There was no stopping it. She retched into the bowl several times, closing her eyes tightly. She hated this but also knew she'd do it again and again. As she puked, she wondered if American Standard had a monopoly on toilets. *It would be nice to read something else for a change.*

As she shifted her weight to get up, she fell backwards into the tub, hitting her head hard against the wall.

Jesse knocked on the door. "You okay, baby? You need help?"

"No, no. I don't need *your* help. I'm fine."

She pulled herself up. As she brushed her teeth, she thought that puking was one step away from death. She lurched into the bedroom and fell onto the bed. Jesse followed her.

He looked down at her and spoke sweetly.

"Aren't you gonna take your clothes off?"

"I can't. The room is spinnin'."

"Here. Gimme your foot." He took off her shoes and gently pulled off her jeans. Then he placed his hand tenderly under her head and slowly pulled off her shirt. He tucked her in and kissed her forehead.

"Jesse, what am I gonna do? How come you never throw up?"

He laughed, "I've had a lot more practice than you."

Maybe all she needed to do was keep drinking, keep practicing, until she got it right.

She heard Jesse leave the apartment. She vaguely

remembered murmuring, "Don't go…please…don't."

But there were no feelings of anger or loneliness now. Terri had passed out immediately after the front door closed.

* * *

Terri and Sharon sat drinking wine on the balcony at Sharon's place. The months had rolled by and it was summer now. Things weren't getting any better with Jesse.

Terri leaned her head back against the apartment house wall and looked up. The summer daylight was lingering but the sky was becoming thick with clouds. The FM radio was playing Maria Muldaur's *"Midnight at the Oasis."*

Terri turned her face to Sharon. "I don't think I can pick my head up. Look. It's stuck to the wall."

Sharon laughed. Terri needed to talk about Jesse. She loved the way Sharon allowed her to go on and on about him without preaching or sounding condescending.

"I don't know why I stay with him. He's so nasty when he drinks and so unreliable. He's been gone since noon with my car. I don't know where the hell he is. What time is it?"

"I think it's about eight."

"Know what he did the other night?"

Sharon looked over at Terri.

"We were in Mike's Bar on Main Street, ya' know, that old man bar, and I *thought* we were having a good time. I mean we weren't fighting or anything. We'd been at the bar for a few hours. So he goes to the bathroom and he doesn't come back. He just left me sitting there."

"Where did he go?"

"The bastard climbed out the bathroom window and he just leaves me there at the bar. This is the kinda shit I put up with. Then we have a huge fight, but when we make up…well…it's really beautiful. It's like drinkin' real sweet water. We made up that night and I had my head on his chest and I was breathin' in deep cause he has this smell…"

"What?"

"Yeah, he's got this smell. I'm not kiddin'. It's usually beer and cigarettes but it's mixed with somethin' else…his own scent. Like musky and sweet. Anyway, I was breathin' him in and I was pretty much in heaven, ya' know? That's when I was thinkin', when we make love after a big fight, it's like real sweet water. Remember when we were little and we were runnin' around your yard on a real hot day, and then we'd go inside and your mom had this beer pitcher filled with ice water? Remember when we drank that water how sweet it was?"

"Yeah, I remember."

"Well, that's what it's like when he touches me after we fight, just like drinkin' that ice cold water. But then we start the whole mess over again. What the hell is wrong with me?"

"I don't know. Maybe it's 'cause he's so good-lookin' and he's…"

Terri threw her hands up. "Yeah, but what good is that if he's a mean drunk? But you're right. He's got somethin'. It's a thaaaaaang."

Sharon's eyes lit up. "Really big one, ay?"

Terri smacked her on the shoulder. "You're bad. It's not that. Well, not *just* that. It's something else, a thing I can't resist. It's not physical, but then *it is* real physical."

"So he's really good in bed?"

"Yeah. The best. He'd do anything to make me feel good. Not a selfish lover at all. But he's got a hold on me. Like that Smokey Robinson song. That's a real sexy song, don't ya' think?"

Sharon sighed, "You're so lucky. Howie and I never had that. And you'll probably never meet a guy who does this to you again. Sounds real nice to me."

"Yeah, nice and scary. I never know what's gonna happen next and it's real scary to want somebody that bad.

It's an addiction. That's what it is. Maybe someday when I'm fifty years old, I'll run into Jesse and that thing will still be there. It's like he owns a piece of my soul or somethin' and he always will."

It started to rain—a few large drops at first and then the sky opened up. They backed up against the wall and watched the downpour.

"Look! Isn't that your car pullin' into the lot?"

Terri walked to the edge of the balcony and looked over the railing, ignoring the fact she was getting soaked.

"Holy shit. That bastard. He lent my car to Romeo. Why would he do such a thing? And why is Romeo comin' in here?"

"Ah. He's probably comin' to see the guys downstairs. Ya' know, those young guys? I think they're shootin' dope."

Terri sat back down. "We're gonna have to follow him when he leaves. I need to get my car." She raised her voice. "That stupid fuckin' asshole."

"Oh, don't get upset. We'll follow him, you'll find Jesse, and you can get your car. Hey, Terri, you ever shoot dope?"

"No. Are you kiddin'? That's a drug I never wanted to mess around with. Why?" Terri knew Sharon well and began to worry.

"I was just wonderin'. Just was always fascinated with it myself."

"Don't get any ideas. Look at Romeo. Why don't ya' ask him? He's a big junkie."

"Mmm. I'd like to get to know him a little better. He's really fine. If dope's so bad for you, why does he look so damn good?"

"Don't talk crazy. Look. There's Romeo gettin' in the car. C'mon, let's go." Terri stumbled as she got up. She pulled Sharon by the hand.

By the time they got in Sharon's car, Romeo was making a right turn at the end of the street toward Main.

They followed him a few car lengths behind. Romeo pulled over and parked the car in front of the Paradise Lounge, a bar in the black section of town. She never went in there but sometimes a few white guys would get wasted and go down and socialize with old high school friends.

Sharon drove around the block a few times. The more they circled the block, the angrier Terri became.

"Let me out in front."

Sharon stopped the car.

"Don't go in there, Terri. You've had too much to drink."

Terri patted Sharon's knee. "Do you think I'd go in this place any other way? Don't wait. I'm gettin' those goddamn keys."

Before Sharon could say anymore, Terri jumped out of the car and went inside. Earth, Wind & Fire's *"Shining Star"* was blasting from speakers somewhere at the back of the room. She saw nothing in that bar but Jesse. There he sat, Romeo on one side, and a big blond on the other. The girl had her arm around Jesse's neck and was whispering in his ear. He was oblivious to everything around him. Kevin was there too, but Terri never gave him a second glance. She walked up behind Jesse and tapped him hard on the shoulder. When he looked at her, his sluggish eyes gave him away. She tried to remain calm, but could feel the rage building deep inside her like a painful poison.

"What are you doin'?" she asked calmly.

"What the fuck does it look like I'm doin'?" His tone matched his look.

"It looks like you're drunk and driving my car around town. It looks like you're with Romeo and this slutty blond girl. Now give me my keys, *asshole*."

He stood up and raised his hands as if being held up.

"Okay, okay. You want the keys? Here's your fuckin' keys." He tossed them to the ground and they landed at her feet. She felt a sense of shame as she picked them up.

She stared into his murky eyes.

"C'mon, Jesse. Let's go. Get in the car."

"Oh no. I ain't goin' no place with you. You got your keys. See ya' later."

He quietly turned and sat back at the bar. The calmness he exuded when he was totally lost in his drunken state angered her more. She knew the sane thing would be to leave. But there was enough booze in her to do exactly what her emotions dictated. She spoke loudly in his ear as he sat there.

"Get up and get in the fuckin' car."

He quickly got up and grabbed her firmly by the shoulders.

"I told you to get the fuck outta here. You don't belong here. Get out." He released her, but when he did, he gave her a weak shove toward the door.

"Don't push me, you bastard."

Her voice echoed through the bar.

"That's it. That's enough." The older black man behind the bar spoke up. "Go 'wan. Go 'wan now. I don't want no trouble in my place. Take it out on the street. You both gotta go."

Jesse quickly snatched his money off the bar.

"See ya', JJ," Romeo called out as Jesse lurched out to the street.

Terri followed him out and she heard one of the black girls say, "Yeah, he sho' is a pretty white boy, but he ain't nuthin' but trouble."

Terri was surprised to see Jesse climb straight into the car. He fell back into the passenger seat, dropped his head back, and closed his eyes. She jumped into the driver's seat and hurried off, as if she might lose her precious cargo. She needed to talk fast before he passed out.

"Who the hell was that girl?"

Without moving a muscle or opening his eyes, he spoke, "Don't start, Terri."

"No? I wanna know who she was. She was all over you."

"You really wanna know? She's just some fuckin' junkie I buy pot from."

"Yeah? Why was she all over you then?"

"Terri. Shut up and let me outta this fuckin' car."

She kept driving.

"I said stop the damn car, you crazy bitch."

She stepped on the gas and ran a stop sign, fully aware she was pushing things too far. She was drunk enough to do that. She enjoyed disturbing his drunken peacefulness.

"Ya' know, you're fuckin' nuts. Stop this fuckin' car and let me out."

There was a red light ahead. She wanted to run it but there was a car coming. She stopped.

"I'm outta' here." Jesse jumped out and started walking. She started screaming.

"Get back in the car! Jesse!"

The sidewalks were glistening after the storm. He glanced at her briefly and then disappeared into a backyard. She parked, got out and started after him.

"Jesse!" she hollered. By this time she was crying. "Wait. Come back, Jesse!"

Desperation came over her. She wondered why she just couldn't let him run. She could see his silhouette in the next yard. He ran a little further, then turned and stopped, facing her. He raised his hands now gesturing her to come.

"C'mon, Terri. I ain't gonna run no more."

Don't do it. Just let him go. Once her anger surfaced, there was no turning back, no control. She ran at him full force, her arms flailing and her fists ready. He grabbed her wrists, but she threw him off balance. They both fell to the muddy ground. He rolled on top of her and pinned her arms down as she fought to release herself. His face was right in front of hers, his blue eyes shining in the dark night.

"What the fuck do you want from me? Huh? You're fuckin' crazy, ya' know it?"

"Shut up. I hate you."

"No, ya' don't. Listen to me! You gotta know when to back off. You hear me? You gotta know when the fuck to leave me alone."

She was still struggling beneath him. "You're a mean nasty bastard and you don't care about nobody."

"Yeah. That's right. That's what I'm about. Take it or leave it."

She started to cry and turned her head away. She couldn't look at those eyes anymore. They were both quiet for a few moments. She could feel his damp hair on her face. He broke the silence.

"I'm gettin' real tired of this shit." His voice was cracking. He lowered his lips to her ear. "What the hell are we gonna do, baby?"

Then he kissed her hard. The feeling of his body on hers caused a fire deep inside her that was frightening.

She squeezed him tightly as they continued making out, even though they were laying in the mud in a strange backyard.

He whispered in her ear, "I wanna fuck you, baby."

A deluge of confusing emotions hit her at once. She knew at this moment she wanted *him* too.

"C'mon, babe. Let's go home," he whispered in a deep voice.

They got in the car and looked at each other, both covered in mud. They laughed. She watched the dimples crease his cheeks.

Jesse squeezed her leg. "Baby, do you realize we just managed to get thrown out of the sleaziest bar in town?"

She laughed all the way back to the apartment, forgetting her rage and feeling nothing but love and desire.

Chapter 11

The next morning, Terri woke up and was surprised to find Jesse in the kitchen. She usually woke before him. He was bare-chested and his legs were stretched out under the table clad in tight Levi's. He was flipping through the pages of a newspaper with one hand, the other was wrapped firmly around a Budweiser. *"Quadrophenia"* was bouncing off the walls. When she walked by, he swung his legs out from under the table and pulled her down on his lap. She ran her hand through his hair which had now grown down past his shoulders.

"Jeez, Jesse. Let me get some coffee. I need it."

"Still love me, baby?"

"Yes, now let me up."

He held on to her arm. "No. Not till ya' kiss me like you want me real bad."

Was there any other way? She kissed him the way he kissed her last night when they were laying in the mud.

"There. Now let me up so I can cook you some breakfast."

"That was real nice," he said as he released her.

As she busied herself with the frying pan, she glanced over at him. His dark hair was hanging down over his face as he read the paper.

"Why are you drinkin' so early? It's only ten in the morning."

"Don't worry about it, okay? Anyway, it's Saturday. You think you'll be drinkin' today?"

"I guess so. Maybe later. Why?"

"What time?"

"I don't know, Jesse. What's your *point?*"

"My point is…I feel lousy and this beer is makin' me feel good. You feel lousy but you're not drinkin' till later. What does it matter if I want to start feelin' good now?"

Before she got a chance to answer, the phone rang.

"Hi, Jeff. What's going on? Really? When? Wow. I'd

love it. I'll need to rehearse a little. Okay. Thanks. Bye."

She turned to Jesse forgetting about their little discussion.

"Guess what? I'm gonna sing. Next Friday night. At the Rusty Rail. That was Jeff, from our old band. We rehearse tomorrow."

"Wow, baby that's great. I finally get to hear you sing some rock and roll."

"Yeah." She was pleased. Maybe this was just what she needed. She knew her self-esteem was taking somewhat of a beating in this relationship and she felt singing was just the thing to lift her spirits. She put the plate of eggs on the table and Jesse pulled her down on his lap again.

"I'm real happy for you, baby. I can't wait to hear you sing."

She looked in his eyes, thinking of California again. "We're still goin' to California, right?"

"Sure. I told ya'. We'll go together. There's nothin' holdin' me here. I promise."

"Jesse, do you love me?"

"Ya' *know* I do."

"If that's true, do something for me."

"What's that?"

"Stop drinking."

He pushed her off his lap. "Oh shit. Here we go again."

"Why not?"

"Because I don't have a problem with it. You do. You got all the problems. You're the one who breaks shit. Maybe *you* should stop drinkin'."

Their joy was always short-lived. It was a relationship held together by a taut strand of obsession nearly at breaking point. Neither of them understood what was happening to them.

She cleared the table wondering if she were losing her sanity along with her self-control.

* * *

Jesse drove Terri's car to the gig at the Rusty Rail. They sipped from the bottles of Beck's they'd taken along for the ride.

"You nervous, baby?"

"A little, but I'll be okay when the music starts."

They parked the car and Jesse pulled some money out of his wallet. He threw the wallet into the glove compartment.

The club was a small, dingy smoke-filled room with a tiny dance floor. As they walked in, the band was already set up. Sharon and Howie were there and some other locals.

They made their way to the bar and Jesse ordered drinks. They were both on their way to a pretty good drunk. She had never been on stage sober but felt confident that no one was ever aware of that fact.

She kissed Jesse. "It's time to start."

"Sure. Knock 'em dead, babe."

Terri made her way to the small stage and looked over the set list. There were a couple of Bonnie Raitt songs, one Aretha Franklin number, 'Move Over' by Janis Joplin, and a couple of blues songs.

"Ready?" Jeff asked from behind the drums.

"Sure. Let's go."

As always when the music started, the effects of the alcohol seemed to magically disappear. She sang through the set with a confident air, pouring soul and emotion into the songs. Whenever she performed, she was unaware of her surroundings. It was always just her voice and the music. Everything else seemed unreal. But by the time she started the last song tonight, the joy of being alone with the music was intruded upon. She hadn't looked for Jesse at all while she was singing. Now she saw him and it was becoming difficult to concentrate on the words. She lost her feel for the music. Her whole being was focused on just one vision.

Jesse stood backed up against the wall with Sharon in

front of him, her arms around his neck. Their faces were almost touching. Then she saw him slowly wrap his arms around Sharon's waist. Terri could almost hear their laughter over the pulsing amps. She suddenly had no more to give. She couldn't wait for the song to end. When it did, she bolted off the stage toward the bar.

The crowd was kind, despite the fact that she totally detached during the last song. Howie stopped her and handed her a bottle of Bud. "Hey, you sounded great."

She looked at him. Her mind was racing. She pointed toward Sharon and Jesse.

"Don't you see what's going on?"

She never understood Howie. Nothing bothered him. She envied him. He shrugged his shoulders and turned away.

She quickly chugged half the beer. She was losing control. The fact that they were still at it angered her more. The fury and jealousy were too much to hold back. She walked over to them. She tapped him on the shoulder with more force than she intended. He quickly turned to her.

"Hey, Terri. You sounded great."

"How the fuck would you know?" Sharon slipped away and joined Howie at the bar. Sharon's part in this was irrelevant to Terri. Jesse stared at her from his drunken abyss. She knew she had to sweeten her tone to get him to come outside with her.

"I need to talk to you. C'mon." She took him by the hand and he sheepishly followed, too drunk to resist. As soon as they were out in the parking lot, she turned to him.

"What the hell is wrong with you? Don't you even know what you're doin' anymore?"

"What the fuck are you talkin' about now?"

"What? I saw you. You and Sharon up against the wall."

"I don't know what the fuck you're—"

"Stop it! Stop it now, Jesse!" She was screaming. "You're nothing but a fuckin' drunk. You might as well shoot heroin again, cause you're still nuthin' but a fuckin' junkie."

"Shut up. Don't ever say that to me, you cunt!"

"You fucker! Don't you ever call me that."

He looked her straight in the eyes as he calmly spoke.

"I said...you're a *cunt*."

Shaking with anger, she began flailing her arms, smacking him hard across both sides of his face several times. Her handprints showed red on his cheeks as he grabbed her wrists. Upset about being restrained, and though her mouth was dry from the alcohol, she threw her head back and spit in his face.

Suddenly calm, he said, "Terri, relax. Go sit in the car."

She instantly felt foolish. She ran over to her car and jumped in the driver's seat. She was sobbing and laid her head on the steering wheel. Terri wanted all these demons to leave her. Inexplicably, she wanted to tell him she was sorry and needed him to hold her.

Jesse knocked on the car window. She opened the window to apologize, tell him it would all be okay. But before she could speak, she felt it—a sting, not painful at all, yet she found herself lying across the passenger seat. She put her hands over her face. Stunned, she had no idea why she was lying down. Her hands were too wet for just tears. She looked at them and saw blood.

She got out of the car and began walking around in small circles. She couldn't see out of her left eye.

Jesse was walking toward the highway. Then he was surrounded. It seemed the whole bar had emptied and Terri heard someone say "Hit me, you motherfucker. You wanna hit somebody? Hit me."

Terri jumped back in the car. She couldn't see or think straight. She grabbed some tissues and put them over her eye. Just as she was about to pull away, a cop knocked on her window.

"We need to know if you want to press charges, miss."

"Just keep him away from me. I gotta go."

She pulled out of the parking lot and drove home. When she got to the apartment she began packing her clothes. She knew it was impossible to go on living here with Jesse.

* * *

The following evening, Terri sat in the Shea's kitchen.

"Close your eye," Patty told her as she bent over her and applied makeup. "When I get through with you, nobody will even see this shiner."

Terri looked up at Patty with her good eye. Marge chimed in as she dried the dishes. "Well I hope you learned your lesson and you're through with him."

Terri always listened to Marge. She was the voice of reason throughout Terri's teenage years. She had also helped her through the crazy time since her mother died.

"Don't worry. I moved some of my stuff to Sharon's this morning. She asked me to move in."

"Okay. You're done. Here look." Patty handed her a mirror.

"Wow. I can't even see it. You even covered the cut."

Just then Kevin walked in. "So I heard he sucker punched you, ay? I told you he was trouble."

"Yeah, yeah, yeah," Terri replied.

"I've seen guys get a split in bar fights. It's a bloody mess."

She glared at him. "Well, it's over now and I'm fine."

Just then the phone rang. Marge answered. Terri knew it was Jesse.

"No, she doesn't want to talk to you. Okay, I'll tell her."

Marge came back into the kitchen and resumed her chore. "That was him. He says you have his wallet."

"Oh no. I can't see him, Patty." The phone rang again and Terri grabbed it. She just listened.

"Terri, it's me. I'm sorry. I'm leaving tomorrow for Las Vegas. I'm going to stay with my buddy, Augie, for a while.

He'll get me a job in the casino where he works but I need my wallet. Can I come over and get it?"

"My car's parked in front of the house. It'll be open. Your wallet's in the glove compartment. Bye." She hung up before he could respond.

Terri knew having distance between them was the only answer. She figured he knew it too.

"I've gotta go make sure the car's unlocked." She ran out and sat in it for a moment. She pulled the wallet out of the glove compartment. She didn't know why, but she began to look through it. There was nothing much inside except a photo that puzzled her—a picture of two small boys, Jesse and his older brother, Mark. One side of the picture was folded back on itself. When she unfolded it, she saw another small face—a younger boy about three years old. She quickly put the wallet back together and threw it in the glove compartment again. She went back into the house. Tomorrow she'd be free of him. The miles between them would free her of her obsession, but she knew her love for him would never cease.

* * *

Terri had settled into Sharon's apartment and now they hung out together most evenings.

They were sitting at a table in the back room of Howie's drinking martinis. Terri had just put on Jethro Tull's *"Bungle in the Jungle."*

Sharon looked gorgeous as usual, her long blond hair covering her shoulders. Her eyes were glassy from the vodka they'd been drinking for the past few hours but they still twinkled and danced in the light as she laughed at Terri's latest jokes.

"Don't you just love martinis? They give me so much energy."

Terri leaned back in her chair. "Yeah, but you're not gonna dance on the bar again, are you?"

"Ugh. I only did it twice. You never let me live that down. So you still bummed about Jesse?"

"Kind of. I feel part of me is gone. I guess I still love him but I'm ashamed to admit it."

"Why?" Sharon looked at her, puzzled.

"Why do you think? See this purple scar above my eye? It's never gonna go away. Never. Don't you find it sick that I'd love someone who did that to me?"

"Nah. He didn't mean it. He was drunk. He didn't even know he did it."

"Well, I have my pride ya' know. There are some things I just can't let go by and this is one of 'em." She pointed at her eye again.

"Well, you can't just turn love off like a faucet, Terri."

"No, I can't, but I can just ignore it. And with him being in Vegas, it's a lot easier. I don't know. This 'love' thing. I haven't had much luck with it. First, I loved Larry, my ex-husband and he gets weird on me. Then I love Jesse, and I get weird on him. He made me do things I didn't wanna do."

"Yeah, I know what you mean. Look at me and Howie. He acts like I don't even exist. We have no relationship anymore. Just go our separate ways. *You* care about me more than he does."

Sharon was right. The only thing that remained constant was Terri's love for Sharon. It was clean and unconditional, something they both felt but neither of them spoke about. Someday they would.

"Thanks for takin' me in. I really appreciate it."

"Let's make the rest of this summer really decadent. I mean, let's do whatever we want. Make a pact with me."

Terri smiled. "If we do, how we gonna tell the difference between this summer and last summer?"

"Oh, shut up. C'mon. Let's make a blood pact like we did when we were little kids."

"Oh no! I've had enough blood and we're not little kids anymore."

"Yes we are—just little kids in big kids' bodies."

Terri pondered the thought for a while and had to admit, Sharon was right again. Lately she'd been feeling like a child. "Okay. I'm goin' to California before winter anyway, so what the hell? It's my last summer in this crazy town."

"Don't forget. We're blood sisters. We have to re-do the pact."

Sharon ran over to the old dartboard and grabbed a dart. She was so damned crazy.

"Okay, Terri. Here's to the rest of the summer and doing whatever we want. Ready?" Terri watched as Sharon plunged the dart way too deeply into the palm of her hand. Terri was aghast as a spurt of blood shot straight up.

"Jesus Christ!" Terri quickly untucked her T-shirt and placed the end of it over Sharon's wound. She furtively glanced around the bar to see if anyone witnessed their ritual.

"Boy, these martinis really kill pain. That didn't hurt at all. There wouldn't be so much pain in the world if everyone drank martinis!"

"Shit, Share. What the hell!" She gently lifted her shirt off the wound but the blood was still pumping. She ran to the bar and grabbed a handful of napkins.

Sharon leaned back and smiled. "Here, Terri. Your turn."

Terri grabbed the dart and stuck it gingerly into her index finger. She was such a coward. A small dot of blood oozed out and she gently placed her finger to Sharon's still bleeding palm. "Okay, you happy now?"

"Yeah, are you?" Sharon said, smiling.

"Yeah sure. I'm real happy."

"Look, Terri. Romeo's at the bar."

"So what?"

"Well that's where I'm gonna start, with him. He's so fuckin' fine."

Terri didn't want to think about Sharon and Romeo.

She needed to change her shirt. She ran out of the bar quickly with her arms folded to conceal the blood. She looked back and saw Sharon glide up to Romeo at the bar. Sharon was already keeping up her end of the blood bargain they'd just made.

* * *

Terri really liked living in Sharon's apartment. The kitchen was large and airy. Her bedroom was a good size with a big bay window. She'd been sleeping on a mattress on the floor and Sharon gave her a small bureau to use. It beat moving back in with Chick after she left Jesse. She undressed and threw on her sleep T-shirt. She couldn't wait to flop down on the mattress.

As she was about to lie down, there was a knock at the door. She was too intoxicated to move quickly. She made her way to the door and opened it, forgetting she had no pants on.

There stood Angel Quinteira with a bottle of wine in one hand and a brown paper bag in the other. She had the feeling his sudden appearance was in some way connected to the pact she'd made with Sharon. He glanced down at her thin legs.

"Hey, Terri, mind if I come in?"

"Sure. C'mon in." There was nothing she could do now about the absence of her pants. She had to admit, there was something alluring about him. It wasn't so much the way he looked but the way he moved that added to his sensual aura—he had an almost feminine sway.

Angel always spoke in a soft and gentle tone, a contrast to his powerful singing voice. He made his way through to the kitchen.

"I've been seeing you around. Sorry I didn't come over sooner to welcome you." He sat down at the table and poured her a glass of wine.

"Here's to you, Terri. It's nice to have you as a

neighbor."

"Thanks." She touched her glass to his and downed her wine. "What's in the bag, Angel?"

"Oh, I got a few things you might like. You got a small mirror?"

He pulled a large white pill out of the bag and handed it to her. "Here. You like 'ludes?"

"Well…sure…but not all of it." She bit the pill carefully in half, remembering what a whole quaalude had done to her before—the wooziness, the rubbery legs, and falling down.

Pink Floyd's *"Wish You Were Here"* filled the room.

Angel poured some white powder onto the table and snorted it. He handed her a straw. She was just drunk enough this time to try it. He stared at her across the table. "I heard you and your old man broke up."

"Well, yeah. He left town." She hoped Angel hadn't heard the whole story but she knew in this little city, there were no secrets.

Angel nodded his head. "I'm glad."

Terri was startled at what he just said. "What?"

"I said, I'm glad." All the time, he was staring at her with his large dark eyes.

Then he placed a green powdery substance on the table and snorted it. Without caring about what it was or what she was doing, she snorted it too. She knew immediately this whole visit was a mistake.

Angel took her hand under the table. Even through this drug induced haze, she felt a little twinge of excitement. His touch was gentle.

"C'mon, Let's go out on the balcony."

Terri desperately needed a diversion from her constant thoughts of Jesse, and Angel was looking better and better.

Outside, Angel pulled her toward him as he leaned back against the balcony wall. He held her face in his hands as he kissed her closed eyes and the sides of her lips. Then he kissed her full on the lips and she remembered that soft velvet tongue from the night she ran out of his apartment.

The kiss was long, soft, and warm. She knew she wanted more of him.

Suddenly, she fell to her knees. The quaalude had taken over. She would have fallen backward if she hadn't grabbed Angel around his legs. She had to speak quickly before he got the wrong idea.

"Angel. I can't do quaaludes. I can't move when I do them. It's bad. Aww. Your legs are so pretty." She didn't mean to say that and promised herself not to talk anymore.

He grabbed her under her arms and pulled her up. "C'mon. Hold on to me."

She threw her arms around his neck and snuggled under his mane, breathing deeply. He smelled good. She couldn't feel her feet touching the floor as he took her into the living room and laid her down on the couch. He brushed her hair from her face.

"Terri, you should've told me. I would never have given you that 'lude."

"Aww. You're so nice…and you smell soooo good." She didn't have any control over her body or her mouth. "Just leave me here. I think I'm gonna sleep now."

He kissed her on the forehead. "Okay. I'm really sorry."

She heard the door close and drifted off into a coma-like sleep to the sweet sound of Jackson Browne's voice.

* * *

Sharon was sitting at the table the next morning when Terri came into the kitchen. Terri was surprised that the effects of the drugs had completely worn off, but the alcohol was still causing problems. She felt sick. She got a cup of coffee and a beer and sat down with Sharon.

Sharon looked up from the paper she was reading.

"What the hell went on last night?"

"Oh, Angel came over with some wine and a bag of stuff."

Terri was a little embarrassed at seeing the mess on the table. Sharon lifted the mirror with remnants of the green substance on it.

"What's this stuff? Please don't tell me you snorted this green shit."

"Yeah. I think we did."

"Why the hell would you snort something green? *I* wouldn't even do that."

"Oh, *please*. You should talk."

"So what's with you and Angel? Anything happen?"

"Nah. I passed out from the drugs and he had to leave. That's it."

Terri looked over Sharon's shoulder at the paper.

"Let me see something."

She turned to the weather map and checked the conditions in Nevada. Her love for Jesse was ever present and she needed to know if he was safe and sheltered under sunny skies. Sometimes at night she'd look up at the moon and stars and feel comforted at the thought that he might be doing the exact same thing. She hated herself for doing it.

"So...you gonna fuck him?"

Terri was bewildered for a moment.

"What the hell are you talkin' about? Who?"

"Angel. Who do you think?"

"I don't know. I don't know anything. I don't even know why the hell I did all those drugs last night. I got no answers for you."

"Well if you do, you won't be sorry, 'cause..."

Terri interrupted her. "Shhh. Don't. It's much nicer to have sex with someone you love."

"That's a crock of shit. You know what the song says." Sharon began to sing, "*Love The One You're With.*"

Terri cut her short. "Yeah, yeah. I know. What the hell does that song mean anyway? Have sex with whoever's

145

handy?"

"Yeah. And Angel's real handy. He's a regular handyman. Remember that one?" Sharon was in a musical mood. She started singing "*Handyman.*"

Terri broke in again. "You're just dyin' for me to sleep with this guy, aren't you?"

Sharon got up and squeezed Terri's shoulders. "I just want you to start feelin' good. Don't forget about our pact." Sharon started to walk away but stopped in the hallway.

"Hey, Terri. Look there's a note for you by the door."

She picked it up and handed it over. Terri read it.

Dear Terri,

I'm so sorry about last night. I feel awful about giving you those drugs. Please let me make it up to you. Come over tonight at 7:30 and I'll fix a nice dinner for you. I hope you don't mind a vegetarian meal. Looking forward to seeing you again. If you don't want to, I'll understand.

Angel

Terri threw the note on the table for Sharon to read.

"Oh boy! Are you gonna go, Terri? I'm tellin' you, you won't be sorry."

Terri thought about Angel's kiss for a second and felt a little quiver. "I think I will. He might do me some good."

"Oh yeah. He sure will."

* * *

She knocked on Angel's door just before seven forty-five. She didn't want to be too punctual and let him know how excited she was.

"Hi," he said as he opened the door and invited her in. He was wearing his usual cut-offs but no tank top tonight.

Hmm.

His apartment was the mirror image of Sharon's. She

remembered the hippie décor. The place hadn't changed much since the last time she was here, the night of the threesome. Neil Young sang *"Cortez The Killer"* over the stereo as Angel prepared the meal.

"I hope you're hungry. I made vegetables and rice. It's almost ready."

She wasn't hungry at all. She knew why she was there and the intrusion of food and conversation seemed a bit foolish.

As they began to eat, he stared at her over the table.

"I'm really sorry about last night. I didn't know you had a problem with 'ludes."

She swallowed a small mouthful of the food. She really didn't want it. "It's okay, Angel. I'm fine. Totally my fault. You didn't exactly twist my arm."

Their conversation flowed easily about music during the meal. Now Steely Dan's *"Aja"* filled the room with their jazzy sound. After dinner, she sat on the couch. He turned off the stereo and grabbed his guitar. "Here, I'll sing something for you."

He sat on the arm of the couch and strummed a few bars. Then he looked up and began to sing a beautiful ballad he'd written. The melody was haunting. She was mesmerized. His eyes were on her the whole time. When he finished, she was almost speechless but felt the need to get a few words out.

"That was a really beautiful song, the words, the melody…everything."

He put his guitar down and sat next to her. He took her face in his hands and kissed her for a long time, his tongue warm and inviting. She thought again about the night of the threesome. He was with only *one* woman now. She had been drinking before coming over and the alcohol gave her the courage to speak. She decided to lighten the mood.

"So, Angel, Laura's not going to jump out of a closet and join us, is she? Is it just us?"

She peeked around. He didn't smile.

"No, Terri. It's just you and me. I've been a pretty lucky guy but that was in the past. It's over. This night's just for you. I wanna make you feel real good." He flipped the stereo back on, took her by the hand, and led her to the bedroom. Of course, he owned a waterbed and there were erotic posters on the walls with bodies contorted in different sexual positions. Stuck to the front of his dresser was a bumper sticker that said, "If it feels good, do it." Terri was amused. Now Lou Reed was singing *"Take a Walk on the Wild Side."*

As they stood next to the bed, he slowly undressed her. He gently ran his hands over her shoulders, arms, stomach and thighs.

"You're so beautiful, Terri. So beautiful," he said softly as he took her hand. "Here. Lie down." He moved to the foot of the bed. As he pulled off his bandana, his long black hair fell down. She had always loved long hair on a man and she was surprised that the sight of his hair falling all around his shoulders aroused her more. She watched as he removed his cut-offs. He moved his compact muscular body gracefully as he crawled over the foot of the bed.

He surprised her by massaging her feet. Lying there naked, she felt quite vulnerable as he ran his eyes over her face, her breasts, her stomach, all of her right down to her toes. He bent over her and kissed her feet, then her shins. His hair tickled her legs and it was exhilarating. He reached his hand up past her thighs to her most sensitive spot and moved his nimble guitar playing fingers purposefully. He inserted a finger inside her and she could still feel his hair on her legs as he began moving his head further up.

"Ooh, mama. You're so wet."

His voice excited her. Now she could feel his thick hair sweeping over her thighs as he kissed them. By the time his lips were on her lower belly, she could feel his mane sweeping over her center. His movements were deliberate and she feared if he didn't stop, she'd come right then.

Then he moved his mouth up to her neck, his hair softly dragging over her breasts and nipples, like very soft kisses. By the time his lips were firmly planted on hers, and his fingers still playing with her center, she knew she could hold back no longer.

"Come for me, mama. C'mon, baby." The waves of pleasure started. He whispered in her ear. "That's it, mama. C'mon. That's what I want."

The more he talked, the more her body quivered. He pulled her alongside him and entered her. They moved together in perfect rhythm and he continued to urge her on. Then when he finally reached his own pleasure peak, it was with so much passion, he shouted, "Ohhhhhhh. Fuck. Fuck me baby. Fuuuuck."

He was truly a man who made love with his soul as well as his body. As they lay back exhausted, Terri realized that this was the first time Jesse was completely absent from her thoughts. It made her feel good. Angel was here now.

* * *

When Terri returned to the apartment the next day, Sharon had just sat down at the kitchen table to drink her coffee. Terri slumped down on the chair opposite her.

"Hey, Terri. How was it?"

"How was what?"

"You know. How did you like Angel? Did you—"

"Fuck him? Yes...I did. And I'll say one thing. He's got real nice hair."

"How about the ice, Terri. Did he do that thing with the ice?"

"No. He didn't do the thing with the ice. Maybe next time."

"Well, don't fall for him. You know how he is. And you always fall for everybody you go to bed with."

"I won't. You know how I feel about Jesse. My feelings aren't gonna go away just 'cause Angel's good in bed."

She grabbed the newspaper that was sitting in front of Sharon. "Hey, what's the weather in Nevada?"

It was always the same but she still felt compelled to check. Terri got up from the table.

"I have to go to my dad's and do some laundry."

It had been a while since she visited the old man and she wasn't looking forward to it. As Terri was leaving the apartment, she ran into Romeo coming out of Sharon's room. He was tucking his shirt into his jeans.

"Hey, Terri. Mornin'."

He was a big man and nearly filled the door frame. His eyes were still drowsy from sleep or heroin.

"Oh…hi, Romeo," she answered trying to conceal her surprise. As she passed through the kitchen, Terri gave Sharon a disapproving stare and got a sly smile in return.

Chapter 12

Terri assumed Chick was doing well enough without her. He busied himself at the diner and with his painting. She kind of admired him for his independent ways. He didn't ask for much and had told her several times since her mother died that he didn't need anybody.

Chick's car was in the driveway. Terri was hoping he'd be at the diner.

"Dad?" she yelled as she walked in.

"Yeah, I'm in the bathroom. Be right out." He appeared in the kitchen as she was dumping her clothes into the washer.

"Hey, how's my baby? You're my baby, ya' know." He pointed to his cheek. "Give yer daddy a kiss."

She did as he asked. She felt guilty that she wasn't happy to see him.

He scrutinized her face. "How's yer eye?"

"It's fine, Dad," she said as she turned her face away.

"That dirty bastard. I better not see him around here no more."

"You won't. He's way out west. Did I get any mail?"

Chick wasn't listening. "Well he better stay out there. That dirty son of a bitch. You and these bums you go around with."

"Dad, *did I get any mail?*"

"Yeah, it's on the counter."

She scooped up the letter, instantly recognizing Jesse's handwriting. She'd read it later. She didn't want Chick's loud ramblings to distract her from Jesse's words.

"Dad, I gotta go. I'll be back in a half hour to get my laundry."

"Hey, I thought we'd…"

She didn't let him finish. She jumped in her car, drove to the foot of the mountain, and tore open the letter.

Dear Terri,

I need to tell you how sorry I am for what happened. I'm sorry and thought it would be best if I went away. I hope you'll find a way to forgive me, but if you can't, I understand. Now I'm staying with my brother and his old lady in Colorado. I got a job working on a ranch. Working with horses is great. If you want to write me the address is on the envelope. If you don't, it's okay. I've been thinking of you a lot and still love you.

All my love always,

Jesse.

P.S. I had to leave Vegas in a hurry. Augie was a bad influence!

Terri quickly tore up the letter and tossed it out the car window. She knew if she wrote to him, the torment would only begin again. But she stashed the envelope in the glove compartment anyway.

* * *

Fall was here and Terri's savings had dwindled to three hundred dollars. It was hardly enough to start a new life in California. She had no idea how much cash had passed over the bar and she didn't care to think about it. Howie had since left the apartment, saying he was sick of the freaks and junkies Sharon and Terri hung out with. Terri was still carrying on with Angel on the nights he was available while Sharon hung out with Romeo. The girls sat on the balcony lamenting summer's end. They were well-toasted. Sharon looked down to the parking lot.

"Look, here come the girls. Bet they're going up to Angel's to get some coke."

Terri peeked over the rail. "Angel sure has a lot of female customers, doesn't he?"

"So, it bothers you?"

"Nah. He's good to me when it's my turn."

"Yeah, I know that." Sharon smiled. "This has been some crazy summer. I'm kind of glad it's coming to an end. Isn't it awful what happened to Kevin?"

"Yeah. He's damn lucky he didn't kill himself. It was only a matter of time before somebody drove through Dugan's Market. It's in a really bad location. He scared the Puerto Rican guy behind the counter half to death. It was a mess, groceries and glass all over the place."

"What's gonna happen to him?"

"Well, since it's his second DWI in—"

"Wait a minute. His *second*?"

"Yeah, he got his first just three weeks ago. He had just crossed the bridge. He closed his eyes at the red light and passed out. The light turned green and the traffic was all tied up. The cops came and arrested him, I guess for sleeping drunk at the light! The judge will probably force him to go to A.A."

"Oh god, that's awful. Why don't they just shoot him?"

"Yeah. He's such a nice guy. I've known him since he was ten. Ya' know, Share, this summer has been fun but look at me." Terri unsnapped her jeans. "I'm gettin' fat. My face is all puffed up. All we did all summer was drink Beck's and eat fast food. I went to my father's the other day and, ya' know, he always tells it like it is. So he says to me 'Hey whaddya' been doin'? Your face is all puffy. You look like a squirrel storin' nuts for the winter.' Isn't that horrible?"

"Yeah, Terri. Me too. Look." Sharon patted her jeans. "Maybe Beck's is fattening."

"Hey," Terri said with a mischievous gleam in her eye. "You think Angel is doin' those *two*?"

"There's only one way to find out." Sharon slugged down the rest of her beer and held up her glass. "C'mon."

"No, we shouldn't."

"Why not? He'll never know."

Terri kneeled on the couch facing the wall adjoining Angel's apartment. Sharon placed the glass on the wall and had her ear tight to its bottom. Terri watched her anxiously. Sharon listened for a few seconds. Then her mouth dropped open. Terri got her answer. Sharon's eyes widened.

"That's enough," Terri whispered. "Stop now!" Then she added slyly, "So what's goin' on?"

Sharon lowered the glass and whispered, "He's doin' them all right and one of 'em is real noisy."

"Oh shit. I'm goin' over there tomorrow night and now I'll be real uncomfortable. Fuck. We shouldn't have spied."

"Who cares?" Sharon said and put down the glass. "You're goin' to California anyway. C'mon, let's go back out to the balcony."

They grabbed more beers first and sat back down outside.

"When you goin', Terri?"

"I don't know. My money's runnin' short again. I might have to delay the trip till later in the fall. Maybe even after the holidays."

Sharon smiled. "That's okay. I get to keep you here longer! But remember I told you, when you do go, you can stay with Sandy. Her boyfriend Ben and his roommate are real nice. Give her a call before you get out there."

Terri loved Sharon's sister, Sandy, and knew if anything went wrong out in California, Sandy would be there for her.

"Ya' know what? I got a letter from Jesse a while ago but I tore it up and threw it out. We were supposed to go to California together. I just can't shake him. Hey, how are ya' doin' with Romeo?"

"Great. I just love him. He's not such a bad guy."

"Do you really love him or are you..." Terri was reluctant but she needed to ask. "Sharon, are you shootin' dope?"

"I gotta tell ya' 'cause you're my best friend, my blood sister. Yeah, I did it a few times. It's okay. I only do it on the weekend."

Terri patted Sharon's knee. "Please be careful. It's not like pot or drinkin' ya' know."

"You said it. It's not like drinkin' at all. Ya' know how

ya' feel after a few drinks? All tingly and numb and warm all over? When you shoot dope, it's so fast. You don't have to wait. All those great feelings but a hundred times better. Know what I mean?"

Terri didn't want to hear anymore about how dope felt. The dreamy-eyed look on Sharon's face as she described shooting heroin was making Terri uncomfortable.

"Hey, I'm gonna meet Romeo later at the Paradise. You wanna come?"

"No. I'm just gonna stay home tonight and go to bed early for a change. This summer is wearin' me out."

Terri did just that. It was a rare occasion for her to stay in and get to bed early. She always felt a little sense of pride on nights like these.

* * *

With some misgivings, Terri knocked on Angel's door. She held the remainder of a bottle of wine she had popped open a little earlier. Angel looked beautiful, his hair falling over his bare chest. He seemed excited to see her.

"C'mon in, babe."

Angel rarely cooked her dinner now but he always offered her cocaine. They sat on the couch and he began the coke ritual, cutting it up delicately with a sharp razor. Terri thought about the look on Sharon's face while she listened through the beer glass to Angel having sex with the two girls the night before. She knew she had no reason to be jealous. She was in love with someone else. Nevertheless, Angel's escapades bothered her. Even though sex with him was totally gratifying, it was starting to feel wrong.

Neil Young's "*Needle and the Damage Done*" was playing as they talked about poetry, music, food, and spirituality. He was well-versed on a number of topics and conversation was never difficult. He was beautiful inside and out, sweet, kind, and always a selfless lover. So what if he had a few vices?

They were quiet for a few moments and then she said, "So you've been really busy this week, haven't you?"

He turned to her with those large dark eyes and placed his warm hands on her shoulders.

"Listen. I like you, Terri. I care for you a lot, probably more than I've cared for any woman in a long time."

Oh boy. Here comes a load of bullshit.

"But I have to be honest with you. I've got a lot of women. I know it's a problem. It affects every aspect of my life. I mean, I love women...a lot of women. It causes difficulties, I know."

She appreciated his honesty and felt placated. In fact, his sincerity was disturbingly arousing.

"Well, I guess you can't control the way you feel. Thanks for being so honest."

"I tried to change. Believe me. I was married once a long time ago, but it wasn't fair, the way I am. I'm just not a one-woman man, but if I was, I'd want somebody like you." He took her in a warm embrace and kissed her deeply. Then he took her by the hand and led her into the bedroom.

She was confused, but she wanted him. She rationalized it was just as unfair to Angel, because she always had Jesse on her mind. After all, they were just pleasuring each other. There had never been anything else. She followed his lead. As they walked by the stereo, he turned it up much too loud. Robert Plant was singing "*Whole Lotta Love*."

"Isn't that kind of loud? Can you turn it down just a bit?"

"Sure, babe."

He turned back to the stereo and dialed it down. When Angel made love, he talked, and Terri didn't want to miss one word, not one moan or groan. His passion was infectious.

"How's that? Better?"

He did aim to please her in every way.

They undressed and fell onto his waterbed. He began kissing her and running his warm hands all over her body, using those magic fingers. By now, Jimi Hendrix and *"All Along the Watchtower"* was playing through the speakers in Angel's room. To be making love with this captivating man to the strains of her favorite guitar solo was like opening the perfect gift. She was giddy from the wine. All her misgivings about coming here tonight had evaporated. Hendrix was doing what he did best and so was Angel. He pulled her on top of him gently and looked into her eyes.

"Baby, you know what I like."

Then he very gently pushed her head downward. She began kissing his chest, and ran her tongue over his nipples, moving lower. She suddenly wished this had been her own idea. After kissing his stomach, she moved on to his groin. She briefly visualized Sharon's face listening through the glass. Then she suddenly thought about Jesse. Before she knew it, it started. Deep from inside her, a flash of anger. It was surfacing and there was nothing she could do about it.

She lifted her head and took a deep breath. It didn't help. Terri jumped out of the waterbed and began gathering up her clothes. As she got dressed, Angel's eyes looked larger and darker than ever.

"What's wrong, mama? You okay?"

"I gotta go," she snapped at him as she zipped her jeans.

"Why baby? What's wrong?"

"I'll tell you what's wrong." She looked at the bumper sticker on his dresser, the one that said *If It Feels Good, Do It*. Then she began to angrily poke the sign with her index finger. "Ya' see this sign? See it?" She raised her voice as Angel just stared. "Well it doesn't feel good anymore. So I'm not doin' it. Get it?"

Then she ran out of his apartment slamming the door. She knew this was the end of her and Angel. She wondered how she'd avoid him in this crazy house until she left for California.

* * *

Terri's week had dragged on uneventfully until she went to the mailbox one night after work and found another letter from Jesse.

Dear Terri,

I can't say I blame you for not writing but I thought I'd try again. I'm still working on the ranch. I was working with the horses the other day and "Layla" came on the radio. I feel that song says it all. I've been thinking of you every day. I love you a lot and it's getting pretty lonely out here. Write me if you want.

Love, Jesse

Her heart was pounding as she read the letter. She desperately tried to recall the lyrics of *"Layla."* She wanted to tell Sharon how happy she was. She burst into the apartment and ran down the hall to Sharon's room.

"Sharon, look what I got."

As she pushed open the door, Romeo was removing a needle from her arm. Sharon's head fell back on the pillow, her eyelids fluttering. Romeo looked at Terri.

"Hey, Terri. Sorry. I didn't know you were here…"

She looked at Sharon's face. "Is she okay?"

"Sure. Hey, Sharon, say something to Terri so she knows you're okay."

Sharon's soft voice spoke, her eyes only half-opened. "Sure, Terri. I'm good. See?"

Terri looked away glumly and went to the kitchen table. She knew there was nothing she could do about Sharon and Romeo. She turned her thoughts to Jesse. She began to write:

Dear Jesse,

I'm sorry I didn't write sooner. I admit I was really mad after what happened. But I've got to be honest. Things just aren't the same around here without you. I'm going to listen to "Layla" again. I miss you. After that night at the Rusty Rail, I tried to forget about you but the fact is, I still love you. I don't think it'll ever go away. That's about all I can say.

Terri.

* * *

A couple of weeks had passed since she mailed the letter. She'd come home late from the bar one night and flopped onto the mattress. She'd been drinking all night and without the diversion of Angel's skilled lovemaking, she'd been feeling lonely.

She passed out quickly that night, but was awakened by loud knocking on her bedroom door. She could hear Sharon's voice distantly calling her name. She thought she was having another weird dream.

"Terri! Open the door." More loud knocking. "Open up."

Finally, she roused herself from her drunken sleep. She yelled to Sharon.

"Yeah, I'm here. What's wrong? Come on in."

The door burst open and Sharon was standing there with Jesse on her arm.

"Look who I found at the bar."

Terri sat up on her mattress. Her mouth dropped open and her eyes widened. "Oh my god!" She'd never been so happy to see anyone in her life. She had a hard time catching her breath. She felt almost sober.

Jesse had a big smile on his face and she thought he was the most beautiful sight she'd ever seen. His brown waves were falling down past his shoulders and his blue eyes seemed darker than before. He quickly knelt on the mattress and they embraced. He held her so tight it almost hurt.

"I'm gonna leave you two alone," Sharon said with a smug look as she left the room.

"Oh my god, Jesse. I missed you so much. I love you. I don't want you to leave again...ever." She started crying.

He was still squeezing her tightly. He lifted her chin and looked in her eyes.

"No, babe. Don't cry."

Then he kissed her for a long time and it was just like that sweet water again, only this time much sweeter. He held her tight and whispered in her ear.

"I'm not goin' anywhere, Terri. I'm stayin' right here with you. And we're goin' to California if you still want to. I got some money."

She looked in his eyes. The way those eyes enchanted her was frightening.

"Sure, Jesse. I still wanna go. But first, I've got some things to tell you. I've been pretty bad this summer. Jesse, I—"

He placed a warm finger over her lips.

"Shhh. I don't care. I don't wanna hear. I'm back and it's all over."

Then he pulled her down on the mattress and ran his hands under her sleep shirt, gently brushing them over her back and her breasts. He made love to her long into the morning hours. As she held his naked body close to hers, she knew her fate was sealed with this man, no matter what consequences she faced. She was willing to risk anything to try with him again.

Chapter 13

Terri and Jesse had said goodbye to everyone. Terri was looking forward to seeing Sharon's sister, Sandy, in California. It had been a long time since they'd seen each other. Saying goodbye to Sharon was hard, but Chick was another story.

"Jeez, that was terrible how your dad was cryin'," Jesse had said after they pulled away. "I feel kinda bad for the old guy even though he treated you so shitty. He really looked pathetic standin' there cryin' in the driveway."

Now they were on the road. Jesse's plan to get them to California as fast as possible was working. Terri was driving and her eyes were on the sky. She held her face as close to the windshield as she possibly could. Every star was a shooting star tonight as she drove through the vast Utah desert. The stars darted this way and that leaving brightly colored patterns in the night sky. The moon was full and cast a pinkish glow over the huge rock formations they were passing.

Terri wished she hadn't done a whole tab. With acid, half had always been enough. Every vision she witnessed was beautiful, yet extremely distracting while driving. She had sharp pains in her lower back, probably from whatever the acid was cut with. The pain was bearable only because of the show before her. She tried to lean back in her seat, hoping relaxation was the answer. She soon found herself with her face close to the windshield again. Her gaze moved from the shooting stars to huge jackrabbits jumping in front of the car. As they hopped by in slow motion, their eyes cast pink beams of light in front of them. Pink seemed to be the color of the night, chosen by the drug.

She became fearful of hitting one of the desert animals. She thought they'd not only damage the car but knew seeing a squashed rabbit or coyote would turn a good trip bad. She was well aware that her mind was taking pictures, but she became vexed at the huge rock formation to her left. It just wouldn't go away. It was as if a large hand were picking up her car and placing it a few miles back on the road, over and over again. Her logical mind told her that her psychedelic mind was taking over, but logic didn't help her much.

Jesse had dozed off and she didn't want to wake him. He'd done his driving time, thirty-six hours of it. He'd crashed hard after a long two-tab trip. She just couldn't lose the vision to her left so she pulled over. Her heart was beating fast. She leaned back, closed her eyes, and tried to relax.

The show went on. Perfect, multicolored flowered patterns danced behind her eyelids. They were soothing but she felt she couldn't drive anymore.

"Jesse. Jesse." She pushed his shoulder a few times.

"Whaaaaat? Arrrrrgh," he growled and turned toward the passenger window.

"Jesse, please. You gotta wake up. I don't think I can drive anymore."

"What?" Now he turned toward her, opening his eyes. He woke up quickly, the acid probably still in his system.

"Jesse. You gotta see this desert. I mean. The animals. There are jackrabbits jumping in front of the car as big as wallabies."

"What the fuck are wallabies?" He sat up in his seat and looked around.

"They're little kangaroos. Oh, never mind. I'm sorry. I'm just too freaked out to drive...and these damn rocks."

"Yeah, aren't they great?"

"Yeah, but they keep following me."

"Terri, relax. It's just the acid. I'll tell you what I'm gonna do." He reached in his pocket and pulled out a baggie. Then he took two purple tabs out and popped them in his mouth. He took a swig of warm beer. "Okay, Terri. Get out and let me drive. Jeez, babe. The things I do for you."

Terri sat in the passenger seat unable to sleep. Soon, morning's pale yellow glimmer blanketed the desert, accompanied by a dark pinkish haze. Terri didn't know if the pink color was real or not.

Jesse looked over at Terri and his black pupils told her that the show was just beginning for him. He gave her a high five.

"Look at this place, Terri. Fuckin' A! California here we come."

* * *

Terri sat against the wall in the tiny studio apartment they'd rented in the small town of Monte Rio. As planned, Jesse and Terri got as close to the Pacific as they could. But this little town was a haven for misfits and the sunny yellow apartment house they settled in was now like a prison cell. They'd been here about eight months but their honeymoon with California ended when the money ran out. The joy she'd felt each time she walked on California soil had given way to despair, as work was hard to find. There was a gas shortage, but they didn't have to wait in long gas lines, because they had no money for gas. Jesse would hitchhike to the nearby large city and wait to be chosen to dig ditches for minimum wage.

But today was going to be a great day. She found out she'd been hired at the state hospital as a typist. Sharon's sister, Sandy, was coming to pick her up to take her to lunch to celebrate.

Terri been stranded in this room for too long and missed the company of friends. And Sandy was a good one. Like Sharon, she was beautiful. Also, like her sister, she loved to have a good time. Terri and Sandy had had no trouble renewing their friendship. Even though they hadn't seen each other in years, they fell back in to a close bond the moment Terri arrived.

She was filled with excitement at the thought of eating real food, instead of the grits and cold cuts they'd been living on. They'd eat at the Blue Onion, a great vegetarian place on the Russian River. Sandy and Ben's roommate, Alan, was the chef there. Terri had met him when she first arrived.

Today it wouldn't matter if Jesse didn't come home after work. She planned to stay out with Sandy as long as she could. As she sat on the floor waiting, she paged through the magazines she borrowed from a girl she'd met in town. Terri walked two miles the day before to borrow them. Reading magazines and listening to the stereo were the only two things she could do to keep her sanity. Now she was listening to Bruce Springsteen. She stopped reading for a moment. She enjoyed the pictures of Asbury Park he was painting in her head.

She glanced over at the small kitchen table and the broken kitchen chairs piled in the corner of the room. Jesse had smashed the chairs last night in a drunken rage. There was also a hole in the wall next to the table. Soon Sandy would be here and she wouldn't have to look at the mess anymore.

Terri jumped up as soon as she heard Sandy's car, opening the door before Sandy had a chance to knock.

They hugged.

"Terri, how are you doing? Sorry I haven't been around in a while. I've been working a lot. It's so great to see you."

Terri was filled with gratitude and invited her in.

"Hey, what happened to the chairs?"

"Eh. Jesse got mad. He was drunk. C'mon, let's go. I gotta get outta here."

"Yeah, let's go. Alan's working today and I know the bartender. We'll get a few free drinks."

* * *

As they sat at the bar enjoying their drinks, Alan popped his head out of the kitchen.

"Hey, Sandy." His face brightened when he saw Terri.

"Hey, Terri. Long time no see. How are you?"

"I'm fine. Great. How are you?"

Alan smiled at her sweetly and said, "I'll make anything you girls want today. Just let me know."

Terri felt better than she had in a long time. She had a drink, a good friend, and was finally going to eat some healthy food. A sense of joy washed over her. She'd just finished her first drink and the hangover from last night began to fade, along with all her worries.

"I think Alan likes you."

"What? What the hell? What is this grade school? You mean like a girlfriend?"

"Yeah, that's it." They both giggled a bit.

Terri waved her off. "Well, what about Jesse?"

"Shit. That won't last."

Unlike Sharon, Sandy wasn't fond of Jesse.

"I don't know if it will or it won't," said Terri. "Things are kind of bad now, but we're both under a lot of stress. He's working real hard and we still have no money. He's drinking a lot more and a lot faster. He's getting real messy if you know what I mean."

"What happened last night? Why did he break those chairs?"

"It's a long bizarre story, Sandy, but I'll try to make it short."

"Go on. We have all day."

"Yeah. Isn't that great?" She started the tale. "There are these nice people in town. They're younger than us and have a little girl about two. She's real cute and this couple told Jesse if we gave them a ride to San Jose, they'd buy gas, buy us beer, and give us twenty bucks. Of course, he said yes. He'd been drinkin' before we left for San Jose with them. It was a pretty long drive, maybe two and a half hours. Halfway there, he's a real mess. So he keeps making these poor people buy him more beer. He was drinking so fast.

"Then I said, 'Let me drive. You're wasted.' So he gets

really pissed off. We start fightin' and he's all over the road. He wouldn't pull over. The mom starts cryin' and holdin' onto the little girl. Jeez, you'd think we were ax murderers. He finally pulled over and we got out. We were screamin'. Then Jesse starts pushing me and I shoved him. The mother was clutching the baby, and the baby is cryin' now too. The mom wanted to get out and hitchhike. Imagine that, Sandy? She wanted to hitchhike with a baby rather than ride with us.

"So I drove the rest of the way to San Jose. On the way home, Jesse takes the twenty bucks and says 'Pull over at a store.' I pull over 'cause he was threatenin' me, and I said, 'We need that money for food. If you get out of this car I'm leavin' you here.' So he went in the store and I left him there. He walked home.

"I guess it was a long walk. When I opened the door, he was standin' there all wet 'cause it was rainin', and boy, was he mad! He threw the six-packs down and started breakin' chairs and screamin' at me. Jeez, what an asshole."

Terri left part of the story out and never admitted how drunk she had gotten drinking the free beer. She also forgot to mention that she smacked Jesse a few times while driving back from San Jose, recalling how hard it was to keep the car on the road with your left hand while whacking someone's head against the passenger window with your right.

Terri finished her third drink. There was one more thing she left out. She was still in love with him.

Terri felt miserable when Sandy dropped her off. It was about eight-thirty and she didn't want to go back to the apartment. When she walked in, Jesse had the stereo turned up full blast. He was stretched out on the bed, mouthing the words to "*Love, Reign O'er Me*." He fixed his eyes on her.

"Where were you?"

"I was out to lunch with Sandy. Can you turn that music down? You listen to that same album constantly!"

He got up and went over to the stereo and turned it down. He looked her up and down and said, "Kind of a long lunch, huh?"

"What the hell do you care? You're never here anyway. I've been cooped up here long enough. I deserve a day out."

"Oh, *you* been cooped up? That's too bad. Maybe you should try diggin' ditches."

"Well, you had fun last night didn't you? Breakin' up those chairs and punchin' a hole in the wall."

He looked over at the chairs on the floor and the hole in the wall.

"Why don't you just go fuck yourself," he said as he walked out the door.

Terri changed into her night clothes, got into bed, and cried. Her contempt for him faded as she envisioned herself with her new job, making it alone without him. But then he'd redeem himself again.

* * *

Terri and Jesse sat in one of the sleazy Monte Rio Bars. For a tiny town, it had lots of bars, four in all. The misplaced inhabitants needed somewhere to lose their loneliness.

Terri had been working at the state hospital for about six months. She hadn't had a taste of alcohol or a taste of Jesse in the last month or so, having decided to quit drinking altogether. She wanted to show him she could do it, and was hoping maybe he'd follow her lead. She was feeling particularly pleased with herself tonight. It hadn't been so difficult to abstain from alcohol, and staying sober made it easier for her to resist Jesse. She didn't know why she agreed to come to this place with him. She sipped a coke.

Jesse had one hand wrapped around a vodka and club and one hand on her knee.

She glanced at him. "Have you thought about lookin' for a job at all lately? I noticed your trips to the unemployment office have stopped."

He took a long swig from his drink. Hank Williams lamented in the background, "*I'm So Lonesome I Could Cry.*"

"C'mon, Terri. I brought you out tonight so we could have a good time. You always gotta start."

"We could use some money. Don't you get tired of doing *nothing* all day? I did."

"I don't do nothin'! Here!" With that he slammed a hundred-dollar bill on the bar.

Terri's eyes widened. "Where'd you get that?"

He gave her a dour look and removed his hand from her knee.

"Use yer imagination."

"No. I wanna know. Where'd you get that money?"

"You don't need to know everything. That's the trouble with you. You wanna know things you shouldn't and you wanna change things you have no business changin'."

He took a few more long gulps of the drink and ordered another one. It was funny but when he drank, Terri could almost taste the vodka. He suddenly changed the subject.

"Terri, don't you think I know what you're doin'? You're out with Sandy all the time. You keep avoidin' me. Now you sit here not drinkin' like you're so high and mighty. What're you tryin' to prove anyway?"

She began to wonder about that herself. Her month of sobriety had made no impression on him at all. Her reasoning became unclear and she began to feel she was only spiting herself.

"I'm not tryin' to prove anything. I just wanted us to stop fightin'." She leaned over and whispered in his ear, "I don't wanna fight with you anymore." Kissing his neck, she whispered again, "I just want us to be okay. I don't want us to hurt anymore." She moved away from him and waved the bartender over.

"I'll have a vodka martini with Smirnoff Silver, please."

Jesse smiled, dimples creasing his cheeks.

"Jeez, babe, when you fall off, you really fall off."

They laughed as Jesse moved his hand further up her thigh. Terri downed the martini. She ordered another drink. The vodka warmed her down to her toes. She felt herself transcend into a more natural state, something she'd missed—relaxed, content. She was exactly where she wanted to be. It was almost closing time. Jesse ordered more drinks.

She got a good whiff of him as he leaned over and whispered to her.

"When we get home, I wanna show ya' somethin'."

Terri felt a fluttering in the pit of her stomach at the thought of what he had in store.

Back at their place, Terri was filled with anticipation as she got ready for bed. She'd had enough alcohol now to lose her inhibitions and she didn't feel that heavy drunken feeling. It was that perfect plateau, that free floating state of anesthesia, one she'd lose if she continued to drink. But Jesse's plan didn't include any more alcohol.

When she walked out of the bathroom, she saw him setting up the large mirror from their bureau on the little end table right next to the bed.

"What are you doing?"

"C'mere, Terri." He pulled her toward him and kissed her long and slow, removing her T-shirt.

They fell onto the bed, still kissing. He took her face gently in his hands and looked into her eyes. He pulled off her pants.

"Did ya' ever see yourself come?"

"What? No...I...I—"

"Well, you're gonna see it. You're real beautiful when ya' come and I want you to see it."

She knew it would be real soon.

He removed his pants and worked his magic with his

nimble fingers and warm mouth. It happened fast and she was a bit embarrassed. He was above her now and with his agile fingers working delicately, her body began to move in waves.

He lowered his head and whispered to her. "Look in the mirror, babe."

She turned but she could only see him. The sight of Jesse making love to her was most spectacular. She wanted to look away but couldn't.

He pulled her close and she cried. The image in the mirror brought on a flood of emotions, mostly love. And uncertainty.

* * *

Two weeks later, Jesse headed to Monte Rio to call his mother. He called her every Saturday and she told him all the hometown news. Terri was anxious for him to return because they were going to tour the Sonoma Valley wineries. Things had been fairly quiet since he made love to her in front of the mirror. They were fighting less.

When Jesse returned, she was busy cleaning the bathroom. She was on her hands and knees by the toilet.

"Terri."

She looked up at him standing in the doorway. She could see something was wrong. His blue eyes had turner darker.

"What?"

"Come out here." He turned around and went over to the bed.

"Wait. I have to finish this."

He walked back to the bathroom.

"Sharon's dead."

The Ajax she was holding clattered to the floor. She stared at him.

"What? That can't be, Jesse. That can't be true."

"It's true. She OD'd yesterday. They...uh...found her in her apartment. It looked like somebody tried to revive her in the tub and then just left her there."

She let out a shrill wail.

"That bastard, Romeo. That fucker. I knew somethin' bad was gonna happen."

She thought of Sharon, vivacious and beautiful. Glimpses of their childhood flashed through her head. She saw Sharon's freckled face, as she reached down to pull Terri up into their favorite tree.

She was lying on the floor, sobbing and yelling. "Oh, my god, nooooo. Nooooo. Sharon, Sharon."

Jesse knelt down, pulled her up and held her close. She was soaking his shirt with her tears. He squeezed her hard.

"I really loved her, Jesse," she yelled. "I really did. I wanted to see her again. I wanted to see her...oh my god..."

"I know. I know just how ya' feel." He thought of Flynn and how he died. "You need to get in touch with Sandy. Ya' know how she must be feelin'."

He took her face in his hands and brushed her hair off her forehead.

"C'mon. Let's get a drink. Let's go to the wineries. You still wanna?"

Her voice cracked. "I don't know, Jesse. I just don't know."

* * *

In the months that followed Sharon's death, Terri had gone on what her mother would have called a "bender." No one was held accountable for Sharon's death—she was just another heroin overdose. Terri dealt with it the only way she knew how.

It was a Friday evening and she was driving home from Riverview, a restaurant Alan was in the process of buying. The deal would soon be finalized. She'd been drinking all day with Sandy.

It was the second time Terri had called in sick this week. Last week it was three times. When she got back to the apartment, the smell of pot permeated the whole room. Jesse was at the table drinking a beer. He was listening to *"The Real Me."*

"Hey, babe. You been gone a while."

She glared at him and headed to the bathroom.

"Yeah, so what? Why are you listening to that fuckin' album again?" She slammed the bathroom door. When she came back into the room he went straight back after her.

"Called in sick again today, huh?"

"So what? My friend died okay?" She turned down the stereo.

"Yeah, it's okay with me but you're gonna lose your job if you keep it up."

She came toward him.

"And that would be awful for you, wouldn't it? I mean...there'd be no money comin' in so you couldn't sit around here smokin' pot all day, right?"

"I guess you're loaded."

"*I'm* loaded? Take a look at your eyes. Just look at them. You've been wasted since I met you."

"Oh, shit. Here we go. Listen, I need to use the car. I been stuck here all day."

"No. I'm going back out with Sandy. I'm supposed to meet her at the Onion."

"Well, I'll drive you there and she can drive you home."

Terri felt her face grow hot. "NO! You're not usin' my car. It's my car. Got that?"

"Ya' know. You're really some bitch."

She stood right in front of him. The words she used now seemed to come from someone else. From this point on, it seemed as if she were viewing two strangers.

"You know what? I don't like you anymore. You know what you are?"

He just stood in front of her and stared.

"You're a fucking burden. Yeah, that's right. A burden. You can go straight to hell with that group of dirtbags from town but I'm not going with you. Got that? Junkie."

She grabbed Quadrophenia off the stereo and broke it over her knee. She went to grab the second record from the double album but Jesse got to her first.

He grabbed her by the shirt and rammed her into the apartment's entry door. It was a French door with multiple panes of glass. She heard the glass breaking behind her. He picked her up and slammed her against it again.

"What? What the fuck did you say I was? You dragged me out here. I bust my ass working for you. Now you got a job and you gotta say that?"

Terri was only aware of one thing at this moment. She wasn't scared.

"You shouldn'ta broke that album." He wasn't screaming anymore.

No, I probably shouldn't have.

He grabbed their alarm clock and slammed it down on the bureau.

"Five minutes. You hear me? Five minutes to get outta here. If you're not outta here in five minutes—just get the fuck out."

"No. I'm not leaving. You leave. Go home," she screamed.

With that he grabbed her and pushed her out the door.

"You're one crazy bitch. I said you're the one goin' and you're goin.' Get the fuck out and take your fuckin' car too." With that he smacked her in the face. She fell down onto the driveway. Next, came her clothes, landing in heaps around her as she lay there. She held her cheek. It stung. She was in shock. She knew this feeling and thought it was good. It was the numbness she needed right now. She started grabbing her clothes.

"I gotta go. Oh shit. I gotta get outta here." She threw her clothes in the trunk. She just wanted out.

A police car pulled up behind her. *Shit. Who called the police?*

The officer approached her. "Having a problem here, miss?"

"I gotta go. I just gotta go."

"C'mon back inside first, miss. Maybe he's gotta go."

Two officers entered the apartment while Terri placed the last load of clothes into the car and closed the trunk. By the time she was back inside, the cops had Jesse up against the wall in handcuffs. He looked right in her eyes. She felt sick. A brief sense of pity welled up inside her. She glanced at the cops. They were way too cheerful.

"He's coming with us, miss. Say goodbye to the little lady, punk." Terri watched them drag him out the door and throw him into the back of the police car.

She stood in the driveway as the car pulled away.

"Wait. I'm no lady. I broke his favorite album. I..." She started to cry.

She sat on the bed. Her thoughts were hazy. She got herself a beer and tried to calm down. She went to the bathroom and began gathering up her cosmetics. She'd go to Sandy's and stay there until she knew what to do.

About fifteen minutes later, there was a knock on the door. It was the cops with Jesse. They brought him into the room, uncuffed him, and threw him on the bed.

"We don't think he'll bother you again, miss. Look. He's meek as a lamb. Just call us if you have any more trouble with him."

Jesse looked different. His face was swollen. His wrists were red from the cuffs. She wanted to throw her arms around him, tell him she was sorry, make love to him. But she didn't want to prolong their misery any longer.

He sat up and looked right through her.

"I'm not gonna hurt you anymore, Terri. I'm goin' home. Can you give me bus money?" He rubbed his wrists where the handcuffs had bruised them.

"Sure, I'll give you money. Uh...they didn't hurt you did they?"

He flashed a big drunken dimpled smile.

"Those guys. Nah. I'm used to it."

She went to the door and turned back to look at him

one last time. She felt a heaviness in her chest.

"I'm gonna go stay with Sandy tonight. So...I'll see ya'."

"Yeah, Terri. I'll see ya' sometime."

* * *

Terri and Sandy sat sipping their drinks on the large soft pillows on the floor. They were at a dance club called The Winery. Terri was telling lies.

"So when is he leaving?" Sandy asked.

"I don't know. Who cares? I say good riddance. I'm glad it's finally over. He was just draggin' me down."

"Yeah, I knew that. He was never good for you. You need somebody sweet and nice, not a drunk."

"Well, not somebody too nice. I don't want anybody boring ya' know? Anyway, I'm through with men for now."

"We better go, Terri. It's almost closing time."

"These damn California bars. They close so damn early. I can't get used to this."

"C'mon. We got a long drive home."

"This damn state is too big. I'm gonna try to get a goddamn beer for the ride home."

Terri was successful getting one for the road. But on the way home, the road was giving her trouble.

"Sandy, you awake? I think you better drive. I'm havin' a hard time seein' the road. It's so dark. Don't they have any streetlights around here?"

"Okay. Just make the next right."

Terri couldn't wait to let Sandy drive. She'd been fighting to keep the car on the road since they left the club. She made the right turn as Sandy instructed, but something was wrong. No brakes. She was about to tell Sandy the brakes had failed when she realized they were airborne. The next thing Terri saw was something like a spider web in front of her, the windshield. And then there was water.

Her feet were soaked with cold water. She started to cry.

"Terri. C'mon, we gotta get out of the car."

"I can't. My door's all smashed."

Sandy pushed her door open, grabbed Terri by the arm, and pulled her out the passenger side.

"Where the fuck are we, Sandy? Is this a fuckin' swamp?"

"Nah. I think we landed in a vineyard. C'mon the water's not deep." Sandy pulled Terri up the side of the steep ravine that led to the road. Terri was amazed at her levelheadedness in the midst of chaos.

"All my stuff is down there, my clothes, the leather jacket my sister gave me, everything." The more she thought about her stuff, the more she cried.

"Don't worry about it now. We'll get it tomorrow. We gotta find a place to call Ben and Alan."

They started down the dark road, guided only by moonlight, as dogs barked in the distance.

* * *

When Terri woke up the next day on Sandy's couch, her whole body ached. She tried to lift herself, but it was too painful. She just lay there with her eyes closed. *Shit. Ouch. Even my hair hurts.* She tried to move again. She heard Alan walk over to the desk and make a phone call.

"Hey, man. How ya' doin? How are things out on the Island? Yeah, that's right. Soon I'll be the new owner of Riverview. The deal is almost done. You gotta come out here. You gotta see the restaurant. Yeah, right on the ocean. Yeah…yeah."

Terri must have dozed off again but caught the end of Alan's conversation.

"We had a little excitement last night though. Sandy's friend, Terri, is here. I told you about her right? They had a little car accident. We had to pick them up. Took them to the hospital. They're fine though. They were real lucky. So sounds like Terri's gonna be staying with us a while. Her boyfriend's going back to New York. He was a real fuck. So this is good news. She's sleeping on the couch right now. I just walked by and I got an angel sleeping on my couch. An angel with two black eyes."

Oh fuck, no. Two black eyes?

She waited for Alan to finish his phone call so she could sneak into the bathroom and check her face. Just then she had a remarkable thought.

I've got nothing. Absolutely nothing.

But then she smiled. Things couldn't possibly get any worse and there was only one way to go…and that was up.

Chapter 14

The plain shingled house looked the same, the roof a bit more worn from the harsh valley winters. It was always a welcome sight but this time, Jesse felt his life was over. He opened the door and threw his bag down. "Ma, you here?"

"Jesse? Is that you?" she called from upstairs.

"Yeah, I'm back." Again. Always back here again with Annie, after he'd lost everything. He was a bit older now and losing hurt more. He knew he lost Terri that night in that dismal apartment they shared in California.

Annie rushed toward him and hugged him. She looked older too.

"Come in the kitchen, son. So good to have you back. Are ya' hungry? Want a cup of tea?"

"Got any beer, Ma?"

"No, Jesse. Ya' know I don't drink it. Sit and tell me what happened. After ya' called, I was so worried. Why would ya' come home in such a hurry now? Just because ya' had a fight with Terri?"

He looked her straight in the eyes.

"Ma, it wasn't just a fight. It's me, Ma. It's me."

Tears started to roll down his face.

"I'm just like him, Ma. I got that curse like ya' said. I can't do this anymore."

He continued to cry as she pulled him on to her shoulder.

"It's me. You understand what I'm sayin'?"

"I know, son. I know. Believe me. You're not like him. You're not a bad boy. Ya' know how *he* was."

"Ma, I hit her. You understand what I did?" His voice got louder. "Just like he did to you. I hit her and it wasn't the first time. I *am* like him."

She hung her head and cried.

"Oh, what did I do to you boys, puttin' up with that man?"

He lifted her chin. "Ma, it's not your fault. I know you must've had your reasons."

She took his hand in hers. "Jesse, that's just the way it was for a woman. There was no other way. When you took a husband, it was for life. Now things are different."

"Look at me, Ma. I'm a drunk and I don't wanna be a drunk anymore. I'm callin' Mark. He'll tell me what to do. And Ma, soon we gotta talk. Me and you. We gotta talk about Danny."

She gave him a grim look and quickly left the room. "Call your brother, Jesse."

He dialed his brother in Colorado.

"Mark, it's me, Jesse."

"Hey, Jesse. How are things in California?"

"I'm not in California. I'm back home with Ma."

"Why?"

"Cause I'm a fuckin' drunken asshole. That's why."

"What?"

"You heard me." He started crying again. "Mark, please. Tell me what to do. I can't stop drinkin' and I don't know what to do."

"You know what to do. Pick up the paper and get your ass to a meeting. I been waitin' a long time for this, Jesse. I'm real happy to hear ya' talk like that."

"Happy? You're a sick fuck, Mark."

He wiped the tears from his face as they both laughed.

"I don't think those meetings are gonna help me."

"Jesse. Listen to me. Just do what I'm tellin' ya' to do. Today. This is probably one of the best days of your life, but you don't even know it. Promise me you'll do it."

"Okay. Okay. I'm gettin' the paper now. I'll call you later."

"You do that. Call me after you go."

Jesse grabbed the paper and looked under the A.A. section. He found a church nearby with an eight o'clock meeting. He made himself a cup of tea and grabbed a handful of cookies. He hoped these would sustain him until he got to the church.

* * *

As he stood in front of St. Paul's, he was edgy. He wanted to turn and run. Go buy a six-pack and maybe hike up the mountain. He was frightened and his stomach churned.

The side entrance to the church led to the basement where the meetings were held. A few men were standing there talking. They all greeted him with a cheery hello. He didn't appreciate the uplifting greeting. He walked into the sparse room and stood in the back. Then he felt someone's hands on his shoulders.

"Hey, JJ. How's it goin'?"

He turned around to see Kevin.

"Holy shit! What the fuck are you doin' here?"

"Oh, I been in these rooms for a few years now."

They hugged and Jesse felt a sense of relief to see a familiar face.

"Yeah, and I feel great. You heard the story of how I drove through Dugan's store, right? The DWI's?"

"Yeah, I heard about that."

"Well, I haven't had a drink since then. The judge kind of forced me in here. But it turned out to be a good thing—the best thing that ever happened to me."

"Really?" Jesse was confused.

"Just keep comin' here and as time goes by, you'll get it. C'mon, let's sit down. The meeting's about to start."

Jesse took a look around the room. There was a poster with the twelve steps on it. He'd learned a bit about them in rehab, but they never made any sense to him. They still looked like some sort of nonsense language. A young girl at the front of the room began to speak. She was pretty, probably in her early thirties. Jesse was happy to see everyone in the room looked normal. She began speaking. "My name is Carolyn and I'm an alcoholic." She continued with her own story, her childhood, her drinking history, and her life today. When she finished, everybody clapped. Jesse did too and felt a little better by the end of her talk.

As he stood outside smoking with the others, an older man asked, "Is this your first meeting?"

He didn't feel like talking but felt he had to answer.

"Yeah, yeah it is."

"Welcome, kid. Keep comin' back." A few other older guys said the same thing. He was suspicious. These people were too happy and too kind. He wondered what their angle was.

"C'mon, JJ. We're goin' to the diner. That's what we do now." Kevin smacked him on the arm.

"Okay." Jesse had nothing else to do, so he jumped in Kevin's car and they all took off for the Interstate Diner. Jesse and Kevin took a table by themselves. They ordered and began to talk. It was a conversation that was different from any he'd ever had.

As Kevin spoke about his drinking, it was as if Jesse were hearing himself. The more they talked, the better he felt.

"Listen, you're going to need a sponsor and I guess I'm it. You don't know anything about staying sober. You only know how to be a drunk. Somebody's gotta help you learn how to do it. Do you think you want this? I mean, do you wanna stay sober like me?"

"Yeah, I want it real bad."

"Then listen to everything you hear in the rooms. Keep comin' to the meetings, and take suggestions. In other words, just do what you're told. And, JJ, you gotta tell your story just like that girl did tonight. I know it's not easy, but you gotta do it someday."

"Are you fuckin' kiddin' me? I'll try, Kev. That's all I can say. I'll fuckin' try."

Kevin and Jesse left the diner and drove around for a while, looking at the decrepit old town where they grew up. Jesse felt like he had been part of its decay.

"Listen, I'll pick you up for a meeting tomorrow," Kevin told him as he dropped him off. "Be ready at seven thirty."

"Okay. See ya' bro."

Jesse went in the house, called Mark, and told him everything about his night. He watched some TV and went to bed. As he was listening to James Taylor's *"Walking Man"* in his room, he realized he hadn't thought about a drink the whole time he was with Kevin.

* * *

As the months passed, Jesse followed almost all of Kevin's suggestions. Now he was on the phone to Mark, waiting for his ride to the meeting.

"Yeah, tonight's the night. How the fuck am I gonna do this, Mark? I put it off for as long as I could. I don't like talkin' in front of people. I don't know what to say. You fuckin' guys didn't tell me this was gonna be so hard."

"Listen, don't worry about what you're gonna say. It'll just come. You'll do fine. Have you taken a look at the steps?"

"Yeah. Kevin's helpin' me with them."

"So you know what's next then?"

"Yeah, I know what's next and I don't fuckin' like it."

"Well I didn't like it either, but I did it. You wanna drink again and go back to bein' a fuckin' asshole, or God forbid, doin' dope again? Face it, Jesse. We're just like the old man. That poor fuckin' bastard. At least we have another chance, right?"

"Yeah, Mark, right. Hey, I gotta go. Kevin's here."

He jumped into Kevin's car.

"Hey, JJ. You ready for this?" Kevin laughed.

"Yeah, I guess so. What's so fuckin' funny?"

"We're all in the same boat. That's what's funny. It'll help you a lot more than you realize."

"But do I have to tell them everything? I mean,

everything?"

"No, just tell your story. But soon you'll have to tell me everything. You know that, right?"

"Yeah, I know."

They talked on the way to the church. Kevin filled Jesse in on what was going on in his life. Bowie sang *"Star Man."*

"Hey, did you hear I started playin' again?"

"Bass or lead?"

"Lead this time. Got a real nice Fender Strat. I hooked up with a few other guys and this time it looks good. We might be ready for a gig in a month or so."

Jesse's mind wandered back to that night he'd heard Terri sing for the first time. It was a disturbing memory, one he'd tried to extinguish along with the others. He wondered if he'd talk about it tonight.

"So what about you, JJ?"

He only heard the end of Kevin's question.

"I said what are you gonna do? How's school going? Never thought you'd wanna be a nurse."

"It's great. I'm doin' good. It's a great way to meet chicks, too. I met a nice one the other day. I'll be seein' a lot of her in class."

"Take it slow, JJ. You still got a lotta work to do. It'll take a bit of time before you can handle a relationship."

He realized Kevin was right, but this time, he figured he'd ignore Kevin's advice.

"So, Kevin. While doin' all this work on myself, you think it's okay if I at least get laid?"

* * *

Jesse's mind was racing and his mouth was dry as the chairman of the meeting went through the usual formalities. He was shaking a bit and it reminded him of the hangovers he'd had in the past few years that could only be remedied with another drink. He was glad this was just a case of nerves. He was thinking about the time in their apartment when Terri had first seen him take a morning drink. Then he heard his name called.

He walked up to the podium and began.

"My name is Jesse and I'm an alcoholic. I wanna say I'm real nervous and shaky, but it beats a hangover."

Laughter filled the room. Jesse was still amazed at the amount of joy at these meetings, and realized a bit of it had been rubbing off on him over the past months.

"I'm up here 'cause I'm an alcoholic, but I'm also up here 'cause Kevin's makin' me do this." More laughter.

"And it's about time. I want to thank Kevin for helping me through this. It's been hard but I'm feelin' better every day." He cleared his throat and began the story.

"I grew up with an alcoholic father. He drank ever since I can remember. He was probably a daily drinker, but the thing about him was he was a real mean drunk. He used to hit my mom and if we got in the way, he hit us too. He also shot our dog in a drunken rage, and did some other bad things. But I guess I'm here to tell my story, not his.

"I started drinkin' real young. I was about ten. I'd fetch drinks for my dad, so when I did, I got some for myself, whether it was whiskey or beer. He was a beer and shot man, so I just drank whatever he was havin'. The alcohol made me feel real good and all those fears I had, even the fear of my dad, they just disappeared with the first buzz. I didn't do so good in school 'cause I drank, but I made it through. I was drunk most of my time in high school.

"It was a lot easier to talk to women when I was half-loaded. I got married right out of school. I kept drinkin' throughout my marriage, and lots of nights I just didn't come home. After a while, I fell in with a crowd of guys who shot dope. I know this is an A.A. meeting and I'm not gonna stay on that subject too long, 'cause alcohol is really the drug that got me here.

"What I want to say is, if I'd been sober, I might have

thought twice about stickin' a needle in my arm. But I did and ended up strung out. So I shot heroin and drank for about two years or so. During that time, I was a liar and a thief, and stole from people I loved. I jumped through a glass door, wrecked a few cars, things like that. I was also with my best friend when he got hit by a train. And that hurt so much, I just did more dope. Needless to say, my wife left me.

"I kicked heroin and thought I was on top of the world, but I kept drinkin'. The dope was behind me, but now the drinkin' started causin' lots of problems in my personal life. But I didn't recognize it at all. The next girl I was with…she drank a lot too, but I don't blame her, havin' to put up with me. We moved in together and I just stayed out a lot. When I did come home, I just wasn't nice. I'd take her car and almost wrecked it a few times.

"I started getting' hangovers that hurt so much, I'd drink in the morning for relief. I thought it was a gift that I could drink so much. My mom said it was a curse, and she was right. It's amazin' you can drink for so long and your mind tells you that it's okay, even though you're havin' blackouts and doin' all kinds of crazy shit. That's the insanity of the disease I guess.

"Well I started to get worried about my drinkin' after I first hit this girl, the one I lived with. I loved her a lot. So here we were one night outside a bar, and she's got blood all over her and her eye is split open. I'm standin' there in a drunken stupor and a voice is sayin' *'You did that. Get the hell outta here. You did it.'* So I did what any cowardly drunk would do. I left town. It never occurred to me to stop drinkin'. So anyway, later I got back with this girl. I don't know why she took me back. I like to think 'cause she was just as sick as I was."

More laughter filled the room.

"But it happened again. I hit her again. Then I came here and this is where I been ever since. It's hard to believe that hittin' someone I loved would bring me to my knees, but it did. A little voice was sayin' *'You're just like your daddy, you fuckin' asshole. Do somethin' about yourself.'* 'Scuse my language but that's what that voice said, and that's how I ended up here.

"So thanks to this program and my sponsor, I'm in school. I have a good job at the VA Hospital and it feels so good to help out the guys over there. I'm amazed every day and thank my Higher Power that I heard that little voice. I gotta thank Kevin. I love ya', man. He's the first man I ever said that to, but it's true. So thanks a lot."

Jesse went back to sit down, but before he did, Kevin stood up and gave him a hug. Jesse leaned over and whispered in Kevin's ear. "What a fuckin' relief, man."

Kevin patted him on the back.

"You sounded good up there, JJ. You're a natural born speaker."

* * *

Jesse strutted down the pale yellow hallway of the VA Hospital and greeted the Vietnam vets as he passed each one.

"Hey, Carl, how ya' doin' today?"

"Hey, JJ. Yo, when you come back down, bring me a Playboy will ya'?"

"You got it."

He went up to the commissary to see his mom. He always stopped by to see her before his shift. She'd gotten him this job and he was grateful. He was grateful for a lot of things lately. He was greeted by more vets, young and old. He'd been getting to know them well now, the ones who called the VA Hospital home.

His mom was at the counter she'd worked behind for twenty-seven years. He felt bad she still had to work because her sons were fuckups. He swore that after he finished school, he'd pay her back.

"Hey, Ma." He leaned over the counter and gave her a kiss. "Gimme a coffee and a buttered hard roll. You have time to sit with me awhile?"

He'd been so busy since he'd been back in town. With school, work, and going to meetings, he seldom had time for her anymore and was feeling a bit guilty. She didn't seem to notice that though. She'd been so happy since he'd stopped drinking. That was all that mattered to her.

"Oh, I might have time for a quick cup of tea. Go sit down and I'll join you for ten minutes."

He sat and watched her bustle around behind the counter, and a sense of peace came over him. The feeling was fleeting but it was something he hadn't felt in a long time, and he knew he'd always remember this moment. She came over and sat down.

"Ma, I been so busy, we haven't had a chance to talk."

"Oh, Jesse. I know. You're so busy with school and your meetings. I want to tell you, son, how proud I am. How long has it been now, over a year?"

"Yeah, Ma. I feel real good. I met a nice girl at school. We been goin' out. I'll bring her to meet ya' soon."

"Oh, that's wonderful. What became of Terri, dear? You think about her much?"

Did he think about her much? It struck him funny. Only every single day since he'd left California. But he wasn't going to tell her that.

"Well ya' know, Ma. She has somebody else so I guess we just weren't meant to be. She met a guy out there I heard. I guess she's happy and I'm happy. So that's it."

"Well dear, I heard her father is upstairs on the ward you're working on this shift. I don't know what's ailing him, but I just thought I'd tell you before you go up. You'll most likely see him up there."

He thought about how the old man hated him. Jesse hoped Chick was senile—maybe he wouldn't remember him. That would make the ordeal of seeing Chick Micelli again a bit easier to bear.

"Yeah. I'm sure I'll see him. He was some piece of work."

A group of people came in. Annie waved to them that she'd be right there.

"I hope he's not too sick. Look, I've gotta get back behind the counter. Have a good day. See you tonight."

"Bye, Ma." He gave her a peck on the cheek and picked up the magazine he'd promised Carl.

Taking the elevator up to the third floor to start his shift, he wasn't looking forward to seeing Chick. He didn't want to think about Terri, and Chick would only bring back painful memories.

"Hey, Jesse," one of the nurses greeted him. "Are we glad to see you! We've got a real live wire in room 281. He's been keeping us busy."

Jesse knew exactly who they were talking about.

"Oh yeah? Is his name Micelli?"

"Yes. How did you know?"

"Oh, just a hunch. Why is he here?"

"He's got stomach problems. Having some tests in the morning, probably an endoscopy. He'll be here about a week. He can't keep anything down so he's on liquids and he's real crabby."

"Yeah, I bet," he mumbled as he started his rounds. *Maalox for room 281.* He decided to save that room until the end.

The last time he saw Chick was the day he'd left for California with Terri. He remembered Chick crying in the driveway as they pulled away. He wondered if time had mellowed the old man at all. He was about to find out.

As he approached Chick's room, he could hear his booming voice.

"I don't take shit from nobody and I'm not gonna take it from you. I'm turnin' on the TV. Don't bother talkin' to me no more." Chick was yelling at the man in the other bed as Jesse entered the room.

"Is there a problem in here, guys?"

"Yeah! That son of a bitch told me to shut up. That's what! And I don't take no shit from nobody." He looked right at Jesse now, his face flushed. Jesse knew from experience the other guy was probably right. He was thrilled Chick hadn't recognized him so far.

"Who wants the Maalox?"

"I do," said Chick. He was still flustered from hollering at his neighbor. "Over here."

Jesse walked over to his bed with the medication.

"I can't eat nothin'. I got heartburn all the time and I keep hawkin' everything up. The other night at the diner, I threw up right in the booth. But the waitress cleaned it up. They're gonna give me another hose job tomorrow."

Jesse chuckled and remembered how funny Chick was those nights he'd spent with Terri drinking and smoking pot in her basement.

"What?" Jesse said, trying to conceal a smile.

"A hose job. Ya' know. They're gonna stick that tube down my throat and clean everything out. I shouldn'ta ate those fuckin' artichokes the other night. Ever since then, everything got stuck."

Jesse was having trouble holding back his laughter. He handed Chick the medication cup. He studied the old man's face as he gulped down the Maalox. He noticed he hadn't changed much at all. The only difference was that Chick had some gray in his thick black hair.

Now that he was past the hurdle of facing Chick again and was actually enjoying the banter, he decided to ask the obvious question. He took the cup from him and said, "So, Chick. You remember me?"

The old man squinted one eye at him. "Yeah. I remember you. You think I'm senile? I know exactly who you are. It hasn't been that long ya' know."

Chick was right. What seemed so long ago to Jesse was probably just a flash to the old man.

"You went to California with my daughter."

"Yeah, that's right." Jesse was becoming uncomfortable now and started organizing the meds on his cart. But Chick still had more to say.

"You still drink beer? You were always drinkin' beer."

Jesse looked right at him now.

"No, Chick. I don't drink anymore."

"Good. Cause if you kept drinkin', you woulda ended up an alkie. I seen that happen to a lotta guys."

Jesse grabbed the cart and turned to leave.

"Listen if you need anything, just buzz the nurses' station okay?"

"Okay. Hey, kid. What're ya', a nurse?"

Jesse was in a hurry to leave, but looked back at the old man. "Not yet, but I'm workin' on it. Hey, by the way, my name is Jesse."

Chick didn't respond. His eyes were glued to the TV.

Chapter 15

Terri awoke with a stiffening jolt in the early morning hours. This had become commonplace for her after a night of heavy drinking. She didn't remember when the hangovers had turned into this almost unbearable state. She knew what to do. It was a clear sunny Northern California morning. She walked into the kitchen. The small cottage Alan bought sat on a hill facing the Pacific. They'd moved out of the house they'd shared with Sandy and Ben about a year after Alan bought the restaurant. They were reaping the rewards of Alan's creative cooking style and the scenic location of his restaurant.

She grabbed a quick bowl of cereal. Then she grabbed a beer. After about four beers, she'd be ready to go to the restaurant to start her day. Alan always slept in due to his late nights at Riverview. He was a workaholic and she had alcohol. Their obsessions provided a perfect balance to their relationship.

Terri was in charge of the restaurant's bar. She did the ordering and some bartending. She settled into their new lifestyle with a contentment she hadn't felt in a long time. Alan had wooed her and won her with kindness and good food. Although she missed the passion she shared with Jesse, she didn't miss the turmoil.

Alan was even-tempered, sweet, and nurturing, but what impressed her most was that he wasn't a drinker. He immersed himself in his work and that caused him to close his eyes to all her shortcomings.

She drove up the winding highway until she could see Riverview. It sat up high on a yellow and green hill overlooking the exact spot where the Russian River kissed the sea. The small building was round, encircled by tall windows so that anywhere you were seated, you were guaranteed an ocean view. The bar was situated in the center of the restaurant and this is where Terri had spent a good part of the last couple of years.

At around ten in the morning, she'd open up the bar and take inventory. Then she'd fix herself a drink and wait for Alan. This was the only time Alan could spare. They'd talk a bit about last night's profits or the escapades of some of their more interesting customers. Then he'd disappear into the kitchen. Invariably, he'd pop his head out at around one to ask Terri what she'd like for lunch.

Today, Terri decided to call Patty Shea. Other than Chick, she hadn't heard from home in about six months and the news her father had didn't usually interest her. She hoped to catch Patty at home. Someone was always at the Shea's house.

"Hello."

"Hey, Patty. It's me, Terri."

"Hey. How's everything out there?"

"Things are great. Alan's doing real good with the restaurant. I help out with the bar and all. I quit my job at the state hospital and just work at the restaurant now. It's so pretty here. The place overlooks the ocean. What's new with you?"

"Got a job at the hospital. Nursing is real hard work, but I like it a lot."

"How's your mom and everybody?"

"Great. Kevin quit drinkin' and he's in a band. They opened up the ski lodge and his band plays up there. We're always there. The disco scene is gettin' worn out. Live music is back. And guess what? My mom is going to art school. She's taking up commercial art."

"Wow. That's great. I'm so happy for her. I'd love to hear Kevin's band. So Kevin doesn't drink anymore? That's something. He could really dump 'em, as my dad would say."

"Yeah, and guess who else stopped drinking?"

"Who?"

"Your old boyfriend."

"Jesse?"

"Yeah. And he's going out with Michelle Brewer. You

remember her? She's younger than us."

Terri remembered the pretty blonde. She felt like someone had punched her in the chest. He stopped drinking for this girl, but couldn't stop for her?

Terri's attention span had shortened, but she managed to finish the conversation. She was thrilled Marge was going to school, but couldn't get her mind off Jesse and the blonde.

After she hung up, she made another drink. She frantically tried to recall this girl Michelle, but the only thing that stuck in her mind was that she was straight, not a drinker, not a druggie, just a nice normal girl. She was small and petite, one of those exceedingly sweet girls with a soft voice who smiled a lot. And Jesse not drinking! That hit her hard. Why did he drink so much when he was with her? Did she really drive him to it as he'd told her all those times? The only thing she could come up with was that this girl was good for him, and she wasn't. She felt small.

Just then, Amber, the afternoon bartender, came out of the bathroom ready to start work.

"Hey, Terri. How's everything? I left something for you in the bathroom."

"OK, thanks, Amber."

Terri was a bit hesitant to start with cocaine so early, but after her talk with Patty, she was feeling low. She hoped a couple of lines would make things right. She headed for the bathroom.

The restaurant business was rife with cocaine use due to the long arduous hours and the busy bar scene. It was the late seventies and nobody believed the drug was addictive.

She came out of the bathroom temporarily anesthetized, and fixed herself another drink.

"Okay. Guess it's gonna be a long night," she told Amber. Just then Alan popped his head out of the kitchen and called to her.

"So what can I make you for lunch, my sweet? I

marinated some salmon. How about grilled salmon over a nice salad?"

She wasn't hungry. She was still thinking about Jesse and the cocaine had diminished her appetite.

"No thanks, Alan. I'm not very hungry yet."

"Okay, but let me know before four, cause it's gonna be busy tonight."

She knew he'd be busy from four until closing. The coke was enabling her to drink more and the day seemed to fly by. Before she knew it, Sandy was sitting next to her at the bar. Her shift had ended at six. Terri became more maudlin as they sat and talked.

"What time is it anyway, Sandy?"

"It's nine-thirty."

"Jeez, where the hell did the day go?" She was slurring her words more than usual. "Hey, do you know Michelle Brewer? You remember her?"

"Yeah, I remember her from high school. Why?"

"She's got Jesse and he doesn't drink anymore. That's why. Why couldn't I have Jesse not drinkin'? Why did we have to go through all that shit? Ya' know what I'm sayin'? She's gettin' all the good stuff and I got all the shit."

"Yeah. Doesn't seem fair does it?"

"No, it's not and I'm pissed."

Alan came out of the kitchen and called Sandy over. Terri watched them talk. Drunk as she was, she knew Alan was talking about her. Sandy came back in less than five minutes.

"C'mon, Terri. Let's go."

Terri was irritable. She'd been drinking and doing coke all day on just a bowl of cereal.

"Wait a minute. He wants me outta here, right? Sandy, am I right?"

"Yeah, but so what. Let's just go somewhere else."

"I'll go somewhere else, but first I'm gonna tell him a thing or two."

"No, Terri. Don't. Let's just go."

"You wait here. I'm not gonna do anything. I'm just gonna get us some champagne. That's all."

Terri went behind the bar and grabbed two bottles of the best champagne in the house. She went and knocked on the kitchen door. One of Alan's chefs opened the door.

"Where's Alan? Can you send him out here?"

Alan peeked out of the swinging kitchen door. Terri poked him in the chest as she talked.

"You don't have to tell my friend to take me home 'cause I was leavin' anyway. And I'm takin' these with me."

She held up the two bottles, turned around and walked away. Alan just let her go without a word. He was too busy to argue now.

"C'mon, Sandy. Let's go to the Winery. There's music there. Do you mind driving?"

After they started down the road, she pulled a small bag of coke and a coke spoon out of her purse and began snorting it. They never made it to the Winery, because Terri passed out in the car and Sandy took her home.

When Terri woke up at five in the morning her body was shaking. She got up, fixed some coffee and had a couple of beers. She fell asleep on the couch after the beers cured what ailed her. Waking up at nine, she was shaking again. She downed three more beers and headed out the door. She stood frozen on the doorstep when she realized her car wasn't there. Then she sat on the steps and started to sob. She went back inside knowing she wouldn't make it to the restaurant today.

When Alan walked into the kitchen, with sleepy eyes and rumpled hair, she was sitting at the kitchen table.

"Hey, my sweet."

"Alan, I don't know where my car is."

"Don't you remember? You went with Sandy last night. Your car's still at the restaurant."

She took a long gulp of beer and, with that, dropped her head into her hands and started crying again.

"What's wrong, Terri?"

She'd never blacked out before. She didn't want to talk to him about it.

"I don't feel good. I'm sick and I have a headache. I guess I overdid it last night."

This was probably one of the loneliest moments of her entire life.

"Yeah, that's all it is. Just a little hangover. Just take it easy for a while and watch the cocaine. Tell you what. I'll go in late. I'll make some sandwiches and we'll go over to the redwood forest for lunch."

She was beginning to worry about going back to the bar day after day.

"Alan, maybe I should go back to my old job. I mean this is your thing, the restaurant. Maybe I don't belong there at the bar and all. Maybe I need my old life back. Know what I mean?"

"No. Not really. I thought you hated office work."

She felt boxed in, like her life wasn't her own anymore.

"Listen, Terri. You can do whatever you want. The restaurant is doing well. You can stop working altogether. Maybe we'll get married and have babies. Not right away but in a while. Think you'd like that?"

Now she really felt backed into a corner. Alan was so good to her, she went along with him. She was feeling too sick and too weak to think or make any decisions.

"Alan, you're so sweet and I love you. I really do."

She tried to convince herself that what she was saying was true.

* * *

The back room of the Interstate Diner was filled with laughter. Jesse and Kevin sat in a booth alone. They needed to have a meeting after the meeting.

"Look at all this fuckin' cream cheese," Jesse said as he scraped most of it off his bagel. "Guess who's a patient at the VA Hospital?"

"Who?"

"Terri's father, that fuckin' crazy guinea."

Kevin chuckled. "Oh yeah? He's a riot. Terri used to tell us stories about him. My sisters love him. He's a funny guy."

Jesse agreed. "Oh yeah, he's funny, but he's got some chip on his shoulder. Some temper too. He doesn't get along with too many people. There's this poor old bastard next to him. One minute Chick's tellin' him a joke, the next, he's tellin' him to shut the fuck up. He's sure got a lot of resentment—against who I don't know."

Kevin took a sip of coffee and subtly changed the subject.

"Speakin' of resentments, you started writing?"

"Yeah, yeah. I'm writin'. But I don't know how fearless and searchin' this moral inventory is gonna be, ya' know. I mean, I don't see how tellin' you all my deep dark secrets is gonna help me."

"JJ, all I know is it works. I did it and I don't know when, but any resentment I had against anybody just left me after I did it. They say you're only as sick as your secrets. How far along are you?"

"Well, it's kind of slow goin'. See, I got lots of those secrets you're talkin' about so this might take a while."

"You better stop fuckin' around. You know this is important. Just do it and when you're done writin', call me and we'll just get it over with. You don't wanna go back, do ya'?"

Jesse shook his head. "No, I never wanna go back. I feel too good. Hey, listen. I was in the commissary and this feelin' came over me. It was like a peaceful feelin'. I was just watchin' my mom, drinkin' coffee and I...I don't know. I don't think I ever had that feelin' ever."

Kevin took a sip of coffee. "I know exactly what you mean. It only lasted a little while, right?"

"Yeah, it was short."

"Well, it's gonna get longer if you stay sober and do these steps. It's that thing that drunks don't know anything about until they get sober."

"Then I'll be lookin' forward to it."

Kevin said firmly, "Well, JJ, you ain't gonna get nothin' until you do the work."

* * *

Jesse loved his new schedule. He'd always been full of energy. He thought that's why he drank so much. He'd always felt like a clock that was wound too tight, and the alcohol would relieve the tension. Now with work, school, meetings, and writing his fourth step, he felt each day had its own purpose. When he woke up he'd quickly set his priorities. It was also great to wake up without a crushing hangover and just drive around without fear of the cops. He felt a new sense of freedom, no longer restricted by his addiction. He didn't know when, but the desire for a drink had left him a while back.

He walked to the nurses' station to start his day, feeling nothing could move him from the joyous space he was in. He greeted the nurses as he got himself a cup of coffee.

"How's everything, Jesse?" a nurse greeted him.

"Couldn't be better."

"Oh, you need to take Mr. Micelli down to surgery. He's next on the schedule."

"Okay. On my way."

He walked into Chick's room.

"Good morning guys. How's it hangin'? Hey, Chick, you ready for your hose job?"

Chick was sitting up in bed watching TV. He didn't look like a man in distress.

"Yeah, damn right I'm ready. I been waitin' three days to get in there so I can start eatin' again. You can't live if you can't eat. It's hell to be sick."

Jesse rolled a gurney up to Chick's bed. "You need help gettin' on this thing, Chick?"

"Nah, I don't need no help. I can make it." He hopped onto the gurney with the energy of a much younger man.

As Jesse pushed him down the hall, Chick started.

"That bastard in my room is a pain in my ass. Ya' know, he told me to shut up. He's got some noive. I'm not takin' his shit. If I wanna talk, I'm gonna talk."

"Oh yeah. I know that, Chick."

They rolled up to the operating room waiting area and Jesse sat down on a bench next to Chick. Jesse was reluctant but wanted to ask about Terri again.

"So how's Terri doin' out in California?"

"Oh, she's doin' real good. She lives with a nice guy. He's a Jew and he owns his own restaurant. You gotta hand it to those Jews. They really know how to make good. Now I don't have to worry about her no more. He can take care of her. She don't call me much though. As long as she's doin' good."

Jesse knew Terri had been living with Alan, but he didn't know about the restaurant part. Chick made it all sound so mundane. He remembered his relationship with Terri was anything but that. Chick's loud voice disturbed his thoughts.

"When the hell am I gonna get in there?"

"Just a minute. I'll check with somebody."

Jesse came back with the bad news. "I think we're gonna be here a while. There's some kind of problem in the operating room."

"Jesus Christ," Chick hollered. "I can't wait here all day. They always make you wait in this fuckin' hospital."

Jesse grabbed a magazine and tried to read, but the old man couldn't be ignored. The next thing he knew, he was talking about being drafted.

"And they drafted me when I was thirty-one and I had to start my life all over again with nothin'. Those bastards. When I was in the army, my brother tried to steal my house from me. He was a no good son of a bitch. My sisters were no good either. They tried to get all my mother's money."

Jesse said sarcastically. "What year was that? 1943?"

"No, it was 1942," he continued. "But I made it. I made a nice livin' and we had a nice house. I had nothin' when I was a kid. I had to wear my sister's shoes and everybody laughed at me. I didn't even have a father. He walked out when I was thirteen. Said he was goin' to pay the gas bill and never came back. Yeah, I grew up without a father. My uncle and cousins used to kick the shit outta me growin' up."

Jesse's good mood was dwindling. "I'm gonna go see what's goin' on." He came back disappointed. "It's gonna be a while longer."

"Those dirty bastards," Chick yelled. "Hurry up in there. I'm a sick man!"

Jesse had had enough. That joyful space was he was in had been intruded upon and he didn't think before he opened his mouth. He spoke to the old man softly and clearly.

"You know what? You got a real bad attitude, Mr. Micelli."

"Hey," Chick began to protest. "You can't—"

Jesse continued, "Oh yeah, I can. 'Cause you're stuck on this gurney with me standin' over you and you're gonna listen to me now. Ya' know you got a chip on your shoulder bigger than your fuckin' head. I was like you too and it didn't get me anywhere. Now I go to a place every week where I'm tryin' to learn to lose all my resentment and I gotta sit here and listen to you.

"You think you own misery? You think you're the only guy who ever had to suffer? How about these poor young Vietnam vets in here without legs? Do you care about those guys? Did you ever care about the other guy? No, 'cause you're too busy thinkin' about yourself.

"So your father left you when you were a kid. Well, I never had a father 'cause he was a fuckin' drunk who beat the shit outta my mother. He died when I was twelve and I was so happy he croaked, I got shit-faced on the whiskey he left behind. So *that's* where I came from. Maybe there's a reason your daughter got as far away from you as she could."

Jesse knew right away he'd been out of line. He sat down quickly and opened the magazine. He peeked over at the old man and saw that his chin was quivering.

Then tears started to roll down Chick's face. Jesse got up.

"Oh no, Chick. Jeez. I'm really sorry. Don't do that. I didn't mean anything. Wait. I'll be right back."

He ran down the hall and came back with some tissues. He patted the tissues on both sides of Chick's face.

"Hey, I'm really sorry. Please stop cryin', Chick."

Jesse wasn't used to seeing a man cry.

"It's okay, kid. Don't pay attention to me. I'm just an old man talkin' too much I guess."

Jesse patted Chick's hand.

"Hey, kid. What's your name anyway?"

Even though he had told Chick his name before, Jesse replied quietly, "Jesse. My name is Jesse."

A nurse popped her head out of the operating room entrance.

"We're ready for you, Mr. Micelli."

As the two nurses rolled him into the operating room, he called back to Jesse, "Hey, Jesse, will you be here when I come out?"

"Sure, Chick. I'll be right here."

* * *

Jesse made good on his promise to be there when Chick came out of the operating room. He was there again when Chick had some exploratory surgery three weeks later. Now a doctor was here with the results. Jesse was making a bed. The old man seemed to mellow a bit over the last few weeks and Jesse had come to enjoy their time together. He listened as he worked.

"Mr. Micelli, I'm Dr. Patel. I need to talk to you about

the results of your last surgery."

Jesse glanced over and noticed Chick was giving the doctor his undivided attention, a courtesy he never gave anyone else.

"Yeah, Doc?"

"Well, there's a large mass in your abdomen and it's attached to some of your organs. We took a biopsy and it turned out to be lymphoma."

Chick's facial expression didn't change. "Is it cancer?"

"Yes, it is a form of cancer but in a man your age, with some radiation and chemotherapy, we have a chance of shrinking the mass. Maybe we can get it under control."

"Well, I don't give a shit what it is. Just get rid of it. Whatever ya' have to do, I'm with ya', Doc."

Jesse was startled at the way he handled the news. The doctor seemed a little surprised too. He'd probably never gotten a reaction like that from any other patient.

"Well, Mr. Micelli, your attitude is very good and that will help when we start the treatments."

"Damn right," Chick said. "The mind controls the body."

"Good. Good." The doctor patted his knee and left the room. Jesse tried to look busy.

"Hey, Jesse. Ya' hear what I got?"

"Yeah, Chick. I heard. But you sure took it well. Maybe that'll be the key to getting better. Are you gonna call your daughters?"

Jesse hoped Terri would come back when she heard the news. He missed her terribly. The old feelings were still there. He wondered what it would be like to make love to her sober.

"Nah, I'm not callin' them yet. I'm gonna see how I feel first with that medicine. I think I'm gonna beat this thing, kid. Hey you wanna play a game of pool? You got time?"

"Yeah, sure, Chick. Let's go."

The pool table was just a few doors down the hall.

They'd played together a few times in the last few weeks. Jesse always listened to Chick now. His ramblings were starting to make more sense and Jesse felt he could glean a bit of wisdom from the old guy.

* * *

Chick broke and sunk three balls. Then he ran a few more. He looked over at Jesse as he played. "So your old man was no good, huh kid?" Jesse was sitting on a bench next to the table.

"Well, it wasn't so much he was no good. He was a drunk. You never know what a drunk can be till you take away the booze. He might have been a nice guy. We never got a chance to find out. Chick, you ever been a drinkin' man?"

"Nah, not me." He walked around the table sinking balls as he talked. "But my wife. She loved to drink. When we were goin' together, she was always drinkin.' Sometimes I used to have to carry her outta places. And she loved to dance on the bar. Everybody loved my wife. She was a beautiful woman. Oh, you dirty bastard," he blurted out as he missed a shot. "Your turn kid."

Jesse approached the table with that confidence Terri was first attracted to. "Tell me more about your wife." He wanted to hear about Terri's mother.

Chick was sitting down watching Jesse play. "Oh yeah. When she had the kids, she didn't drink so much anymore. Sometimes at Christmas or late at night she'd have a shot or two."

Jesse looked up. "She drank whiskey?"

"Oh yeah. She loved scotch too. Then when the kids got bigger, ya' know, when the little one was nine or ten, we'd go out every weekend. She loved to go to bars. And when she drank, she was like a different woman—happy and real affectionate. When we'd come home, she'd go in and kiss the kids and tuck 'em in. My wife wasn't usually like that, but when she had a few drinks, she was different. I loved when she got that way. I'd nurse a few drinks, but mostly I just loved watchin' her cause she got real happy. She'd get drunk and sometimes really sick the next day, but then she'd take a nap and she always cooked dinner.

"Ya' know, kid, sometimes when you really love a woman, even if they do wrong, you stand by 'em. I knew people talked about how much she drank, but I didn't care. I had to go along with it 'cause she was my wife. Know what I mean?"

Jesse hadn't been shooting at all. He was mesmerized by Chick's story about his wife. "Yeah, Chick. I guess I know what ya' mean."

"Go ahead, kid. You're not shootin'."

Jesse ran off the rest of the balls and sunk the eight ball.

"Yer good, kid. I'm gettin' tired. I'm goin' back to my room. Come and see me later, okay?"

"Okay, I will." Jesse left the pool room, his mind filled with thoughts of Terri

* * *

"Hey, Chick. You're goin' home." Jesse came in to help Chick with his things. "We just have to check you out. Is anybody picking you up?"

"Nah. My brother's in Florida for a couple of months. He's been taking me wherever I need to go since I don't have my car anymore. I'll take a cab."

Jesse felt bad for the old man. He didn't realize until this moment that he was totally alone.

"Hey, listen. I'll take you home. They'll let me out of here for a little while." Jesse went over to the nurses' station to see if it would be okay. The nurse gave Jesse Chick's discharge papers. "C'mon, Chick. Let's go."

Jesse wheeled him to the elevator.

"I don't need this damn wheelchair. I can walk, kid."

"Well it's hospital policy. I have to wheel you out."

"I can't wait to get the hell outta here. I miss my house, ya' know."

"Yeah, I'm sure. What happened to your car?"

"Ahhh. I had too many accidents. Ya' know I hit a kid on a motorcycle on Main Street. He didn't get hurt though. He got right up and all these kids were standin' on the corner, and they said 'That old man did it.' They were all pointin' at me. Nobody feels sorry for an old man. So I couldn't drive after that."

Jesse was trying not to laugh as he thought of the poor guy on the motorcycle. He helped Chick into the car and returned the wheelchair. Jesse got in his old Plymouth Valiant. It ran like a top.

"How do you like this beat up piece of junk, Chick?"

"At least you *got* a car," Chick replied.

"You're gonna need to go to treatments a few times a week. How 'bout I take you? I have to come here anyway."

Chick looked over at Jesse.

"You'd do that for me?"

"Sure, I'll do it. I'll give you my phone number so you can remind me."

"Thanks, kid. You're a good boy." Jesse pulled in the driveway thinking of his first date with Terri, when they hiked up the mountain.

"I'll walk you in."

"Nah, Jesse. That's okay. See you in a few days. Thanks, kid."

Jesse called Kevin that night. There was something in the old man's honesty that made him ready. "Hey, Kevin. I'm ready whenever you are. Okay. See ya' then."

He pulled the wire bound notebook out from under his bed and finished writing.

Chapter 16

Jesse looked out the kitchen window at the green mountain that loomed in front of him. It usually gave him a sense of peace but that tranquility wasn't there for him tonight. Cream's *"White Room"* was playing on the stereo. He lit his fourth cigarette. He'd never been a chain smoker but he needed the comfort. He was preoccupied with the wire bound notebook sitting on the kitchen table. Tonight was the night Kevin would hear everything in that notebook—every resentment and every shameful secret Jesse had been carrying around since he was a kid. He was making a pot of coffee when he heard Kevin knock.

"C'mon in, Kevin. It's open."

"Jeez, JJ. It smells like a meeting in here. How many packs did you smoke?" Kevin wasn't a smoker. Jesse waved him off.

"Shut the fuck up. You know I'm not lookin' forward to this."

"Nobody likes it but you can't go on until you get through this. Just think of it as a big hill you have to climb. Things get a little easier on the way down. Like climbing that mountain over there. Always nicer coming down."

"Okay, okay. Fix yourself some coffee, Kev. I'm not gonna wait on you."

Kevin's straight blond hair reached down his back and was tied neatly in a ponytail. "So how are things going with Michelle?"

Jesse didn't feel like making small talk. "It's okay but, listen, why don't you just start readin' the notebook. I don't have to read it to you, do I?"

"No, you should, but I won't make ya' do that. I'll read it and we'll just talk okay? Remember I'm not here to judge you. I'm an alcoholic just like you and I probably did all this same shit." Kevin sat down at the table with his coffee. Jesse tossed the notebook at him.

"Here, I'm goin' outside for a smoke. It's pretty long."

"It's okay, JJ. See you in a while."

Jesse ran down the stairs and sat on the back porch. As he waited, his thoughts turned to what he'd written about Terri in the book and the way he still felt about her. He was concerned about still having those feelings, and now Kevin would know. He knew Kevin would probably want to talk about Flynn's death. Jesse didn't mind. He didn't feel that much guilt over it anymore. But the other incident haunted him, the one he didn't even write down. He needed to tell Kevin the whole story face to face. He couldn't wait until this night was over.

He went back inside and sat at the table. Kevin was still reading. "Aren't you done yet? Jeez, it wasn't that long."

"Hold on. Just a couple of more pages."

Jesse paced around nervously. He looked at the mountain again. He thought about making love to Terri in the old trolley stalled on the mountain. It helped get his mind off the notebook.

"Okay JJ. C'mon sit down. This is a really good fourth step. I can see you were real honest. It's okay. I did lots of these things too, the stealing, the lying. Drugs and alcohol make you do a lot of things."

"Did you read about Flynn?"

"Yeah. I never knew the whole story. I knew he was hit by a train, but I didn't know the part about the bad heroin. It must've been hard on you. The way it all went down."

"Yeah. The cops made it worse. They were tryin' to get to me. You know how they do. But I never did tell them where we got the dope. I knew they had nothin' on me. But ya' know, I still hate to hear that train whistle. I fuckin' hate it, Kevin."

"Believe me, you'll feel better after tonight. C'mon, let's go to the diner and celebrate your fourth step."

"No, Kev. Wait. There's somethin' I didn't write in the notebook I gotta tell ya'. I couldn't write it down. I just couldn't. That's okay, right?"

"Yeah, JJ. Sure, go ahead."

"Well...uh. You read the part about my dad, right? I mean, I know ya' did 'cause he was the first one on the resentment list. He was a real mean bastard. He was a drunk ever since I can remember. He used to beat my mother and he'd beat us too. Well, that part you read but..."

He looked down and ripped a small piece of paper out of the notebook. As he continued to tell the story, he began tensely twisting and folding the paper.

"I never told you this. I never really talked about it to anybody, not even my mom." He hesitated and swallowed hard. "I had a little brother named Danny. When I was about eight, me and Danny were playin' in the road in front of our old house. He was only three. I was supposed to be watchin' him. I used to spend lots of time with Danny to help my mom out. I really didn't mind 'cause I loved the little kid. I don't remember a whole lot about him but he had these real big blue eyes and lots of freckles. That's what I remember most, his eyes.

"So my mom and dad were in the house having a real big fight. It was early evening, just after dinner, a nice summer night. Ya' know, when it's just startin' to get dark. I was up in a tree. I just naturally climbed up there when they fought, just a habit I guess. I felt safe up there, free. All of a sudden, my dad comes staggerin' outta the house. He was drunk as shit and he jumped in the car and starts it. I screamed at him to wait 'cause Danny was behind the car in the road. He was so drunk and he...he...ran him over. He dragged him up the street. I don't know how far. He killed him."

Jesse put his hands over his eyes. His voice was beginning to crack. "Oh fuck, Kevin. I didn't wanna do this."

"It's okay, JJ. It's okay. If it's too hard for you, you don't have to."

Jesse took a deep breath and wiped the tears off his face. "No, I gotta finish it now. I just remember his body goin' up the road and then the car took off and he was just layin' there way up the road." He wiped his eyes again. "I don't remember a whole lot after that, but I guess I ran in the house and told my mom. I told her I saw the old man run him over. She ran out and made me stay inside. I guess the police came and then the ambulance but here's the bad part. When she came back in the house, she says, 'If anyone asks who hit Danny, you say you don't know.' She begged me to do it.

"So I did and we never ever talked about it again. There were rumors and shit around school that my dad killed his own kid but I stuck to the story. I wanted to do the right thing for her, ya' know. To this day I can't fuckin' figure out what her reasons were. I haven't even thought of it myself until I had to do this fuckin' fourth step. I shouldn't have even been in that fuckin' tree. And I don't feel better now like you said I would." He got up to get some paper towels and wiped his face.

"Jesus Christ, JJ. First of all, you gotta forgive yourself. About your brother, about Flynn, everything. You gotta know you didn't do anything wrong here. You gotta let these things go right now, here and now. I can't believe you and your mom never talked about Danny."

"We didn't. As the years went by, it was just like it wasn't real, like I never had a little brother. Mom doesn't even have a picture of him hangin' up in the house. I gotta talk to her about it, but not now. I'm not ready."

"No, JJ. You're right. In time, you'll feel better. I promise. C'mon. Let's take a ride. You did a great job tonight."

In the car on the way to the diner, Jesse felt his first slight sense of relief, like seeing a bit of sun through the clouds.

"So I'm done?"

"Yeah. Now you can take it easy for a while." Kevin squeezed Jesse's shoulder as he drove. "Hey, I didn't know you still felt that way about Terri. That's news to me."

Jesse didn't mind talking about Terri now that the worst was over. "Yeah. Well, she's been on my mind a lot. And Michelle...she's nothin' like Terri, ya' know. She's straight and really good to me, but yeah, I still have feelings for Terri, even though so much bad shit happened. If I ran into her, well, I don't know what I'd do."

"I have an idea what you'd do. You'd fuck her, you asshole."

"Oh yeah, at least I'd try."

They both laughed but then Kevin added seriously, "JJ, you don't know what shape she's in. You've been sober quite a while. You know she's got a problem. She's just like us."

"Yeah, I know. But I have a feelin' if I ran into her, even if she was strung out on dope, I'd go right back to her. I know it's sick."

"Yeah, it is. But the thing is, JJ, we *are* really sick."

* * *

Jesse climbed the narrow stairs to the tiny attic. He knew enough time had passed since his fourth step and he was ready for this moment. The memories the attic held would hurt. But it was time to move on and make amends to people and Danny was first on the list. He pointed the flashlight into a cardboard box of family photographs. He found a copy of the faded snapshot he kept in his wallet— a picture of all three brothers. He turned the photograph over. His mother had written their ages on the back: *Mark 14, Jesse 8, Danny 3.*

He looked at the front again and studied Danny's face more closely. He felt his throat tighten as he reached into the box for more photos. He found them—a picture of Danny laughing, sitting upright in a wagon, pictures of himself and Mark on bikes with Danny balancing on Mark's crossbar, and all three of them at a birthday party.

He hurt but he knew it would hurt more not to look. He picked out a few of the larger pictures and went downstairs to his old room.

His mom was grocery shopping and he expected her back soon. She'd probably figure he had just come over for his usual Saturday morning visit. He knew this visit would be different. He was placing the pictures in frames he had bought when he heard the door slam.

"Ma, that you?" He ran down the stairs to greet her.

"Hi, Jesse. What're ya' doin' here so early?"

He took the grocery bags from her arms. "I came to see ya'. Any more groceries?"

"Just a few more bags, dear."

He ran out to get them. Annie was unpacking when he came back in. He stopped her.

"Hey, Ma. Sit down. I put some coffee on and I wanted to talk to you about somethin'."

"Wait. Let me put these things away."

"No, Ma. Come and sit down. This can't wait."

"What is it, Jesse? Don't tell me you've taken to drinkin' again."

"No, Ma. Nothin's wrong. Things are goin' real good as a matter of fact. Things are great, but we have to talk." He sensed she already knew.

She got up to get some coffee and brought them both a cup.

He waited for her to face him again. He wanted to look in her eyes. As she sat across from him sipping her coffee, he began.

"Ma, this program I'm in…well…there comes a time to sort of make things right with people. Ya' know what I mean?"

"I do. Make amends, ya' mean."

"Yeah. That's exactly it, make amends. It's time for me to do that with a lot of people. Like you, Ma."

She raised her hand to stop him.

"Oh, Jesse. You don't—"

"Ma. Be quiet and listen to me. I do have to make amends to ya'. I want to say I'm sorry for stealin' from ya' and a lot of the awful things I said. You been nothing but good to me, Ma. You been too good, and I want to thank you for steerin' me in the right direction. Ya' saved my life ya' know."

"Oh no, Jesse. Any mother would've done what I did. The love a mother feels for their children...well, there's nothin' like that kind of love."

"I just needed to say these things and now the only way I can make it up to you is to keep on changin'. It's hard, Ma, this program I'm in. I gotta keep changin' all the time or else...well, I don't ever wanna go back. But part of this changin' and growin' is bringin' things out in the open, and not keepin' any secrets."

She fidgeted in her seat. He felt nervous bringing up Danny, but he knew it was time.

"Ma, I want to show you somethin'. Wait here." He ran up the stairs as fast as he could and came down with a framed picture of the brothers and handed it to her.

"Here. I'm doin' this for him, and for you. I know it hurts, but look at it. We gotta talk about it, Ma."

He watched her as she studied the picture. Tears welled up in her eyes.

"Oh dear God. Jesse, get me some tissues." He did as she asked. He felt tears coming too, but he needed to talk. He'd cried more since he'd gotten sober than he probably had in his entire life.

"Ma, I had a brother. I'm not gonna pretend anymore that I didn't. We both know how he died. We can keep it that way, just between us. But I need to ask you a few things. That okay with you?"

"Sure, son, sure. Whatever you want."

"Why Ma? Why did you cover up for dad? I need to know."

She looked at him with the same piercing crystal blue of his own eyes. She composed herself as she talked.

"Jesse, I don't like to think about that day, but I'll try. My first thought wasn't to cover up for him. I needed you to stay inside that night. I didn't want the police to know you saw what happened. I was really tryin' to protect you at first. I thought maybe by keeping you out of it, in time you'd forget too. When I look back, I guess that wasn't the right thing to do. I didn't want to believe it myself when ya' told me. When the police came, they asked me if anyone had seen what happened. I said I didn't know. I couldn't tell them, Jesse. I told them you were inside the whole time, even though I knew you were up in that tree. I couldn't let them talk to you. You can understand that, can't you?"

"Yeah, Ma. I understand that part of it. But what about him? I mean, Dad. You just let him back in this house after that? I really don't get that part. How could you do that, Ma?" He grabbed some tissues and wiped his eyes as he listened for the answer he needed to hear for so many years.

"Your father didn't come back for a few days after that. He had gone out on a binge like he did so many times. But that time, I didn't even bother tryin' to find him. Oh, he was probably over on the other side of the river. He used to go there to drink and visit whores. I really didn't care if I ever saw him again after that night.

"But the few days he was away, I had a chance to clear my head a little and think about what would happen if I told the police he killed Danny. No matter how many times I went over it, I felt that no good would come of it. He'd be in jail and you and Mark would have to live with that. My only prayer to Mother Mary every day was for you. That you'd be okay. I hoped the years would be kind to you and erase the memory—the awful thing you'd seen. I know you've had it very hard. I know you have and I'm sorry."

"It's okay, Ma. Go ahead and cry. I'm okay now. See?"

He waited a few seconds because he didn't want to

upset her more. Then he asked.

"Ma. What about him? You never told the old man he killed Danny?"

"Yes, I did tell him. It was one of the last conversations I had with him. We hardly spoke to each other again after that. But I knew something even before Danny died. I knew your father was dyin' too. I knew this disease would be takin' him soon. I saw my own father die the same way. It was happening all over again. I could see it in his eyes and in the way his mind was goin'. He hadn't been eating, just drinkin'—drinkin' all day, every day.

"So he was here in this house, but only physically. I could go on because I knew he'd soon be gone. And when I say we didn't speak again, I mean exactly that. I kept him away from you for those remaining years. I don't know if you ever noticed. I knew I had to do that. And for myself, I would talk to Father Sullivan. Do you remember him?"

"No, not really."

"Father Sullivan was a great blessing to me. I told him the whole story and he said, 'You've certainly had your cross to bear in this life, Annie. You followed your heart and don't ever feel you made the wrong choice.' And I prayed about it every day, Jesse. Right or wrong, that's how I got by.

"And your father? He had his own hell to live in after he'd found out what he'd done. He drank all the more. But even now I don't hate him. Lord knows I hated livin' with him, but I didn't hate *him*. I never told you this, but once a long time ago, maybe when you were five, your father went to the place you go to."

"Dad went to A.A.?"

"Yes and he stayed in there for about a year or so. Oh, you should have seen him then. He was different when he was sober. He was kind, sweet, and thoughtful. There was a fine man underneath all that drunkenness. He showed me a side of himself in that short time period that I would never see again. And when it came time for him to make amends to me, what a wonderful time that was. He wrote me a beautiful letter. Someday I'll show it to you. We were happy for a short time."

Jesse gazed at his mother, his mouth open. "I guess you felt bad when he went out and drank again, huh?"

"Yes. Things got bad after that. He was a lot worse. So you see, I do know somethin' about this disease and your program—more than I let on. Thank you, son. Thanks for listenin' to me."

He got up and kissed her forehead. "Thank *you*, Ma." He ran upstairs and got the rest of the framed photos.

"Look at these." He gave them to Annie. She looked at each one of them. "I want to hang them up, Ma. For Danny. Let's hang these up, okay?"

"Okay, Jesse, do that. I want to look at my three beautiful sons."

* * *

Six months had passed since Jesse's fourth step and he was on his way to Chick's. He'd become fond of the old man and now looked forward to his visits with him.

Jesse knocked on Chick's screen door. The inside door was always open. No one answered but he could hear the TV blaring.

"Hey, Chick. You in there?"

"Yeah, Jesse. C'mon in."

Jesse hadn't seen or heard from Chick for the three days since his last chemo treatment. When he went inside, Chick was lying on the couch. He was pale and weak. Jesse noticed how thin he'd gotten.

"What's the matter. You okay, Chick?"

He sat up and spoke slowly, "I don't think this medicine is doin' me any good kid. I think it's makin' me sicker. Look at this." Chick rolled up the sleeve of his polyester shirt.

Jesse looked down and saw that Chick had dime-sized dark brown spots up and down both arms.

"Yeah, Chick. I know. That medicine is nasty."

Chick pointed to his bald head. "And I can't stand this. I used to have nice hair, ya' know."

"Yeah I know ya' did. Listen, let's go over to the VA and see what's goin' on. Maybe your blood count is off and they can fix it. That's probably what's makin' ya' weak." Jesse felt bad for the old man. He'd come to enjoy listening to all the tales Chick would tell about the old days. He especially liked hearing Chick reminisce about his wife.

"Hey, kid. Before we go to the hospital, think we have time for a little ride?"

"Sure, Chick. I think we have some time."

"Will ya' take me for a ride through the cemetery? I'm worried they might admit me to the hospital again and I just wanna drive by my wife's grave. Okay, kid?"

"Sure. Sure it's okay."

As they drove to the cemetery, Jesse began thinking about Danny. Maybe he could stop by his grave. He'd gone a long way in dealing with the loss of his little brother. It might not make him bleed as much now. Chick's voice broke in on his thought.

"Hey, kid, you ever hear of Rudolph Valentino?"

"Who?"

"Rudolph Valentino. He was the greatest actor that ever lived. The best! He was Italian, ya' know. His real name was Rodolfo Gugliemi. He made a lotta movies and then he died real young. I think he was only thirty. Yeah, his appendix busted. His funeral was mobbed. There were riots all over. He was the greatest screen lover that ever lived. Never heard of him, huh?"

"No, Chick. Never have." Jesse liked the Valentino story. He smiled over at Chick.

They approached the cemetery and drove under the arched entrance.

"Keep to the left, Jesse."

Jesse followed the road as it made a large circle around

the head stones.

"Keep goin' all the way to the top and then stop. There it is. I see it. Right there."

Jesse stopped the car.

"There. See. Genevieve Micelli. I feel bad I can't get out. I feel too weak. Ain't that a nice headstone? It cost me five hundred clams."

Jesse tried to stifle a laugh. Chick always did that to him. He gave Chick a few minutes to look.

"Okay. Ready, Chick?"

"Yeah. It's a shame. She was a beautiful woman. I miss my wife."

"Yeah, I know ya' do." Jesse pulled the car up a little way. He knew just about where their graves were, although he'd never visited them. He stopped the car and got out.

"Wait here a minute, Chick. I gotta see somethin'. Be right back."

He walked around briefly and then he saw it. It read *Thomas McLaughlin*. And right next to it a small headstone with the inscription, *Daniel McLaughlin*. He walked over to his father's grave and got down on one knee. He wanted to say a short prayer but began talking instead. "You poor son of a bitch. You only got a small taste of what I got now and you lost it. You blew it. Look at me, Dad. See me? I'm okay. I'm sober. I've got what you lost, but I'm gonna keep it. I'm gonna be okay and so is Mark. And you know what? Just thinkin' about how you lost it, ya' don't know how much that's gonna help me." He made the sign of the cross and went over to Danny's grave.

He knelt down and spoke. "Danny, it's me, Jesse. I'm sorry I was up in that tree. I'm really sorry." With that, he got up and walked back to the car. When he got in, Chick noticed his eyes were wet.

"Yeah. It's rough, kid. Losin' people. When you get old like me, you get used to it. Who were ya' prayin' for?"

"My dad. And my brother too. I had a little brother. He died when he was three. Guess I been missin' him ever since, but I never knew it."

Chick looked genuinely sympathetic. "That's awful, kid. That's really a shame. Sorry."

"Thanks. Guess we better get to the hospital. You ready?"

"Yeah, I'm ready, but I gotta tell ya' what I did. I got worried 'cause I was so sick and I called my daughters. I didn't want to get them upset but I'd kinda like to see them, ya' know, in case anything happens."

Jesse perked up. "Don't worry, Chick. You're gonna be okay. Uh…so is Terri coming back? I mean, are your girls comin' to see ya'?"

"Yeah. Sarah's comin' from the city, she's been here a few times already. But I was surprised the little one's comin' from California. I guess she wants to see me," Chick said proudly.

"When? When is she comin'?"

"Let's see. What's today, Monday? She's comin' this Friday I think. That's right, this Friday."

Jesse drove Chick to the VA Hospital wondering what it would be like to see Terri again.

Chapter 17

Planes made Terri sick and anxious. She drank four Beck's before boarding. She needed another drink for the stomach churning takeoff but they wouldn't serve her one. Now she'd been in the air forty-five minutes and was still waiting. She saw a stewardess approach.

"Excuse me," she said and raised her hand as if she were in grade school. "Can I get something to drink?"

The stewardess answered sweetly, "We'll be serving lunch in about twenty minutes and we'll be serving drinks then."

Shit! That's a long time.

Terri persisted. "Can't I just get a little vodka and club soda now? Is that okay with you?"

"I'm sorry, we're not ready to serve drinks yet."

Oh fuck it!

She'd just have to wait. She grew more irritable as she thought about how her father had managed to interfere with her life of leisure in California by getting sick. Just when things were going so well. Sarah had urged her to come home thinking that Chick might die soon. Terri doubted that. She leaned back in her seat and thought about their conversation.

"Terri, I know you don't want to, but he's down to a hundred pounds. He looks so weak. The medication disagrees with him. You can do what you want but...you never know. Don't you want to see him again before he dies?"

Terri had a fleeting thought that she would have rather gotten a phone call that he died than to have to go through this. He'd always been so dynamic and she wasn't looking forward to seeing him weak. It wasn't his style. And she didn't want to hear about all his misery. She knew he'd go on and on.

She was still waiting for the drink when her thoughts turned to Jesse. She'd probably run into him and that would prove interesting. She had no idea what her reaction would be.

"Did you order the pasta?" the attendant asked as she held a tray out to her. She snapped out of her daydream.

"Yes, and can I have a vodka and club soda? And make it a double." Terri was afraid she wouldn't get another drink and it was a long flight.

* * *

Terri threw her arms around her sister when she saw her waiting at the airport. They hadn't seen each other in quite a few years. Terri's relationship with Jesse had caused a small rift between them.

"Sarah. You look great."

"So do you. California must agree with you."

"Yeah. I started jogging out there. I was getting fat 'cause Alan's always cooking."

"Ha! Sounds good to *me*."

As they drove upstate, it felt good to be together again and to catch up on everything. Sarah lit a joint as they drove. "So you finally met a nice guy?"

"Yeah, Alan is real nice but…" Terri let her answer trail away. "How about you?"

"Nah. Same old shit. I keep real busy at work. I don't have time for men anymore. They're a pain in the ass anyway."

"You can say that again. Hey, stop at the next deli so I can get some beer."

"Alan sounds nice. Daddy's thrilled you have a Jewish boyfriend. He brags to everybody."

"Oh yeah? I can just hear him now." Terri could really imitate her father well and she started in. "Yeah. She's livin' with a Jew. He owns his own restaurant. Those Jews are smart cookies. Now I don't have to worry about her no more."

Sarah laughed. "That's *exactly* what he said!"

"So how is he, Sarah? Did you see him?"

"Yeah, I was up there a few weeks ago. He seemed okay then but I guess the medicine is getting to him. I hate that VA Hospital. It smells, and daddy's always fighting with every guy they put in the room with him."

"Yeah. So what else is new? If he's still doin' that, he can't be *that* sick. I'm a little pissed. Here I was in California havin' a great time and now I have to come back to this shit-ass town."

"Stop complaining. It's only for two weeks."

"Yeah but…" Terri was worried about running into Jesse. "Listen, Sarah. Remember Jesse? You didn't like him. Remember?"

"Of course I remember him! That asshole. He hit you."

"I know. But he's back here now and I know I'll run into him."

"So?"

"Well, I don't know how I'm gonna feel about it. That's all."

"Oh no. Not that shit again. The bad boy syndrome. Why do we do this? I thought your boyfriend out there was so nice. Why do you wanna screw that up?"

"Well, he's kind of got me boxed in. Know what I mean?"

"No."

"He's got a lot of plans for me just like the plan for me to manage the bar in his restaurant. I mean, I think I'd like to be consulted a little more when someone's plannin' my life, ya' get me?"

"No, I don't. I think you just wanna get mixed up with that other one again. You better stay away. As Daddy would say, 'he's no damn good.'"

"But I heard he doesn't drink anymore. How about that?"

"I don't know. I don't like him."

"There's a deli. Stop there. I need a beer after that awful plane ride."

* * *

The girls still had the keys to their dad's house. Terri hesitated on the small concrete porch before she walked into the apartment. Sarah snapped at her, "C'mon. What're you waiting for? I have to go to the bathroom. Get in, will you?"

Terri opened the door slowly and walked in. She threw down her bags. "Oh god. Look at this place. What a freakin' mess. We're gonna have to clean it before he comes home."

Terri immediately began getting cleaning supplies out from under the sink. She opened the fridge to put her beer away. "Ugh. Look Sarah. Even his eggs are dirty. And I bet the milk is sour. Look at all this rotten food. This is so disgusting. Sarah! C'mon. Help me clean!"

Sarah shouted from the bathroom. "You're a pain in the ass. Give me a chance, will ya'? I'll be right there."

Terri suddenly stopped what she doing and looked around.

"Sarah, where's Peppy? Where's the dog?"

Sarah came into the doorway and leaned against it.

"Didn't he tell you? The dog died. He was cryin' on the phone to me, 'First, my wife. Then my dog.' He was a mess for days. He loved that dog."

"Loved him? He didn't love him the day mommy died. Ya' should'a seen the way he smacked his ass. Poor dog, livin' with him."

Sarah laughed.

Terri wiped down all the countertops and then began to clean the old food out of the refrigerator. The mention of her mother made her recall what it was like just after she died, when Terri thought she had to take care of Chick. It looked like he needed some taking care of now. She thought he must really be in bad shape for the place to look like this. She took each egg out of its nesting place and gently wiped each one with a damp cloth. Sarah was sweeping the floor and looked up just as Terri finished the last egg.

"Why the hell are you cleaning the eggs?"

"They were filthy. I'm not kiddin'."

"You're nuts. Let's get this over with and go to the hospital."

"What did he look like Sarah? I mean the last time you saw him. Does he look the same?"

"Yes and no. He lost lots of weight, but he's still got that same attitude. I mean that hasn't changed at all."

Terri was relieved to hear that. She didn't want to see him go down without a fight. "Ya' think he's gonna die?"

"I don't know. Sounds like the cure is worse than the disease."

They quickly finished cleaning the small space.

Terri opened a Beck's.

"C'mon, Terri. Let's go. He's expecting you and he's real excited. How long since you've seen him?"

"I don't know. Years. And I really didn't see him a lot before I left town. You know how it is. He's so *annoying*."

"Yeah, I know. C'mon. Let's go."

* * *

Terri followed her sister as they approached his room. She wondered if they had to stay longer than an hour. She was looking forward to going to Howie's bar and then maybe to the Lodge to hear some music—anyplace but this VA Hospital. She hated it. The bare yellow walls went perfectly with the strong smell of urine that permeated the hallways. She peeked into his room as he greeted Sarah. He was lying flat in bed with the sheets pulled up to his chin. His face was pale and thin, almost gray, and he was completely bald. He'd gone a long time without wrinkles, but now they were there, and she noticed his sunken temples. The thinness of his face made his nose look much larger. She thought it a pitiful sight. She knew he'd always taken pride in his appearance and these changes were probably hard for him to bear.

"Hi, Daddy."

He turned his head slowly, saw her, and began to cry.

"Look," he wailed as he pointed to his bald head. "I lost all my hair."

She bent down and kissed his forehead.

"That's okay, Dad. It'll grow back. Remember when you shaved your head? Don't cry."

"No! This is different. I'm a sick man! That medicine is makin' me sick."

She looked over and glared at Sarah. Why didn't she prepare her? She just wasn't ready for this.

"Sarah says they're gonna change the medication and maybe you'll feel better then. I missed you, Daddy," she lied.

He looked up at her. "Oh, Daddy's so happy you came back. You look so good. California's nice huh?" He began to compose himself.

She noticed he didn't raise his head at all when he talked. Terri figured he didn't have much time left at all. "Yeah, California is real nice. I like it."

"How long you gonna stay?"

"Oh, about two weeks." She wished she were leaving tomorrow. Coming here every day would certainly be a chore. She didn't know at which point he stopped crying, but it was always that way. He seemed to be able to turn it on and off.

"Two weeks, huh? Then you gotta go back?"

She didn't want to make any false promises; that she might stay longer. "Yeah, I gotta go back to help Alan in the restaurant. I take care of the bar and all."

"I know. You finally got a nice life. Don't worry about yer daddy cause I'm gonna bounce back. I always bounce back and don't you forget it!"

"That's good, Dad." She changed the subject. "So has Uncle Jimmy been helping you out? I mean, takin' you where you need to go?"

"Oh yeah. It's good 'cause he's right next door. And ya' know who else is helpin' me?"

"No. Who?"

"Your old boyfriend, Jesse. Remember you went out there with him? He's been helpin' me a lot. He works here. He's a nurse, I think. He takes me to my treatments and everything. He even takes me to Poughkeepsie to see my nephew, Sonny."

Terri was stunned. She couldn't see them together at all. Chick always hated Jesse. How the hell did this happen?

"He takes you to see Sonny?"

She stared at Sarah in disbelief.

"Yeah, he turned out to be a nice boy. He doesn't drink anymore either. He's a real hard worker too. I call him my adopted Irish son."

I can't fuckin' believe this!

Her jaw dropped open. "So ya' don't call him *The Mick* or *Beer Can* anymore I guess?"

"Noooo. I would never say that. He's good to me, that kid."

She sat down next to Sarah. She'd heard enough about Jesse. She was relieved when Sarah changed the subject.

"Oh, Dad. Uncle Vinnie called me. He told me to tell you he was asking for you."

With that comment, the weak pale figure suddenly came to life. Chick sat straight up and threw the covers off. He turned quickly, his two scrawny legs were dangling over the side of the bed. His gray face began to regain color as the rage welled up inside him. The girls were startled and sat up stiffly in their chairs.

"What? That dirty bastard was askin' for me? You talked to him?" He was shouting now, the way he always did.

"That son of a bitch only came to see me once. I don't wanna hear anything from that dirty fuckin' bastard. He's no damn good. Don't talk to him no more. Ya' know what he did to me forty years ago? He tried to take my house, that's what. He argues about everything. If I say something happened at Ebbets Field, he says it was the Polo Grounds. And the last time I talked to him we had a big fight. He told me you gotta use four sticks for one tomato plant. Suppose I have one hundred plants! I need four hundred sticks. Where am I supposed to get four hundred sticks?"

Chick's arms were flailing now as he continued and his eyes began to bulge behind his glasses. "That stupid bastard. That's right. Four sticks. I told him he was fulla shit. Then he says, 'You're wrong, Chick, because Dominick told me he used four sticks to a plant.' Do you believe that bullshit?"

Terri couldn't believe what she was seeing and hearing. She felt as if she were in a bizarre scene from a Fellini movie. It was the part about Dominick that caused her to lose it. Dominick was a man she'd never even met, an uncle who'd died long before she was born. There was something about the way her father pulled his name out of the past that caused the laughter to erupt.

She jumped up and immediately ran out of the room, unable to regain her composure. She faced the pale yellow wall and began laughing hysterically, her hands covering her face. She couldn't control the movement of her shoulders.

She felt a soft firm hand. A nurse was behind her speaking softly. "It's alright. It must be hard seeing him like that."

Terri buried her face further into her hands. "Thanks," she croaked to the nurse. Then she ran to the nearest bathroom and tried to wind down before going back into the room. The door swung open and it was her sister. They looked at each other, unable to speak through the hysteria. They inhaled loudly now because the laughter had been so intense, it had cut off their air supplies.

"I'm sorry. I had to go. I...I..."

"I know, Terri. I had to leave too. He was still yelling when I ran out."

Sarah couldn't contain herself.

"Sarah, you gotta stop smoking pot before you come here."

"Well, *you* didn't smoke pot and look at you!"

"I can't fuckin' believe I came back from California for this. That guy is *not* going to die. I think he's tryin' to pull a fast one on us."

They calmed themselves and went back into the room, ready to take whatever was coming at them.

"Where the hell did you two go?" Chick hollered as they walked back in. He was sitting up as if nothing happened and he didn't look at all like the sick wasted figure Terri saw in the bed forty-five minutes ago. He was like a new man.

"We had to go to the bathroom." Terri figured getting that anger out was good for him. He almost looked healthy.

"Dad, we're gonna go. I'm tired from the plane ride."

"Aww, that's too bad. I hate to see yous kids go. You comin' back tomorrow?" His mood now seemed upbeat.

"Sure, Daddy. We'll be back tomorrow."

The two sisters both kissed the old man goodbye and left the dismal brick building.

* * *

On the way back to the house, the sisters talked.

"Why don't you stay over tonight, Sarah? Don't go back to the city. We can go up to the Lodge. Remember the old ski lodge? They have bands there now. Kevin's band is playing. Remember Kevin Shea?"

"Yeah, I do. Patty's brother right?"

"Yeah. C'mon. Stay."

"Nah. I really gotta get back to the city. You know I

hate it here and I've been coming up every other weekend to see him since he's been bad."

"Well, he's not so bad now, is he? And did you hear the part about Jesse? How can that be? Daddy hated him. You hated him. Now he's Daddy's adopted son. What the hell? Well I'm going out tonight and I figure I'll run into him, but I'm nervous. Know what I mean?"

"Oh yeah. I know exactly what you mean. Well be careful. You have to go back to Alan. Don't get any crazy ideas."

Terri couldn't stop the crazy ideas from coming.

As soon as they arrived at the house, Sarah got ready to leave for the city.

"Oh, Terri, Daddy said you could use his car."

Sarah grabbed her stuff and smiled at her sister. "Take it easy and be careful."

"Yeah, you said that. You comin' back next weekend?"

"Yeah. Call me and let me know how you made out with Jesse, okay?"

They hugged and Sarah jumped into her rented car and drove off.

* * *

Terri grabbed another beer and walked downstairs to her old room. It was a mess because Chick had been using it as a storage area. She made her way through stacks of boxes and junk to the bureau with the large mirror. She stared at herself. She looked pretty good for a woman who drank so much. She wasn't overweight or puffy thanks to the jogging. Terri hated the thought of staying in this room. She'd never liked it down here and now it reminded her only of Jesse.

She walked to the back of the basement where Chick had done all his painting.

It was still there.

The nearly life-sized naked lady draped across the pink couch. The one that had had Jesse in stiches.

She wondered how long ago Chick had finally finished it. She had to admit, it was really good. She was struck by the fine detail and the use of the flesh tones. Chick Micelli did have his talents, even if social interaction wasn't one of them.

Her old stereo still worked. David Bowie was singing "Young Americans." Terri turned it way up. The beat and Bowie's voice had her dancing around the messy room. She'd always loved Bowie right from the start and admired the way he constantly reinvented himself.

She was excited now to go to the Lodge to hear some live music. It was about ten when she headed over there. She experienced an exhilaration she hadn't felt in a while.

She could hear the pulsating sound of the bass guitar even before she got out of the car. She adjusted the rearview mirror to check herself. She'd always remembered what Sharon said about looking good. She knew he was in there to support Kevin. Jesse loved music just as much as she did. Even if he were there with Michelle, Terri felt she'd handle it graciously.

As she walked through the back door, she stopped short. Jesse was right there with Michelle. They were standing with a few guys in a small circle. She had nowhere to run. He looked at her immediately and she held her breath. Her heart began to pound as she saw the clear blue of his eyes. She swallowed hard.

He had that same strut, that aura of self-confidence he'd always had. His eyes seemed to penetrate her whole being. They grew larger as he got closer. He smiled a huge dimpled smile.

"Hey, Terri, how ya' doin'?" If his insides were churning like hers, he didn't show it.

"Hi, Jesse. I'm doin' okay. Everything all right with you?"

She felt foolish. Making small talk seemed inappropriate. It was remarkable how much restraint she could muster, doing the exact opposite of what she wanted to do. The beer she finished in the car helped and she wanted another drink right away.

He didn't touch her at all but she wished he had. His hair was still long, falling over his shoulders. He stared in her eyes as he spoke, "Yeah, everything's good. You just gettin' here?"

"Yeah, it's late, but I wanted to hear Kevin's band. I heard they're good."

She glanced over at Michelle who was still talking to the other guys.

He bent down to her ear and whispered, "Are you gonna be here a while? I mean, stayin' with your dad?"

Her heart was pounding as his lips touched her hair.

"Well, yeah. I'm stayin' a while I guess."

His lips were so close she could feel his breath on her ear. He said, "Don't leave. I'll be right back."

He walked over to Michelle and grabbed her arm. Terri watched him escort his girl out the door.

Terri ran to the bar, ordered a double vodka and club and quickly gulped down half of it. She tried to make small talk with some of the girls she used to hang out with, but kept her eye on the door. Feeling tense, she went to the bathroom to fix herself up again.

As she headed back to the bar, the was band playing "*Rock the Casbah.*" She saw Jesse standing there, right by her drink. She squeezed in beside him and picked it up.

He turned and looked in her eyes again. His gaze was intense. "Hey, I wasn't sure you'd still be here."

"You said, 'Don't leave,' didn't you?"

"Yeah, but after all that went down in California, I just wasn't sure you'd wanna talk to me."

She wondered how this man could not know what he did to her with those penetrating eyes. How could he look so self-assured and be saying this? Could it be he felt the same way she did?

"Well, I'm still here, but what happened to your girlfriend? I heard you've been going out with her for a while." She looked up at him briefly and quickly looked away.

"Oh, she had to go home. Has to work tomorrow. Yeah, we been goin' out a while. So how's it goin' out there with Alan?"

Suddenly his leg touched hers under the bar and all the surrounding sounds in the room faded. The only thing she was aware of at that very moment was the heat of his leg on hers. It felt like a slow burn increasing in intensity to the point she was having difficulty speaking.

"What? I didn't hear you."

"I said, what about you and Alan? Everything okay out there?"

She felt her throat constricting and her lips quivered.

"Yeah, it's okay." She cast her eyes down at the bar again. She couldn't look at him anymore. She didn't want to reveal her vulnerability.

He bent down and his deep voice seemed to vibrate in her ear. "Listen to me. I'm sorry about everything bad that happened to us. I'm really sorry. I wish I could make it up to you in some way. Maybe I can, if you let me. Let me, Terri."

Tears welled up in her eyes as she looked at him.

"Jesse, what are we gonna do? I can't believe this is happening. You know how we are. It's no good."

He put his arm around her and pulled her close. He gently ran his thumb up her cheek and cleared a tear. He spoke again, almost in a deep growl.

"Don't. Don't do that, Terri. Maybe you had too much to drink. I don't want you to cry." His eyes were getting watery too.

She forced a smile and grabbed some napkins off the bar. "Maybe it is the vodka. But what's your excuse? I heard you don't drink anymore."

"You really wanna know what it is? It's you and me. It's always been you and me." With that he threw both of his arms around her. She buried her head into his chest and returned the embrace. The scent of his body through the thin material of his shirt was like a sedative. She needed to run, get out of there and get back to Alan as soon as she could.

No matter how much strength she tried to muster, she couldn't free herself. It was too late.

"Terri, come home with me. I got a nice place now. Come and see it."

She looked up at him realizing there was no sense trying to make small talk anymore.

He took her hand. They left the Lodge and got in her dad's car. She handed him the keys. Before he started the car he pulled her closer.

"I've been thinkin' about this for a long, long time."

With that, he kissed her just like he always did after all the fights they'd had. His tongue was soft, warm, and familiar. She felt those same feelings all over again and they were better than any drug she'd ever done.

Chapter 18

As Jesse drove her car to his apartment, she sat as close to him as possible, kissing his neck and stroking the inside of his thigh. She kissed his ear and whispered, "I never stopped lovin' you, even when things got bad with us, even when I was with Alan. I never stopped."

She slid her hand further up his thigh and he involuntarily pushed down on the gas pedal. She laughed.

He pulled to a stop in his driveway and switched off the engine. As he turned to her, his eyes locked on hers. She grabbed his hair, pulling his face closer and kissed him hard. He jumped out of the car, opened the passenger door, and pulled her by the hand.

Terri wasn't interested in seeing his place. She just wanted him now.

She wasn't sure if her overwhelming desire was fueled by the alcohol, or if it was just her natural response to him.

She didn't care.

She pushed him gently against the wall, pressing her body to his. She kissed him with a force that took him by surprise. She could feel he was aroused.

"Whoa. Whoa. Terri. Hold on. Do you—"

"No! I can't hold on. It's been a real long time." She ran her hands under his shirt as they kissed. His body was warm and firm. Unable to stop herself, she ripped down the middle of his shirt. Buttons bounced on the wood floor in all directions.

"Terri! What're ya' doin to me?" he whispered. His hands found their way under her sweater. He unsnapped her bra, moving his hands under it and over her breasts. He pulled off the sweater. With the fingers of one hand grasping her nipple, his other hand unsnapped her jeans. His fingers were on her groin, moving in small circles as if he were painting tiny pictures over her skin. He moved his hand further down.

"Now!" she said. "Right now!" She pulled him a bit too

hard by the ripped shirt and they fell in a heap of flesh and crumpled clothing to the floor. She crawled on top of him and helped him as he pulled his pants off. She wanted him inside her. He knew what she needed. Easing her way onto him, she began thrusting her body against his, all the while holding his hands tightly over his head. His deep moaning let her know he wanted this. It wasn't long before he came with a loud shuddering growl.

Their lovemaking had been explosive and urgent, the time away from each other feeding their lust. He looked up at her.

"You okay, baby? What the fuck? Damn, girl. What about you? You didn't even come. Let me—"

"No, I'm okay. Don't. I'm really okay. Too much vodka maybe." She smiled down at him. He pulled her close one more time and then sat up, reaching into his damaged shirt for his cigarettes.

"You ruined my favorite shirt, ya' know. This is fuckin' crazy," he said as he lit up. "I guess we got some explainin' to do, huh?"

"I guess we do. Sorry about your shirt," she said as she nestled her head into his shoulder.

He laughed, those dimples lining both sides of his face. "It's okay. It was worth it. Ya' know, babe. What you said in the car. The same goes for me too. I always did love you—just you. I know I had a crazy way of showin' it but it was the drink, ya' know. We're gonna be okay now. We really are."

She stared into his piercing eyes. "I can't believe this is happening."

He finished his cigarette, pulled her close, and kissed her again, his tongue deep inside her mouth. "You smell good, baby."

She'd been drinking half the day. She knew exactly what he meant. That was the last thing she remembered. Then she passed out in his arms.

* * *

When Terri woke in the morning wrapped in Jesse's arms, she was shaky and confused. She knew he would have no beer in the house and she desperately wanted one. It was eight and she was surprised she'd slept this long. She wished she could lay back down and enjoy the warmth of Jesse's body, but the urgent nagging inside her needed to be dealt with. She got up and began gathering her clothes.

Jesse's eyes were open and he watched her as she got dressed. "What're ya' doin' baby? You're not leavin' so soon, are ya'?"

"Well...I...I'm kind of confused about last night. My head hurts a little and I need time to uh...regroup. I should go see my father."

He grabbed her gently by the wrist. "I have some aspirin in the medicine cabinet. Stay."

She knew aspirin wouldn't fix what ailed her. "I'm gonna call you, Jesse. Tonight, okay? After I see my dad and figure out what's goin' on."

He sat up in the bed and pulled her down next to him. He focused his aqua eyes on hers. "Terri. Don't go back. Stay. I can't let you go back to California. I need to know what you're gonna do. Now."

"I don't know. I hate to hurt Alan, but..." She threw her arms around his neck. "I love you. I'll call you tonight, okay? I promise." She pulled back quickly as she didn't want him to see how shaky she was.

He got up, threw on his jeans and walked her to the door. He leaned in and kissed her long and slow.

"Call me. Don't forget, okay?"

With that she ran down the stairs to her car, passing Kevin on his way up to Jesse's.

The door was still open and Kevin went right in.

"Hey, Kev, what're you doin' here so early?"

He knew Kevin must have seen her leave. "You want

some coffee? I'm just puttin' some on."

Kevin sat down. "JJ. What the fuck are ya' doin', man?"

"What do ya' mean?"

"You know what I mean. What the fuck? What are ya' doin' with her?" He motioned toward the door.

"Listen, Kev. You're my sponsor and I love ya', man, but it's my fuckin' life. I can't let her go back. I changed, but I can't change the way I feel about her. I can't fuckin' help who I love. What the hell am I supposed to do?"

Kevin looked down and shook his head. "You're gonna jeopardize everything you worked so hard for if you start with her. You know that, right? You know what she is. She's just like us. Don't fuck this up, JJ. Michelle's great for you."

"I told ya'. Ya' can't help who ya' fall in love with. You don't know her like I know her. She's strong and good. All the times we fought, all the shit she put up with, she never backed down. Know what I mean?"

"No, JJ. I don't know. What do ya' think? You think you're gonna help her? Well you're *not*. You're fucked up if you think that."

"No, I don't think that at all. I can handle this, Kevin. I just wanna be there for her."

"Yeah, well don't come cryin' to me when things get really bad. Maybe you should get a new sponsor, 'cause I don't wanna watch this. Maybe we've come to the end of the line."

Jesse squeezed Kevin's shoulder firmly. "Don't! Don't drop me, Kevin. It's gonna be all right. Trust me."

* * *

In the months that followed, Chick flourished on the new chemotherapy regimen, and his weight gain was noticeable.

As Chick got better, Terri got sicker. She was happy living with Jesse in his small apartment. Their moving in together caused lots of talk in that small town, but now everyone had gotten used to seeing them around.

Alan had taken it well, busy as always with his restaurant. Terri knew he was destined for success.

It was a gorgeous Saturday morning, but Terri woke up trembling, as always after a night of heavy drinking. Jesse was still asleep. She got up, grabbed her robe, and went to the fridge for a beer. It was just before seven.

About an hour later, Jesse walked into kitchen. She was finishing her third can. It was the first morning she didn't bury the empty beer cans under paper towels in the wastebasket.

She loved the way he looked when he woke up. She flashed her eyes over the length of him. His long hair was messy and he had an impish look on his face. His thin legs looked sexy in the boxers he wore to bed. She studied the fine downy hair on his arms and the hair on his chest. He walked over and started the coffee. She was surprised at how much he loved his coffee. He never touched it when he was drinking. He flicked on the radio. The opening chords of "I Wanna Be Sedated" blasted into the room. Terri loved The Ramones.

Terri watched as Jesse moved around the kitchen in time to the music. She wanted him just as much as she did when she'd first seen him at that pool table. His movements were always fluid, so precise. He moved the way he made love.

Her joy was always tinged with a small dose of misery. A shadow of discontent hovered over her.

He came over and put his hands firmly on her shoulders, and began massaging them.

"How you doin' today, babe?" He bent down and kissed her neck.

She took a deep breath and a sip of beer. "I'm okay."

"So, Terri. How long ya' been drinkin' in the mornin'?"

He sat across from her at the table with his large mug of coffee.

"I...I...uh. I really don't know. Maybe a year or so. If it bothers you, I'll try to—"

He stopped her right away. "It doesn't. You don't have to try to do anything. Not for me. I know what it feels like. Don't you remember? In our first place? Remember how it bothered *you* when I'd crack open a beer in the morning?"

Yes, she remembered how little patience she'd had with his morning drinking. "I remember, Jesse. I—"

He cut her off again and took her hand in his. "Don't worry. I understand. Hey, I'm takin' your dad to the diner. You wanna come?"

"No. I hate that place. And you know how he aggravates me. How do you put up with him? He tells the same stories over and over."

"I like his stories. I think he's a riot. Listen, he'd really like to see you. You haven't been spendin' much time with him."

"No. He's got you. You appreciate him more. Tell him I'll be by later. I'm going out shoppin' today. I'll stop by his place when I'm done. I promise. Thanks for takin' such good care of him. I'm not handlin' this cancer thing of his very well."

She got up and gave him a hug. She went back to bed wondering how much time she would need to straighten up. She was getting tired of drinking herself sober.

* * *

On her way to the mall, she thought that it was a beautiful day to stop over at Howie's bar for a vodka and club. Just one might take the edge off. She walked in to find her new favorite bartender, Angie, behind the bar. She loved to drink with Angie. She could really knock 'em down, as Chick would say. Tower of Power were asking *"What Is Hip"* over the bar speakers.

"Hey, Angie. I'll have a vodka, club and lemon."

"You got it, Terri."

It was noon. She had plenty of time. She was just about done with her drink when a couple of girls she knew walked in. Diane and Carrie. Terri used to hang out with them in high school. Now she heard rumors they were "coke whores." Terri hated that expression and just thought of them as girls who liked to do coke.

"Hey, Terri," said Diane, "long time no see."

They headed straight for the bathroom but then Carrie stopped and turned back to Terri. She smiled.

"Wanna come?"

What the hell? Why not? She followed them into the bathroom. There was an old wooden vanity with a small mirror hanging on the wall behind it. Carrie grabbed the mirror, laid it on the vanity, emptied the coke onto it and began cutting. The mirror was worn and chipped from years of this incessant ritual.

"So, how's it goin' with Jesse? You guys really shocked everybody. It gave us all somethin' to talk about in this crap town for a couple of weeks. The last big news was when he punched you in the eye in front of the Rusty Rail."

"We don't fight anymore. He's changed. He was always a nice guy. He just drank too much." Terri bent down and snorted a line.

Carrie laughed. "Yeah, but *you* don't, right?"

Terri sneered at her. "Shut up."

"Hey I was just kiddin'. I'm a lush too, ya' know."

They went back to the bar but made frequent trips to the bathroom. Terri lost track of time again.

"I was supposed to go shopping, but now it looks too bright outside. I don't think my eyes can take that sun."

"Oh fuck it," Carrie chimed in. "You can shop anytime. Give Terri another drink, Angie."

Terri asked again. "Really, what time is it?"

Diane threw her arm around Terri and whispered in her ear. "You know what time it is? It's time to go to Angel's apartment and get more coke."

They drove over to the big white house. Terri parked the car and sat there. "You go up. I can't go up there."

"Why?" Carrie was curious.

"Well, I slept with Angel and—"

Carrie interrupted her. "So what? Who didn't? Anybody in this car who didn't sleep with Angel, raise their hand. See Terri. We all did. C'mon."

Terri wouldn't budge. "No. I'm not goin' up there." She thought of Jesse. "That's not all I did. I did something else too."

The girls were wide-eyed. "What? What did you do?"

"Well, I was in bed with Angel one night and he did something that annoyed me and…"

The girls were anxious. "Yeah. Go on."

"Well I got mad and I jumped out of his bed and started screaming at him. I just lost it. Picture that. It's embarrassing."

The girls were impressed. "Wow, I never heard of anybody jumping out of *his* bed. I mean he's so fucking good." Carrie licked her lips.

"Oh shut up, Carrie. Go on, I'll wait here."

The girls returned after about ten minutes. "C'mon Terri. Let's go. Angel always comes through, in more ways than one."

They laughed and drove out of the parking lot. "Where to?" Terri asked.

"Let's go to New Paltz."

"You got it."

As the Pretenders belted out *"Precious"* the girls headed off for a night of music, lots of cocaine, and probably more booze than three small women should be able to consume.

* * *

It was about four in the morning when Terri pulled into the driveway. She had no idea how she made it home. The road was like a snake slithering before her and she breathed a sigh of relief as she pulled in.

"Thank you, God," she said aloud. She ran up the stairs, brushed her teeth, threw off her jeans, and jumped in bed. She lay next to Jesse, her jaw clenched. Her brain was fighting to sleep, but her eyes remained open. She knew she was in that surreal space between dreams and reality. Too much coke, too much alcohol.

Then she felt and heard them. Rats! She heard their shrill shrieks and could feel them running above her head, over her pillow. She pulled up the blankets. "Oh God. Stop it. I won't do this again. Just make them go away." She jumped out of bed, ran into the living room and rolled into a fetal position on the couch. "Please make it stop. I won't do it again. God, make it stop."

She heard Jesse's footsteps as he entered the room. "Terri, what is it? Why ya' cryin'?" He sat on the couch and pulled her close to him.

"Oh my God. What did I do? I'm not gonna do it anymore. I promise. I won't do it again."

He held her tightly as she cried. "It's okay, baby. It's gonna be okay."

"I'm so sorry I didn't come back. I didn't go see my father either. I…"

He hugged her and rocked her gently. "Shhh. Shhh. Hold on." He went into the bathroom and ran a warm bath. He came back and took her in his arms again. "What happened, babe? Too much coke, right?"

"Yeah. It's bad. Real bad. I thought there were rats on my pillow. I heard someone knocking at the window. I just want it to stop. Will you walk with me outside?"

"No. I got a better idea. C'mon." He helped her off with her T-shirt and led her to the tub. "Get in. Just lay there awhile. I'll keep the water real warm." He began pouring warm water all over her. "Sit up."

She sat up and he poured water over her head. He washed her hair with shampoo, massaging her scalp gently and rinsed with more warm water.

"Thanks. That feels good."

"That's what I'm tryin' to do...make ya' better. You need to calm down now, but if you wanna stay up and talk after this, we'll do that too okay?"

"Okay." Her lips were shaking. She was feeling a bit better, but a great sense of shame came over her at what she'd done. She felt as if her life were out of control, like a carnival ride she couldn't get off.

* * *

When she woke up the next morning around ten, she felt better than expected. She still had enough cocaine in her system to stave off the crushing hangover that would soon descend upon her. She could hear that Jesse already had Pete Townsend and *"Sheraton Gibson"* playing. She wandered into the kitchen and Jesse was drinking his coffee. He turned to greet her. "Hey, how are ya' feelin'?"

She sat down at the table. "Actually, not too bad. I'm surprised."

He came over and kissed her forehead. "Still buzzin' on that coke I take it?"

"Yeah, maybe. We did a lot. But never again. I'll never do coke again. I'm through. I don't know why I just kept doin' it. It's crazy."

He was leaning against the sink, his legs crossed. He took a sip of coffee. "Well I guess you're just a girl who can't say no." He flashed a big smile, the hollows of his dimples appearing larger than ever.

"Well I can't say no to you."

He gave her a wink.

"But I'll be sayin' no to cocaine from now on."

"Yeah, baby. That's good, but maybe coke's not your problem."

She gave him a puzzled look and changed the subject.

"Shit! I forgot about my dad yesterday. And you're right. That coke's still in my system. I should go over there now, but I just can't."

She knew she needed a few beers.

"Do you think you could go over there and talk to him? Just this once. Tell him I don't feel good. Just tell him anything. I can't listen to him today."

Jesse gave her a disapproving look. It was something he seldom did during the time they'd been back together.

"Okay, okay. But he really wants to see you, ya' know."

"Oh thanks, Jesse. Just this one time. I promise. I'll go over tomorrow." She got up and gently wrapped her arms around his slim waist. "I love you. I'm gonna take it real easy today and I'm gonna stay home and get to bed early…with you."

She kissed him long and slow, and he responded with a deep growl.

She'd already planned her day.

She needed to get a six- pack.

She'd start drinking, and when she felt just a tiny buzz, she'd sleep all afternoon and stay home with Jesse.

She promised herself not to drink after her nap and, for once, she was just fearful enough to keep her word.

Chapter 19

On his way to Chick's, Jesse thought about Terri. Even though he understood her better than anyone else, he knew he was powerless to help her. He felt everything she was feeling. He understood her weaknesses, but could do nothing.

As he pulled into Chick's driveway, he knew he'd have no more room for thoughts of Terri. Chick would demand his full attention. He knocked on the screen door, but there was no answer. Opening the door just a crack, he called in.

"Chick? Chick, you awake?"

"Yeah, Yeah. That you kid? C'mon in."

Chick was in the living room staring at the TV.

"C'mon, Chick. Wanna go to the diner?"

Chick waved his hand to quiet him. "Shhh...Shhhh. Wait a minute. I'm watchin' somethin' here."

Jesse looked over at the TV to find out what the old man thought was so important. It was a talk show.

"Oh no. Don't watch this stuff. These shows are weird."

"Shhh. Quiet. I wanna see this!" he snapped.

Jesse listened and watched as the white-haired host prompted several elderly people to speak. Each one talked about how they'd been sexually abused as children. Jesse watched as Chick stared at the screen in a hypnotic state. After the show was over, Chick turned off the TV and stood up.

"Well, I'll be goddamned. And I thought I was the only one. C'mon kid, let's go to the diner."

Jesse sat down on the couch and his mouth dropped open. "What? Wait a fuckin' minute. What did you say?"

"I said I thought I was the only one that happened to. What's the matter, kid? You don't look so good. We goin' or ain't we?"

"Chick. You mean...what those people were talkin'

about. That happened to you?"

"Yeah and I never told nobody 'cause I thought it only happened to me. Ya' know, it made me feel good to listen to those old people talk. They said what I been wantin' to say all these years. But I never told nobody, not even my wife."

Jesse's mouth was still open. "Jesus Christ, Chick. You're not fuckin' kiddin' me, are ya'?"

"Nah. Why would I kid about somethin' like that?"

"Who did that to ya', Chick...I mean if you don't mind me askin'?"

"Ahhh. A couple of relatives. My uncles, older cousins. I don't really remember who. They used to take me out to the barn and do a job on me. Ya' know what I mean? But don't tell nobody. Okay, Jesse?"

"Okay, Chick. But I thought you said they beat you."

"They did that too. That's the only part I told people. I just left the other part out. But now...now after I heard those old people, I can say it. It's not somethin' ya' wanna take to your grave with ya'. Know what I mean? So don't forget. Silence is golden. C'mon, let's go. I'll buy ya' some lunch."

"No, Chick. I'm buyin' *you* lunch."

The old man tousled Jesse's wavy hair before they got in the car.

As Jesse drove to the diner, Chick asked about Terri.

"So what happened to her? Why didn't she come?"

Jesse's thoughts were far off, still thinking about the little boy in the barn.

"Who?"

"My daughter, that's who."

"Oh, she's...uh, not feelin' good. Ya' know, women's problems."

"Yeah, yeah, yeah. I know. She's sick. She's always sick. Jeez, I love those kids. You'll find out when you have kids of your own. Maybe you'll have daughters like me. Some guys want sons, but I was so happy I had daughters. I didn't give a shit, even when they got real fresh when they were teenagers. No matter what they do, you still love 'em. But ya' know what really hurts? They don't love ya' back sometimes." Chick paused. "That's all I need, kid. Just to know they love me a little bit. Sometimes, they let me know, but not too much."

Jesse stared at the road and thought about what Chick told him back at the house. He caught only the tail end of what the old man just said. "Don't worry. I'll talk to her. I'll tell her you wanna see her."

"She'll come over when she feels better. They're good kids." Chick changed the subject. "Hey, ya' know that medicine they're givin' me for that thing?"

"Ya' mean the chemotherapy?"

"Yeah. That stuff. Well, what would happen if I don't take it no more?"

Jesse knew what would happen but he didn't know how to say it.

"Well, ya' might get sick again. Why?"

"Well, I made up my mind. I don't wanna take it no more. It's makin' me sick, and it's doin' somethin' to my mind. I can't remember things much and I started seein' things."

Jesse knew that the medication that counteracted the nausea sometimes caused hallucinations. He also knew that once Chick made up his mind, there'd be no changing it.

"You wanna talk it over with the girls?"

"Nah. You tell the little one. I don't wanna take it no more."

Jesse knew Chick would do exactly as he pleased.

After lunch, they sipped their coffees.

"Hey, kid. Ya' know I saw somethin' on TV last night. It was on that show *Star Track*."

"You mean *Star Trek*?"

"Yeah. That's the one. The show was about another planet just like ours. They said we all got a double on that other planet, see? And while we're here doin' what we're doin', the other guy that looks like us is on that other planet doin' the same thing. So what I wanna know is, ya' think there's another guy just like me on that other planet, in a diner drinkin' coffee right now?"

Jesse put his cup down and looked Chick in the eye.

"No, Chick. I don't think there's another guy like you anywhere in the whole fuckin' universe."

* * *

During the months that followed the cocaine nightmare, Terri managed to stay away from the drug. She did this by staying home and drinking herself into what she thought was a sound sleep. But tonight Jesse had talked her into coming to the Lodge with him to hear some live music.

They sat at a table not too far from the bar. Kevin's band was supposed to be playing tonight but Kevin didn't show up for the gig. The Lodge was playing recorded music instead. Right now it was Humble Pie and *"C'mon Everybody."* It was midnight and Terri hadn't had her fill of alcohol yet, even though she'd been drinking since about five. She was musing about Steve Marriott's clear strong voice when Jesse interrupted her thoughts.

"Jesus. I can't fuckin' believe Kevin didn't show," Jesse said as he sipped a coke.

"Don't worry about him. He's a big boy."

Terri handed Jesse her empty glass. "Will you get me another one, please?"

"Listen. Maybe we should leave after this one, eh?"

"Why? You dragged me here and now that I'm having fun, you wanna leave."

"Okay. Okay. You can stay if you want but I'm leaving soon." He headed for the bar to refill her drink. He returned, banging her drink on the table and sat down.

"Why do ya' wanna leave?" she asked and took a long gulp.

"Because I'm tired. That's why. But you don't get tired, 'cause you're wired on alcohol. Sorry. I'm just tired. People get tired."

"Well, I was perfectly happy to stay home—"

"Stay home? That's all you been doin'. Ya' stay there and drink till you pass out. Don't think I don't know why you're afraid to go out anymore. I know. Believe me, I know."

"I don't pass out. I'm in my own bed, so I don't pass out."

He said in a raised voice, "Just 'cause you're in your own bed doesn't mean you don't pass out. Oh, never mind. Fuck it. I don't wanna fight. There's no point."

"And I'm not afraid to do anything!" she lied. She didn't get a chance to defend herself, because at that moment there was a commotion at the bar.

"Oh shit!" said Jesse. "Somebody just shoved one of the Kelly brothers and ya' know what that means."

Terri did indeed know what that meant. There were five Kelly brothers and when one started fighting the others jumped in. It was too bad they frequented their favorite hangouts together, because this led to bigger brawls. On some nights, the brothers had no problems with other bar patrons, in which case they'd fight each other.

Terri watched as the fight accelerated. Now about eight people were involved. Three of the brothers had appeared quickly from across the room. Arms and fists flew and bar stools were knocked over as two of the men tangled and fell to the floor.

"C'mon, Terri. Let's get outta here." Jesse stood up and grabbed her by the arm.

She pulled away from him roughly. "No. I don't wanna go." She wanted to watch. There was nothing she liked more than a good bar fight. Besides, she didn't get her fill of vodka yet.

"What? Are you fuckin' nuts? Somebody's gonna get

hurt. Let's get the hell outta here."

"No! I said I'm not goin' with you."

"You're fuckin' nuts. I said we're goin' and I mean we're goin'. I'm not leavin' you here."

With that, Jesse grabbed her and dragged her by the arm to the door. He pulled her down the walkway outside the building, Terri fighting him the whole way.

At the end of the walkway, he saw Romeo having a smoke.

"Hey, Romeo. Give me a hand with her."

Terri pulled and flailed her arms, her hands now formed into fists. Romeo grabbed one arm and Jesse had a hold of the other.

"Get your fuckin' hands off me. Let me go! You fuckin' junkies. I'll be damned if I'm gonna let two junkies manhandle me."

Romeo started laughing.

"Whoa, JJ. She's a wild one when she's mad, ain't she?"

"Yeah, yeah. Just help me get her in the car."

Jesse opened the passenger side and shoved her into the seat, her head accidentally hitting the roof of the car. He jumped in the driver's seat.

She punched him several times. "You bastard. You hurt me. You banged my head. You prick."

Jesse stared her down, his blue eyes turning dark.

"Who the fuck you callin' a junkie? Huh? Who? I wanna know who?"

"Well, I—?"

"Don't do it. You just don't know when to shut up do ya? Now I'm takin' you home. If you wanna drink more, do it at home."

Terri felt more rage building. He knew her too well. It was as if he could see right into her mind. As he drove toward the house, she started again.

"Ya' think you know everything. You're so damn self-righteous, aren't ya'?"

"Just don't talk, okay? Think you can do that? Just shut

up for a while."

"Don't tell me to shut up. I wish I never came out with you tonight. No! Know what I really wish? I wish I stayed out in California with Alan. He was good to me. He let me do what I want. He didn't drag me outta places and bang my head on cars like you."

She rubbed her hand over the bump on her head and it only made her angrier.

"I hate you. You hear me? I hate you."

"So go ahead and fuckin' hate me."

Jesse stopped at a red light. Before he could do anything to stop her, she jumped out of the car. She turned and looked at him once more, but his eyes looked different. There was something there she'd never seen before.

"What're you lookin' at? Don't look at me like that."

She slammed the car door and ran down the street. When she looked back, she saw him standing outside the car calling to her. She ran faster. When she turned again, he was gone. She stopped running and staggered down the dark street. Her legs felt heavy and she had trouble putting one foot in front of the other. Her loss of control only angered her more.

"You stupid bastard," she mumbled. "Take me out and buy me drinks all night and look at me. Shit!"

She lurched down the street mumbling and crying.

She wiped her eyes on the back of her hand as she walked up to St. Paul's Church. It was the church she attended as a child, the church she was married in, an institution she felt had abandoned her after her divorce at age twenty-two. Yet, somehow in her drunken state, she was drawn to it. She ran up the steps to the massive wooden and wrought iron doors and tried the door handle. It was locked. She squeezed the handle hard and pulled roughly at the door until it shook and clattered loudly.

"Open up. Let me in. Shit. It figures." She banged with her fists as hard as she could. "C'mon. Open up. You assholes. It's your fault! Let me in. You jerks. Fucking assholes!"

She thought if she could just get in, she'd be safe. She wanted to kneel down and say a few prayers, maybe light a candle, that's all.

"Open the goddamn door. You want people to come in here and then you lock the fuckin' door."

She fell into a heap in front of the church and sobbed.

"Why are you doin' this to me? Why are you lettin' me do this to myself? Huh? You hear me? Why? It's not right."

She stopped crying. She realized she needed to get up and get out of there. She couldn't fall asleep here on the church steps. She wiped what remained of her tears, but when she opened her eyes, there were four shiny black shoes surrounding her.

"What's the problem, miss? Everything okay? Father Doherty called us and said you were causing quite a disturbance."

She was silent for a moment. "I...I'm okay. I just..."

"C'mon. Help her up."

Each officer grabbed an arm and gently pulled her up. But it was too soon for anyone to touch her. She wasn't ready. It reminded her of what just happened with Jesse and Romeo.

"Oh, no you don't! Don't touch me." She hadn't expected this torrent of anger, nor did she have any control over it. Her hands immediately formed small fists as she swung her arms wildly."

"Uh oh. This one's gonna be trouble."

"I'll give ya' trouble. Get your fuckin' hands off me."

Terri's arms were still free and she pulled and thrashed as the local cops tried to grab hold of her. She felt her fist hit something hard as her arm flew up.

"She hit me! Damn it. Let's cuff her."

"No! Let me go!" Terri fought with all her might as her arms were pulled behind her. She felt the cold steel cuffs being clamped on her wrists. They walked her over to the patrol car.

"Face the car, miss." She did what she was told. The rage was still there, but fear had begun to displace it. Listening to the young cop as he spoke, she felt as if she were in the midst of a crazy dream.

"You're under arrest for assaulting a police officer, trespassing, and disturbing the peace. You have the right to remain silent…"

No. This can't be happening. Shut up asshole. Don't say a word.

She cried on the way to the station. The ride in the patrol car made her nauseous as she swayed back and forth, not able to steady herself with her hands.

At the station, the two officers sat her down on the bench that faced a long wooden barrier.

"Now, you're going to be allowed a phone call, miss. You have a lawyer?"

"Nah." Terri hadn't needed one since her divorce.

"Stand up and I'll take these cuffs off. You okay now, miss?"

"Yeah, I'm okay."

Terri stood up and he unlocked the cuffs. As soon as her hands were free, her rage returned, this time a lot worse. She bolted for the front door but they grabbed her around the waist.

"Nooooo. You can't do this to me. I can't be arrested. I didn't do anything. Why don't you fuckin' assholes leave people alone?"

The cops tightened their grip this time.

"That's it. C'mon. Let's lock her up until she calms down."

They pushed her into a small cell with a small cot attached to the wall.

"You can yell all you want now. Maybe when you calm down, you can make your phone call."

She stared the officer down, resenting the fact that someone so young had thrown her into a cell. She figured now that she was in so deep, she might as well get a few last words in. She hollered with her last bit of strength. She knew she didn't have much time, as all the booze she drank would soon render her silent.

"You fuckin' jerks. Open this door. You can't keep me in here. Open up, I said. I gotta be somewhere. You gotta let me make a phone call. My lawyer's gonna hear about this."

She thought she heard the young officer say sarcastically, "So now she's *got* a lawyer!"

After a short time, she became exhausted. The alcohol, or lack of it, made her sick and weary. She sat down on the cell floor and cried. She could hear voices now fading into the background. Terri flopped over onto the cell floor as she heard bits of the fading conversation.

"....call the state hospital. Not makin' any sense."

No. I'm not crazy. I'm a drunk. Don't. Please. I'm not crazy.

Before she drifted into oblivion, she heard one last voice. "No, she's not state hospital material. I know her. I went to school with her for eight years. She's okay. Oh fuck. Look at this now. Somebody pick her up off that filthy floor and put her on the cot."

* * *

Terri woke up and stared at the unfamiliar wall. She felt so vile, it almost didn't matter where she was. She pulled her knees up to her chest as she tried to ease the sharp pain in her lower belly. Rolling over, the sight of the bars startled her.

Oh God. What's this? God, no!

Then glimpses of the night before began to play in her brain like pieces of a puzzle. Bit by bit, memories of the evening came back—the fight at the ski lodge, the church, Jesse pulling away, the cops. She couldn't remember much after the cops.

Terri was scared and sick and needed to use a

bathroom right away. As often happened after a night of heavy drinking, her body needed to rid itself of the poison. After a few bouts of diarrhea and a six-pack, she'd feel normal again. Terri glanced over at the toilet in the cell. The thought of using it turned her stomach.

"Ohhhh God. Is anybody there? Is there a bathroom here? Somebody let me out. Pleeeease, let me out." She sat up and glanced at the small window, noticing it was still dark out. Doubled over, dizzy and nauseated, breathing deeply was her only relief.

"Hey, Sarge. Sounds like your friend's awake."

Footsteps approached and she heard a vaguely familiar voice.

"Terri, Terri, Terri. What the hell did ya' do to yourself?"

Looking up, she recognized him right away. Charley Hoffman. God, how she used to love Charley. He was the only one who made any sense during her eight wretched years at St. Paul's Elementary. She remembered how he used to make her laugh until she cried. Then they'd both end up in the principal's office, still unraveled. His eyes were blue-gray and he had a huge, never-ending smile that he couldn't seem to control. That smile never sat right with the nuns.

Terri knew he'd been a cop for years. Sometimes they'd run into each other in the bars. "My old girlfriend keepin' outta trouble?" he'd always ask. They had been good friends in school and once in third grade he had given her an old magnifying glass, a token of his affection for her. She'd always kept it.

But they'd gone their separate ways and Terri felt ashamed to see him in her present condition.

"Oh. Hi, Charley. I...I'm...Is there another bathroom in this place?"

"Why? You mean you don't wanna use the beautiful throne in here? C'mon outta there." He unlocked the cell and let her out. "Bathroom's over there, hon. C'mon out and talk to me after you freshen up. OK?"

"Sure, Charley." Even though Terri was mortified at her condition, he made her feel comfortable.

When she returned, Charley was on the phone. "Hold on a minute..." He lowered the phone and motioned toward the bench against the wall. "Sit down over there, hon. Be with ya' in a minute."

Terri did as she was told. She sat with her hands locked tightly under her armpits to stop them from shaking. It was a habit she didn't even think about anymore. As soon as he was finished, he came over and sat down next to her.

"Charley. Am I in any trouble? I...I can't..."

"Are you in trouble? Oh man, Terri. You are in deeeeep shit." She couldn't help but smile. He always did that.

"Really? Oh God. You're not kiddin', are you?" Her memory was jogged again and bits and pieces from the night before flashed through her brain—the handcuffs, her fist hitting the cop's face.

"What's gonna happen to me, Charley?"

"Relax. Relax. You're not under arrest...anymore."

"What? What do ya' mean?"

"Well...ya' hit one of my rookies, Terri, but I had a little talk with him and he's willing to drop the charges. Ya' really shouldn't hit cops ya' know." He wrapped his arm around her shoulder and pulled her toward him for a moment. She felt him kiss her head lightly. "I don't ever wanna see ya' around here no more. Hear me? If I do, you'll really be in trouble. Now, ya' wanna make your phone call? Ya' were supposed to make it last night but ya' passed out."

She felt her face flush. She didn't like that expression. Terri had always thought when she went to bed loaded, she was just falling asleep quickly. But passing out in a jail cell...well she had to admit Charley had her there.

"C'mon over here, Terri. Use my phone."

Terri called Jesse. "Hi...uh...Jesse. I'm at the...uh

police station. Can you come and get me?"

"What? What the fuck? I called everywhere for you last night, everywhere but there. What the hell happened, Terri? Never mind. I'll be right there." He slammed down the phone.

After Jesse arrived, Terri sat on the bench while he talked to Sergeant Hoffman, her hands still locked safely under her arms. She couldn't hear what they were saying, but she found their camaraderie disturbing. She wondered when Jesse had a change of heart about cops. When they were through, they both walked toward her.

"Now listen, Terri. Remember. I don't wanna see you here anymore. My old girlfriend in a jail cell. Tsk tsk tsk." The sergeant shook his head. "Shame on you."

"Thanks, Charley. Thanks a lot. I really mean it."

Jesse gave her a disgusted look. "C'mon. Let's get outta here." She followed him out of the station house.

As they drove home, Jesse was quiet at first but he couldn't contain his words any longer. "Jesus Christ, Terri. I can't believe you hit a cop. What the hell were ya' thinkin' hittin' a cop?"

"Stop sayin' that. I didn't hit him! My hand flew up and his face was there, that's all. That's how it happened."

"Oh Christ, Terri. Stop it! Stop it, will ya'? Your hand flew up. What bullshit!"

The Who's *"Can't Explain"* was playing on the new cassette player in Jesse's car.

Terri stared out the car window and tried to comb out the knots in the back of her hair with her fingers.

She yelled, "Oh my God! Oh God! Ewwwwww! I'm gonna get sick."

Jesse rolled his eyes. "What the fuck is it now?"

"Oh, Jesse. There's something slimy in my hair. Oh I gotta take a shower. Hurry up, hurry up. Go home!"

"What the hell do ya' expect? You pass out on a jail cell floor, and believe me, you're gonna get slimed."

"I passed out on the floor? Passed out? Bullshit!"

"Yeah, lucky for you, you were friends with the Sarge. He had them pick ya' up. He made it real easy for ya' didn't he? If that had been me, they probably woulda beat the shit outta me. Jesus Christ, Terri."

"Oh yeah, I'm real lucky! My luck ran out a long time ago."

"Your attitude sucks, ya' know it? And when are ya' gonna go see your father anyway? Don't ya' care that he's sick?"

"God, I don't wanna talk about him right now. I got my own problems."

"You said it. You got a problem all right. It's all about you. And another thing you should know while you're bein' so fuckin' selfish. While you were out punchin' cops, John Lennon was murdered."

"What? What? No, you're lyin', right?"

"No, I'm not lyin'. He was shot."

"Shot? Where? Who would do such a thing?"

'Right in front of his apartment. He was shot four times. Fuckin' psycho was waitin' by the entrance. In the shadows. Yoko was there but he didn't aim at her. He wanted to shoot John Lennon. His name is Chapman, David Chapman."

"Oh my god. That dirty *fucking* city," she said and slumped down in her seat.

She immediately felt even sicker. She covered her face and sobbed loudly. Then she asked, "Is there any beer in the house?"

"How the fuck would I know?"

"Well, I want some beer."

The tires screeched as Jesse pulled over at the next deli. He jumped back in the car he thrust a twelve-pack at Terri.

"Here. Is this enough? Drink yourself sober and we'll talk later."

She wasn't listening. She just kept repeating over and over.

"Not John. Not John…"

Chapter 20

The news about John Lennon had a paralyzing effect on her that even she couldn't explain. Terri stayed cloistered in the apartment and drank herself into semi-consciousness most nights. Home was now the safest place to drink.

Then Jesse experienced a devastating loss of his own.

Kevin relapsed.

Now it became clear to everyone why he had been a no-show at his own gig.

He was living down by the river in one of the old hobo camps. Jesse was distraught. He needed comfort. Terri didn't have much comfort to give right now, so she cooked him a special dinner. She was still looking for his forgiveness too.

Seated at the dinner table, she finished her glass of wine but found the bottle empty when she went for a refill. She loved to drink while she cooked.

She got herself a beer. Bowie's *"Rock 'n Roll Suicide"* was playing. She swayed to it as she sat back down.

"Want this?" She offered Jesse the piece of veal on her plate that she had hardly touched.

"What'sa matter? Can't you eat that?"

"Well, I'm kinda full."

"Full? You gonna stop eatin' now? What did you eat today? You drink a bottle of wine and you're full, huh?"

She took her plate off the table and started the dishes. She looked over at him as he finished his dinner.

"Listen, I know you're upset about Kevin and I understand. But hey, it's his life. He's in charge of his own destiny."

Jesse slammed his fork on the table and pushed his plate away. He leaned back in his chair and looked at her in astonishment.

"That's what you call it? You think he's in charge of his destiny? And I suppose you think you're in charge too.

Right? Am I right? Kevin picks up a drink and he's livin' in a hobo camp and you think he's in charge, huh? If he was in charge, why the fuck did he suddenly start drinkin'?"

Terri looked over at him as she washed the dishes.

"Maybe he was just thirsty."

With that, Jesse swept the remaining dishes off the table and they shattered as they hit the floor.

"You think that's funny? Do ya'? It's not. It's not fuckin' funny at all. Where the fuck are my shoes?"

A few minutes later he came out with the shoes in one hand and a bottle of vodka in the other. He threw his shoes down and held the bottle up.

"What the fuck is this doin' under the bed? Huh. This is what you call bein' in charge, huh?"

"Well…I could have put it on the end table, but you don't drink so I thought it would be better for you if it were under the bed."

Jesse threw the bottle across the room. He put his shoes on and stood up. "I gotta get the fuck outta here. I'll be back later. If you're still awake, we'll talk. We gotta talk about your father too. You see how sick he's getting' right? I hope you can see that at least."

He was standing in the doorway now, ready to leave. "I need to get to a meeting." He looked at her and shook his head sadly. "And so do you."

His final words sucked the air out of the room. Terri couldn't move. Jesse started to pull the door closed.

"Jesse, Wait!"

"What?" he called back in, his hand still on the doorknob.

"Those meetings. What do ya' do there?"

He closed the door and walked back over to her. He stood in front of her and took her face in his hands, his eyes searching hers.

"Terri. You *really* wanna know?"

"I wanna know, Jesse. I…" She began to cry and buried her head in his chest. "Do they brainwash you there?"

He threw his head back and laughed, "No, Terri. They don't brainwash anybody. Look, if you still wanna talk about it later, we'll talk. Okay? I gotta go."

"Okay," she said and hugged him tight before he left.

She marveled at the thought of being brainwashed out of drinking another drop. Not such a bad idea. But Terri also knew deep down what worked for Jesse could never work for her.

She couldn't fathom a life without alcohol.

* * *

Jesse sat in the same school basement Terri Micelli ate lunch in as a child. He wasn't listening to the speaker tonight though, because he was too busy mutilating his foam coffee cup. Bit by bit, he broke off pieces of the white material and dropped it into the shrinking cup. He hadn't heard one word the speaker said—he was too busy thinking about Kevin, Chick, and Terri.

Jesse finally paid attention at the end of the girl's story, and heard the words he'd been waiting for. He looked up and readied himself.

She was beautiful, tall and willowy with long wavy dark brown hair and Jesse always wondered what kind of a drunk she had been. From what he could glean from her story, she'd been pretty bad. But you could never tell that from her wholesome good looks. That's what Jesse loved about A.A.—the irony.

The girl concluded: "Well, that's enough about me tonight."

Everyone applauded.

"Does anyone have a problem or a topic tonight? Anybody feel like drinking?"

Jesse shoved his hand into the air, as if mere seconds mattered.

The girl smiled at him. "Wow. That was fast. Go on,

Jesse."

He looked down at the cup again. "My name is Jesse and I'm an alcoholic."

"Hi, Jesse," the group replied in unison.

"I...uh... guess it's gettin' to be too much. I'm in a whole lotta pain, and yeah, I been thinkin' about pickin' up. It's like everything's fallin' apart around me and uh...well, you all heard about Kevin. He's gone. He's livin' in a hobo camp. He rides the rails. He *fuckin' rides the rails.* What the fuck!

"Six months ago we were sittin' in the diner, Kevin was really together, had a great job, and a great life, but now he's a fuckin' bum. And then the old man...ya' know, I talked about him, Chick. I can't help it, I just got to like the old guy...and he's dyin'. Every time I see him he looks fuckin' worse. So the process started. I've seen it so many times at my job. He won't be around much longer and my girl...that's Chick's daughter. I dunno if there's anything I can do for her. I found a bottle of vodka under the bed today and she just sits there every night and drinks till she passes out. So I said today, *'What the fuck? Ain't life just fuckin' great?'* and to be honest, the only thing I know will take away the pain is a drink, so that's where I'm at. Thanks."

Each person at the table spoke directly to Jesse. He listened to each of them and with each story, felt a little better.

Now it was Angry Jack's turn. Jack was an older man with white hair and a beefy red face. There was a jagged scar on his cheek from his temple to his chin, but his scarred face in no way matched the way his soul had been ravaged by his disease. Jesse knew he'd find a lot of solace in Jack's words. He always did.

Jack looked directly at Jesse.

"*I* don't feel sorry for ya', kid. I know exactly how ya' feel, but ya' won't get any pity outta me. And don't pity yourself either, 'cause once you start with that crap, you're on your way down. Self-pity is a drunkard's best friend. I know. I lived with self-pity and anger for a long, long time. You been here long enough to know you can't do a damn thing about what's goin' on around you. And ya' know what? As long as you don't pick up a drink, there are no big deals. You just keep doin' what your supposed to do.

"Face the one day you're given. Take a look at Kevin and learn from it. I was like him. Alcohol took me a whole lotta places I didn't necessarily wanna go."

After the meeting Jesse walked over to Jack and the group that surrounded him.

"Jack. Can I talk to ya'?"

Jack left the group and walked Jesse to his car.

"You were right in there, Jack. I need a sponsor now and I was wonderin', would ya'?

Jack bear-hugged Jesse.

"Sure, kid. I'd be honored. Yer gonna be okay."

Jesse jumped into his car, slipped a Hendrix cassette into the player, and drove home to *"Bold As Love."* He marveled at the fact he'd totally lost the craving for alcohol.

When Jesse came back the apartment, Terri was passed out on the couch, a half-filled mug of beer behind her on the end table. He took her shoes off and gently lifted her off the couch, like he'd done so many nights before. This night was different though. He laid her gently into bed, kissed her on the cheek, and whispered, "Yer gonna be okay."

More astonishing than his words was the fact that he really believed them.

* * *

Terri tested the water with her hand as usual before getting in the shower. As she felt the blast of hot water, her body tingled. The details of the night before started coming back to her. John Lennon's music had been playing non-stop on the radio since his death and it set her off on another long drinking bout.

She felt sick and shaky this morning and cursed herself for not grabbing a beer before she got in the shower, a habit she was getting used to.

Then it happened.

As she grabbed for the washcloth, she saw the tiles moving. The wall looked as if it were breathing, rippling in and out with sickening regularity. The glass shower door was buckling. Nausea overtook her. Suddenly, she felt as if the tub were dropping, fast like a runaway elevator—then back up and down again.

She gasped and grabbed the only thing available, the soap dish in front of her. She closed her eyes and held on tightly, hoping it would all be over when she took another deep breath. Terri recalled that the slanted room in the fun house at Palisades Amusement Park had given her this exact same feeling—a total loss of equilibrium.

Terrified, she turned the water off and got out before she was able to wash. She grabbed her robe and steadied herself on the sink.

Oh God. What is this? What is it?

She staggered to the kitchen and grabbed the one beer that was left, gulping it down. She needed more than one. She got dressed quickly and headed for the store, her hair a complete mess.

As she waited in the checkout line at the local grocery, her nausea intensified and then shifted to her lower gut, with severe cramps. She breathed deeply and held the twelve-pack tight under her arm.

Her turn finally came and she handed the checkout lady a twenty. As she held her hand out for the change, coins slipped through her trembling fingers and bounced around on the counter. She tried to pick up each coin, but her shaky fingers were useless. Terri looked up at the lady behind the counter. The lady sensed her desperation.

She picked up the change and placed the coins firmly in Terri's hand. The cashier even went so far as to squeeze

Terri's hand into a fist. "Don't drop these honey, and enjoy your beer."

As this whole scene played out, Terri had the strange sensation of seeing it as an outsider, as if she'd been momentarily removed from herself.

In the car she broke open the twelve-pack and drank quickly. She knew this was her only remedy.

Jesse had been at an early morning meeting and when he walked into the kitchen, Terri was crying and writing. She had just finished her fourth beer.

"Hey, Terri, what's the matter? Hung over again? What is it?"

He sat across from her and looked over at the piece of loose-leaf in front of her. The handwriting on the paper was smeared with her tears. Warren Zevon's *"Desperados Under The Eaves"* playing on the radio only made her sob more.

She looked up and wiped her eyes with a napkin.

"I'm having a real bad day, Jesse." A loud wail sprang from her small body.

"What do ya' mean? Tell me what's goin' on. You wreck the car or somethin'?"

"No!" She began to use her hands as she talked. They were still shaking. "I'm sick. Listen to me, Jesse. Listen to what happened to me today. I...I was taking a shower and, I know this is crazy, but I had to get out of the shower 'cause the walls were moving and the shower door...and I went to the Grand Union and I couldn't hold my change...I..."

"Whoa! Slow down," he said and grabbed her hands. "Just slow down, okay?"

"Jesse, look!" She pulled her hands away from his and held them straight in front of her. They still shook violently.

"Look! Four beers and look at my hands. It won't stop!" She folded her arms to bring her hands under control and continued sobbing.

Jesse looked at her and smiled. "Maybe this is a good day."

"What? I feel like I'm dyin' and you say it's a good day?"

"What are ya' writin'?"

She shoved the smudged paper toward Jesse. "I'm writin' why I don't wanna drink no more." She let out a weak laugh. "It's a nice concise list, don't ya' think? But I don't know how, Jesse. I don't know how to break this cycle. I mean, that's why I made the list. When I feel good in a few days, I'm just gonna start all over again. I needed to write the reasons down, because if I don't, I'll forget all this pain. Ya' know what I mean?"

Jesse looked down at the list as he answered her. "I know *exactly* what ya' mean. Exactly. Hey, these are real good reasons to stop drinkin', especially the one about not bein' able to stop once you start. You think you wanna go to a meeting with me?"

She shook her head. "I don't know. I don't think it's gonna work for me."

He took her hands and she looked into his eyes.

"Jesse. I can't imagine a life without alcohol. I can't."

Chapter 21

That evening Jesse pulled the car up to St. Paul's School. "It's gonna be okay, Terri. Go to the church basement."

"Jeez. I can't believe this. I never thought I'd be going to an A.A. meeting at St. Paul's. I used to eat lunch in that basement. Jesse, I...I'm scared. Why aren't you comin' in with me?"

He turned in the car seat to face her. "Don't be scared. All I can do is drive ya' here. The rest is somethin' ya' gotta do for yourself. Ya' gotta really own it. I know everybody in there. I can guarantee you're in good hands. Trust me." He leaned over and kissed her forehead.

"I do."

"And keep your eyes open for a girl named Kristin. I think you'll like her a lot. Terri, it's really a good thing. You'll see."

Terri rolled her eyes. "Yeah, right!"

Terri dragged herself out of the car and walked toward the door. She passed a man at the doorway and he reached out his hand to her. "Welcome."

She shook his hand quickly, cast her eyes down, and entered the basement.

These people were far from what she expected to see at a meeting like this. She liked something she saw in their eyes. They had a joyful glow. Terri had seen so many eyes glazed over by drugs and alcohol, but these eyes were different.

Everyone sat down at the table and a man started the meeting. He read from a sheet of paper. Terri didn't grasp much of what he said, but a few phrases caught her attention, one of them being *"If you want what we have..."*

As each person spoke or laughed, Terri thought about her childhood in this basement, when there was no talking allowed. She thought about the nuns who stifled their very whispers. She took wicked delight at the laughter in the room now.

The girl Jesse talked about, Kristin, spoke last. Terri was surprised that someone so gorgeous could be an alcoholic.

As the meeting broke up, Kristin came over to Terri and took her hand.

"Hi. I'm Kristin. I'm a friend of Jesse's."

"Hey," Terri said. The girl's hand was warm, and as Terri looked into her green eyes, she felt intuitively they'd be friends for a long, long time.

"We usually go to the diner after the meeting and I'm alone tonight. You want to go get a cup of coffee? I know we'll find a lot to talk about."

Terri felt a sense of relief come over her, like taking off a heavy winter coat on a hot day. "I'd like that. I think I'd like that a lot."

They drove off for the diner in Kristin's car.

* * *

Terri sat in the tub and talked to Jesse as he leaned on the sink. A few months had passed since her first meeting. As she spoke about the meeting she'd just left, there was an exuberance about her. Her hands moved about expressively while she talked.

"You should have been there. This guy…I think his name is Richie…he was celebrating ten years. Just think! Ten years sober! And Jesse, he cried when he got his coin. He stood right in front of me, and I could see his tears fall right on the goddamn floor. This grown man just cried like a baby. Outta joy! What a wonderful thing! I don't even feel like drinkin' anymore. Do you believe that?"

Jesse nodded. "Oh yeah. I believe it all right. So how's it going with Kristin? She's a good sponsor, huh? I knew you'd love her."

"Oh yeah, I do. She's great. I want to stay like this, Jesse. I never want to go back. I'm gonna do everything she tells me to do."

"Don't go too fast now. Take it easy. It'll get better and better."

Terri poured a cup of water over her head and slicked her hair back with her hands.

"You've been goin' to see your father a lot," said Jesse. "He likes that."

"Yeah. It's a lot easier to go there now. The smell doesn't bother me so much. He's gettin' so thin, Jesse."

"Yeah, I noticed. You tell him you don't drink anymore yet?"

"No, but tomorrow I'm gonna tell him. Not that he'll care. I don't think he ever noticed my drinkin'."

She caught him staring intently at her, a faint smile on his full lips.

"Ya' know, Terri. You sure are a pretty woman!"

"Well, thanks, Jesse," she said, a little surprised. He hadn't said something like that in a long, long time. Hearing it sparked something inside her. She didn't know if it was what he'd said, or just the joy left over from the meeting. It didn't matter. She got out of the tub and without drying off, wrapped herself around him. She kissed him slow and deep.

He whispered in her ear. "Ya' know you're getting me all wet."

"Funny, that's what I was gonna say."

Intimacy had been difficult for her the first few weeks of sobriety. She had been so accustomed to losing her inhibitions with alcohol. Now she found drug-free lovemaking a lot better.

She unbuttoned his shirt and her hands moved over his slim body and down to the snap of his jeans.

She kissed his chest and worked her way down.

"I want to make up for everything I put you through," she said as she looked up at him.

He looked down and brushed her damp hair away from her face. "Uh...I never heard of making amends this way…but it's not such a bad idea."

Terri unzipped his jeans, knelt down, and did her best to make things right with Jesse.

* * *

Jesse drove down the road that led to the river and parked the car. It was a steep hike down to the old hobo camps.

It was early evening and he could smell campfires burning. Dogs were scavenging around piles of empty food cans and bottles. Tattered T-shirts and torn jeans hung limply on makeshift clotheslines.

Through the smoke, Jesse could see a group of men sitting around a campfire.

He spotted Kevin right away.

His blond hair was still long, but unkempt and dirty, no longer tied neatly in a ponytail. As Jesse approached, he saw a bottle of cheap whiskey on the ground next to his friend.

"Hey, Kevin!"

Kevin turned to him. His clothes were filthy and he was wasted.

"JJ? What's goin' on, man? C'mon over here. Meet my friends." He got up and gave Jesse a hug. Jesse could tell he hadn't bathed in a while.

"Kevin, can we talk? I miss ya' man. I really miss ya'."

"We can talk. Sure."

"I mean…away from these guys." Jesse motioned toward the dirty unshaven men around the fire.

"No," Kevin told him. "These guys are my brothers, man. Whaddya want?" Kevin's eyes were barely focused on him.

Jesse felt his chest tighten. "Like I said. I miss ya', Kev. We all miss ya'. Ya' know, your family is goin' nuts worryin' about ya'. Your sisters talk to Terri about you all the time. Why you gotta do this to 'em? Come back. I need ya' to come back."

Kevin turned to him, his eyes glassy.

"Back to what? I'm ridin' the fuckin' rainbow, man. I'm livin' life down here. Don't ya' know? I'm on top o' the fuckin' world, man. You're plastic, JJ. Your life and everything out there is plastic. I'm like God in this place. Hear that? God! Look at this!" Kevin held up a can of spaghetti with a spoon in it. "See this. This is life, man. You can't do this. You're stuck in a place I don't wanna go. I'm fuckin' free now."

"What the fuck are ya' talkin' about, Kevin? What the fuck?" Jesse felt a lump forming in his throat. He knew it was no use. He turned to leave.

"Bye JJ. Come and see me again. I got the power. Know that?"

Jesse had trouble holding back his tears as he trudged back up the steep ravine. Kevin was lost.

* * *

Terri walked down the corridor of the VA Hospital and greeted the wheelchair-bound Vietnam vets who had gathered in the hall to catch a few rays of the warm sunlight. Some were reading books or magazines, but they all looked up and greeted her. She looked forward to saying good morning to them now, the same men she used to hurry past. Somehow their appearance wasn't as disturbing to her now and she understood how much they appreciated even just a word or two from her.

As she approached Chick's room, she heard him holler.

"Don't tell me what to do! You can go to hell!"

She took a deep breath and entered the room. Chick's roommate looked like a child who'd just been scolded.

"Dad. What's going on?" She looked at the other man and motioned to him apologetically. "Sorry."

Chick stood by his bed, one hand holding his pajama pants, the other holding on to the bed rail.

"That son of a bitch told me to get a belt." He pointed at the old man. "I don't have to take that from nobody."

"Daddy, get in bed. You look a little wobbly." She pulled the curtain that separated the two beds, but not before waving goodbye to the old man who sat in his chair, wide-eyed and still in shock.

"So what if he told you to get a belt? Why do ya' have to take it as an insult? He didn't say anything bad."

"Bullshit! People don't know how to mind their own goddamn business." Terri helped Chick into bed. He poked his cheek hard with his index finger as he often did. "C'mon. Give yer daddy a kiss. Right here."

Terri bent over and kissed his cheek. His face was thin, his temples sunken from illness.

"Ya' know, ya' look good, baby. Your face looks good. What is it? Did ya' do somethin' different?"

Terri sat down on Chick's bed. "No. Well…yeah I did and I wanted to talk to you about it."

"What?"

"Well, it's a good thing, Dad. I don't know where to start. Ya' know I used to drink a lot and…well, I quit drinkin', Dad. I haven't had a drink in more than two months. I realized I'm a…uh…I'm an alcoholic, and I go to A.A. now. You know Alcoholics Anonymous?"

Terri sat up stiffly, fully expecting that he hadn't been listening.

"What? Are you kiddin' me? Oh baby, you just made yer daddy a happy man."

Terri was astonished. "What?"

"Oh yeah. I could see it. You always had a drink in yer hand. I felt bad, but what could I do? It hurt me. Ya' know, it hurt me to see ya' drink like that. It reminded me of yer mother. She liked to do that, too."

Terri gave herself a moment to digest what Chick had said.

"Daddy, ya' think I got it from her side of the family?"

"Oh yeah. They drank like crazy on that side. And yer

grandfather. He was a mean bastard when he drank. He used to beat them, his wife and all of 'em."

"What? You talkin' about the same grandpa with the handlebar mustache and fedora hat? My grandpa, who used to take me to get fresh eggs and let me chase the chickens around?"

"Yeah. Him."

"But, Dad, he was so nice to me. I loved him."

"Oh, he got nice when he got older. How old were you when he died? Five?"

"Yeah, but I still remember him. He taught me that rhyme. You know. 'Knock, knock. Who's there? Grandpa. What ya' want? A bottle of beer. Where's your money? I left it home. Get outta here you dirty bum.' Gee, Dad. I never knew he was mean."

"Oh Christ! He was so mean when he drank. He used to chase people with a butcher knife up Broadway. Remember when we used to go play pool on Broadway, Terri? You had your own little cue, remember? You used to be so cute walkin' into that pool hall with your little cue and you could *play* too. Everybody used to watch ya' play. I was so proud."

"Yeah, Daddy I remember. I used to love to go there with you. Can I ask you a few things about Mommy?"

"What about her?"

"Well, when I was little, I used to sleep at my friends' houses all the time. Then when I was older, you guys went out almost every weekend. Where did you go?"

"Oh, we went to bars. Your mother used to love to go out to a bar. Her favorite one was across the river. We went out a lot. But your mother loved you and yer sister, and don't forget it. Remember when you and yer sister went to that big farm to hear music? You both ran outta' the house while we were yellin'."

"Yeah, Dad. You mean Woodstock."

"Yeah, that place. It was a goddamn mess. Your mother was watchin' it on TV and she was cryin' the whole time yous kids were gone. Ahhh. Ya' never listened to yer mother. She told ya' not to go there."

"I know, Daddy." But Terri wanted to hear more about her mother's drinking. It was like finding the final piece of a puzzle that had been missing for years. She took solace in the revelation there was a reason for her affliction and she wanted to hear more.

"Dad, you think Mommy had what I have? You think she was an alcoholic?"

"Oh no. Don't say that about your mother."

"It's not a bad thing if it was true. Listen it wasn't her fault. It's a disease people didn't even know they had in those days. You know how lucky I am?"

"Oh yeah, baby. You were always lucky. Remember when we used to go to Saratoga? You'd pick a horse and it would come in. You were a lucky kid."

"Yeah. I'm real lucky. Ya' know I told Sarah about my problem and she said she didn't think I was so bad. How is it that you noticed and she didn't?"

"Hey, I'm yer daddy. I notice everything, and don't think I don't."

"Thanks, Dad." She kissed him again. "So how are you feeling? Do you want a new pair of pajamas or anything? These are a little big."

"Nah. I don't want nothin'. I'm okay. Don't worry about me 'cause ya' know yer daddy always bounces back. Hear me? I'm gonna bounce back! That thing I had…ya' know. Well it's gone. Ask them on the way out when I'm gettin' outta here, okay? How's yer job? How's that nice boss you told me about? That was good of him to give you your old job back."

"Mr. Katz? Oh he's great. I owe him a lot. He's been good to me."

"And Jesse. He's so good, Terri. You got a nice boy there, even if he is Irish. You take good care of him. He's good to me."

Terri blushed as she thought about the way she took

care of Jesse last night.

"I...uh...I know, Dad." She stood up. "Listen I'm gonna get goin'. I gotta—"

"Oh, c'mon. Can ya' stay a little longer?"

She sat back down without hesitation.

"Yeah. Yeah, Dad. I can stay as long as you want."

As Terri and her father began talking about old times, she realized the urgency was gone, that nagging need for a drink, replaced by something else. Something she wasn't yet used to.

Chapter 22

Terri got a call from the social worker at the VA Hospital who asked her to stop by. Bob Davidson had always been kind and helpful but now there was a problem. She knocked lightly on the open door to his office. He looked up when he heard her and waved her in.

"Mr. Davidson. What's going on?" She was angry.

"Terri. Sit down. Calm down. As I told you on the phone, it seems your father's been fighting with everyone here. The psychiatrist who evaluated him wrote in his report that he's combative and he needs to be in the care of the psychiatric unit at the Bronx VA."

"That's bullshit, Mr. Davidson! My father was *always* feisty. He's been like that since I was a kid. They can't send him down there! I live up here. I'll never get to see him."

Terri gathered herself. "Mr. Davidson, my father is *dying*. He wants a spot in the nursing home right here and that's where he's going."

"Terri, I can't get him in the nursing home. There's a waiting list...and the psychiatrist..."

"Fuck the psychiatrist! Do I have to call my sister? You'll be hearing from her and her New York lawyers. I want my father in that nursing home so get the paperwork ready."

She stormed out of the office and down the hall to Chick's room. He was in bed watching TV and brightened when she entered the room.

"Hey, Terri. I didn't know you were comin' today."

She sat in the chair next to his bed. "Dad, everything okay? I heard there was a doctor here to see you. That right?"

"Yeah. That's right. One of those head doctors was here. When he first came in I thought he was a real doctor. Then he started askin' me a lotta questions about grandma and grandpa, about when I was a kid. So I said, 'Get the hell outta here. It's none of yer goddamn business.' I woulda chased him out but I was stuck in this damn bed 'cause I can't walk no more."

"Good. I'm glad you told him off. Well, I can guarantee he won't be back. Sarah's gonna take care of it." Terri always envied Sarah's guts. No one could tell people off like her big sister. She knew if Sarah got involved, Chick would definitely get in the nursing home. "And Dad, they're gonna move you to the nursing home here. You still wanna go there, right?"

"Oh sure. It sounds nice. You said I can go outside there, ain't that right? That I can go outside if you take me in the wheelchair?"

"Yeah, Dad. You can go out and get fresh air."

"Terri, you payin' my bills and takin' care of my checkbook? Ya' keepin' track of my social security check?"

"Yeah, next time I'll bring it, Okay? So you can look at it."

"Oh, you don't have to bring it...and Terri, if you need any money, take what you need. I don't need any money in here. Take whatever you want."

"Thanks, Daddy. Thanks a lot. Oh Jeez, I almost forgot, I brought you some books. Look at these."

She handed him three large hardcover books, biographies with lots of pictures.

He looked down at the books and started to cry.

"Don't cry, Daddy. They're just books."

"Oh, Terri. You know I love the Pope. And look at this, Michelangelo...and Rudolph Valentino! Where'd ya' find these? Jeez, Valentino. He's been dead a long time."

"There's a new book store in Poughkeepsie. You can find a book on anybody."

"I'm gonna look at these as soon as you leave. They're real nice. That Pope John. Ain't he somethin', Terri? Why would that dirty bastard wanna shoot him? That was a damn shame."

"Yeah, Dad. Everybody loves the Pope."

"He's the greatest Pope that ever lived. I don't give a

shit if he is Polish. He's terrific!"

Terri stayed longer than she expected. She was enjoying her visits with Chick more and more. She was making her amends without even trying.

* * *

Terri went home and called her sister in New York.

"Hi, Sarah. Listen they want to move Daddy down to the psychiatric unit at Bronx VA. You gotta call them and stop them."

"What? Are they crazy? What did he do, go and hit somebody?"

"No, Sarah. He didn't do anything. He's just being himself, ya' know. I tried to tell them he was always like that. I think he's starting to get on their nerves. Please call and tell them to get him in that nursing home. Please."

"Okay. I'll talk to my lawyer. Don't worry."

* * *

Sarah was as good as her word. Chick was now where he wanted to be, the VA nursing home.

As Terri walked down the hall toward her father's room, she stopped in her tracks. On both sides of the hallway there were several sketches of the Pope and Rudolph Valentino. She looked at them wide-eyed, her mouth open.

A nurse called to her, "See your father's drawings? We had no idea he could draw. Aren't they wonderful?"

Terri was flabbergasted. "Yeah. He always painted and sketched, but I didn't know he'd start again. This is amazing."

"He's really something," the nurse replied.

"Yeah. He's somethin' all right."

Terri walked into Chick's room. He had pulled his wheelchair up to his new roommate's bed and was shoving a newspaper clipping toward the man.

"Look, Lefty. Read it. It's Joey Manero. He died. Don't ya' remember Joey Manero?"

The old man gave Chick a hollow stare.

"C'mon, Lefty. You remember him. Joey 'Eggs.' Remember why they called him Eggs, Lefty? Remember? He always ordered eggs when we used to run around together. Every place we'd go, he ordered eggs. Ahhhhhh. Here." Chick put the clipping in the old man's hand and closed the man's fingers tightly around it. "You read it later."

He wheeled himself backward, saw Terri, and smiled.

"Hey, Dad. What were ya' doin'? Tryin' to make that old guy remember somethin'?"

"Ya' know who that is?"

"No, Dad. Who?"

"That's Lefty Carlin. Don't ya' remember? He used to come in our store."

"Oh yeah. I remember him. He must have Alzheimer's disease."

"No, he ain't got a disease. He's senile!"

Terri smiled. "Yeah, I think you're right."

Chick looked over at the old man and shook his head.

"Poor bastard. That's a damn shame! He can't remember shit."

"Hey, Dad...those sketches outside. They're beautiful. When did you decide to start drawing?"

"Yesterday. I said, 'If I can't walk, I'm gonna draw. I'm not gonna just exist.' So I got a pencil and some paper and started. Ya' know, it made me feel good. I felt good all day 'cause I drew those pictures, and I'm gonna draw more too."

"That's great, Daddy. Want me to get you some good paper?"

"Yeah, bring me some paper and I need some charcoal, pencils, and...those things you rub with. You know what I mean, those blenders."

"Yeah, Dad, I know. I'll get some at the art store. So you still like this place, Dad?"

"Yeah. How long I been here, Terri? About two months?"

"About that."

"Is Sarah coming up this weekend? I really wanna see her."

"Yeah. She's gonna keep coming every other weekend. You wanna go outside in the courtyard, Dad? It's a beautiful day."

"Yeah...Yeah, take me out there."

She pushed Chick across the courtyard and stopped in the shade of a large maple tree. It was a hot day but the air seemed extra fresh, a contrast to the stale air inside. Terri knew it must have smelled really sweet to Chick.

He looked contented for a dying man. "Ya' know, Jesse comes to see me every day."

"He likes you, Dad. He thinks you're great."

"Ah, he's a nice boy, even if he is Irish. Goddam shame about his little brother."

"Whaddya mean? He ain't got a little brother."

"No, of course he don't. He died. He was only three."

Terri suddenly had a flashback to the photograph she saw in Jesse's wallet all those years ago, the day he left for Vegas. She remembered the image of the little boy, how it was folded back and kept out of sight.

"Daddy, how did he die? I need to talk to Jesse—"

Chick cut her off.

"Nah, ya' don't. He'll tell ya' when he's good and ready," Chick said firmly. "You should hang on to Jesse. Look for some kinda security. You and yer sister, you gotta get some security. Know what I mean?"

"Yeah, Dad. Don't worry. I'm secure. I'm more secure than I've been in a long, long time."

"Your mother used to worry so much about yous kids. She was crazy about her kids. When we used to come home late at night...we used to stay out late, ya' know.

Well, she'd run right into your rooms and fix the blankets and kiss you both. I used to love to watch her do that."

"She did? That's really nice. I'm gonna write Mommy a letter someday."

"A letter? Why? She's dead."

"Because it's good to write. It's healthy. I'll feel good when I do it, just like you feel good when you draw."

"That's nice, Terri. That's a nice idea." Chick looked over at a couple of Vietnam vets in wheelchairs across the yard. "Look at that. That's a shame. Look at those poor kids. The government really shit on them after they fought in that war fer nothin'."

"Dad! That's what I tried to tell you when I was in high school, but you screamed at me. Remember?"

"Yeah, well that was then. I met a couple of 'em and talked to them. I can change my mind can't I? When I was in the war, we knew who we were fightin'—Mussolini, Hitler. We felt like we knew those guys and we wanted to beat 'em. But these poor guys. They didn't even know who the hell the enemy was. They got a bad deal. Look at 'em. So young with no legs. I can't walk, but I'm an old man. That's a damn shame. Goddam government."

"Daddy, did you fight? Over in England and France?"

Chick perked up. "Ya' mean did I see any action? Nah. But don't think it wasn't dangerous! I mean bombs were droppin' all over the place. But I hated leavin' your mother. Christ we just got married and I got drafted. I wasn't young either. I was thirty-one. Had to start all over when I got out."

"You did a good thing though, Dad...I mean..." Terri patted his hand. "Thanks. I know it must have been hard."

"Terri, ya' know. You're a good goil. You were always a good kid."

The more time Terri spent with her father, the more she liked him. And rather than think of all those years she wasted, she decided to make the best of the time they had left together.

Chapter 23

Jesse looked over at Terri as he drove.

"You nervous?"

"No, not at all. I'm happy. I'm amazed. I'm...I don't know what I am. God! One year without a drink. Kind of in shock I guess. It went by so fast."

"It's been quite a time for you. I'm proud of you. When you get that coin tonight, it's gonna feel so good."

Terri squeezed his thigh as he drove. "I know. I really can't wait. Oh yeah, the nursing home called. They said something about some papers my dad has to sign tomorrow. The 'DNR' papers. You know about them right?"

"Yeah, it's just a standard thing at this stage. Ya' know, so they don't hook your father up to machines. Nobody wants to be hooked up to machines...Terri...it won't be long now."

Terri stared out the window.

"Yeah, I know. He seems so good though. He's eating and all, but the doctor said the cancer is in his liver. Jeez, Jesse. Right now, I don't know whether to laugh or cry."

"You'll probably do both when you get that coin in your hand."

He pulled into St. Paul's school parking lot. They sat and listened to the end of Ry Coder's *"Jesus on the Mainline"* before getting out the car.

* * *

Terri and Jesse sat at Chick's bedside and Terri explained as best she could the meaning of the papers he was about to sign. A new doctor was standing across from them. Chick had told Terri about him—*one of them Jap Orientals.*

"Dad, when you sign these papers, you're saying you don't want to be hooked up to machines that will breathe for you and keep you alive. It says if you pass away, you don't want to be revived with tubes and stuff."

Chick was propped up on pillows, pen in hand. The doctor placed the papers on a book, waiting for Chick to sign. Chick looked at the papers and then at Terri.

"Wait a minute!"

Terri recognized the cockiness in his voice right away.

"Maybe I don't wanna sign this. I wanna know, how long can I live on those machines?"

Terri breathed in but didn't breathe out. Part of her wanted to grab the papers and cheer. Then she let out a breath, and logic prevailed.

"Dad. You don't really want to be hooked up to a machine, do you? I mean, remember when Mommy was sick, you wouldn't have wanted—"

The doctor ungraciously broke in.

"Mr. Micelli. I am very busy today. You must sign these papers. You are terminal. You have terminal liver cancer. It would be foolish not to sign these papers."

Terri gasped. She wanted to pull the papers away and tear them up but when she looked down, Chick was reluctantly dragging the pen over the paper. She noticed his chin quivering. The doctor snatched the papers and walked out.

She looked at Jesse and said, "That dirty fuckin' bastard."

Terri ran out of the room, Jesse was one step behind her. By the time she was in the hall, the doctor was disappearing around a corner.

She ran after him and screamed, "Hey, you. Dr. Chung. Ya' fuckin' asshole."

Jesse grabbed her arm.

"That dirty bastard. What kinda doctor is he?" she yelled.

Jesse held her tight. "C'mon, your father's alone. He's upset. Let's go back in."

When they returned, Chick lay there staring, his chin

still quivering slightly, like a little child's. He looked up at her.

"Terri, was that you yellin'? You never swear like that. Don't be mad. Anyway. Why would he say that—about my liver?"

Terri had no idea how to respond at first. She didn't like the look of the upset little boy slumped in the bed, she wanted a bit of the *old* Chick Micelli again.

"Don't listen to him, Dad. He's not your regular doctor. Just forget it. Ya' know, these doctors. They're always in a hurry. They just say anything. Listen, when I come tomorrow, you want anything special?"

"Yeah, can you bring me a dish of pasta fagioli? I love your pasta fagioli. Ya' know, Jesse, she makes a good dish of macaroni."

Jesse smiled and patted Chick's hand. "Oh yeah, Chick. I know that. She's a pretty good cook. Just like her mother, huh?"

"Oh yeah. My wife could cook. She was terrific. Ya' know, Terri, I been dreamin' about your mother a lot...all the time now."

"That's real nice, Dad. Listen, tomorrow I'll bring you the pasta. Okay? You feel better?"

"Yeah. Don't you worry. You know yer daddy's gonna bounce back."

She bent down and kissed him on the cheek. She knew it would take a lot more than the threat of impending death to break Chick's Micelli's spirit.

* * *

As she spooned the pasta into Chick's mouth, Terri noticed how everything about him had become smaller, except his nose. His skin was still smooth and taut, but the concavity at his temples and the grayness of his skin was unsettling to her. She knew that each day, she'd lose a little bit more of him.

Chick grimaced as he swallowed a spoonful of his favorite dish. He shook his head and motioned for her to take the bowl away.

"What, Dad? You don't want anymore?"

"Nah. It tastes funny."

Terri wiped his mouth and quickly removed the bowl, realizing that food was no longer to be a part of his world. Now his comfort was her only concern.

He rested his head back against the pillows and nodded off. Sleep was becoming more frequent. He needed to rest, but she knew with just one touch of her hand, he'd wake up and smile at her.

She was drawn to the small sleeping man and longed for just a bit more of the father she once knew. Terri reached out and gently squeezed his shoulder.

His tired muddy eyes opened and he smiled.

"Daddy, I'll go back to work while you sleep."

"No. No, Terri. I wasn't sleepin'. I was just dozin' a little. Ya' know all the Micellis do that. We all like to sleep. You and your sister, you were always nappin'. You still like to nap, Terri?"

Terri was relieved at the strength in his voice.

"Yeah, Dad. I still do."

"Oh yeah. Hey did I ever tell you the funny story about your Uncle Dominick?"

"No, Daddy. Tell me." Terri moved her chair closer to the bed and gave him her full attention.

"Oh, this is a good one. We were eatin' at Aunt Frances' house. It was some holiday, I don't know, Easter or somethin'. Dominick was late for dinner. He was comin' for coffee later. So he knocks on the door and everybody was sleepin'. Everybody. Jeez there musta been ten people there. Nobody answered the door. So he looks in the window and starts bangin' on it. So he figures we're all dead. He thinks we're poisoned…so he…"

They both began laughing, but Terri could see how difficult it was for him.

"So he calls an ambulance. He didn't even check us. Then he found out we were all just sleepin'. Ain't that funny, Terri? See, we all love to sleep."

"That's a riot, Dad. That's a good one."

She patted his hand. Chick rested his head on the pillow but Terri didn't want to lose him. She tried to conjure up some happy memories to keep him with her a little longer.

"Daddy. Remember those great vacations we took to the beach, when we used to go to Connecticut with Aunt Nilda and Uncle Frank? I used to love—"

Chick turned and lifted his head slightly off the pillow. Terri saw a bit of fire in his eyes.

"Aunt Nilda? That dirty sonofabitch! I couldn't stand that woman. The worst thing we ever did was go on vacation with those two bastards. You know what she had the noive to say?"

Terri smiled. Tickled at Chick's reaction, she had a hard time sitting still. Chick Micelli was still in there.

"What, Dad? What did she say?"

"She said you were a pain in the ass. You were only five then. I said 'Don't talk that way about my kid. You think your kids are so hot? Your daughter's the pain in the ass.'"

"Gee, thanks, Dad. Thanks for sticking up for me."

"Yeah, the noive of that bitch, pickin' on a little kid. Your aunts hated kids...except Aunt Vi. She liked ya'. Christ, they even hated their own kids. I never went on vacation with those bastards again after that. Saratoga. Now that was a nice vacation. Remember when we went to Saratoga racetrack?"

Terri remembered the whole excruciating week in Saratoga. While her parents played the horses, she spent most of her time with a kind black woman who sold fried chicken near the entrance to the track. After the thrill of picking horses had worn off for Terri, the woman kept the little girl entertained and well-fed.

But now Terri needed to placate the old man.

"Yeah, Dad. That was a great vacation. Remember we went to a museum there and saw Diamond Jim Brady's stuff?"

"Oh yeah. And you loved to play those horses, Terri."

"Sure, Dad. I loved that," she lied.

Chick grabbed her hand and held it tightly.

"Oh, Terri. We had a good time, didn't we? I mean…we had a nice house. I was a good father, right?"

She looked in his dark sunken eyes.

"Yes, Daddy. Of course you were. Don't ever think otherwise. You were the best!"

He smiled and his eyes filled easily. Chick Micelli's tears were real and had always been real. He brightened before he spoke.

"Ya' know. When I was a kid, I went to school in one of those one-room schoolhouses. One day, I jumped right out the window, 'cause I didn't like school. The next day the teacher says to me 'Giovanni, you're never gonna amount to anything in this life. You're just like the caboose at the end of the train.' And I never forgot that, Terri. But see, she was wrong. I proved 'em all wrong. Ain't that right? Give Daddy a kiss right here!"

He poked his cheek with his scrawny finger.

Terri stood up. She bent down and kissed his pale cheek. "I better get to work. Mr. Katz is waiting."

"Can ya' stay just a little longer, Terri?"

Terri sat on the bed and ran her fingers over his sunken cheeks.

"Sure. I'll stay."

She waited until he was asleep and then quietly slipped out of the room.

* * *

Terri started coming to the nursing home each morning before work. As she walked down the hall this morning, she heard a faint sound that got louder as she approached her father's room. It was a moan, interspersed with a gurgling sound. It never occurred to her that the sound was coming from her father until she walked into his room.

He reached to her with his arms the moment he saw her. His mouth was open but he was unable to speak, his eyes spoke for him. There was a desperation there she'd never seen. His breathing was labored.

"Daddy. Oh my god."

She ran out to a nurse.

"Help. My father. He can't breathe. It sounds like he's drowning. Help him. Hurry up."

The nurse took Terri by the shoulders.

"Calm down, dear. We just need to suction some of the fluid, that's all. He'll be okay after that. Wait right here."

She called for help. Two more nurses arrived and hurried into Chick's room. When they emerged smiling, Terri sighed.

"You can go in now, Terri. He's much more comfortable."

Terri reached out for the nurse's hand.

"I just want to say thanks. You've all been really good to him. I know he's a tough patient. Is he in much pain?"

The nursed grabbed Terri and hugged her.

"No. We won't let that happen. We just gave him a shot of morphine. Whenever he needs it, we'll give it to him."

Terri rushed in. When Chick turned to her, she knew he'd soon be gone.

"Daddy."

He motioned for her to come closer, his crooked finger moving slowly.

As she moved her ear to his lips, he whispered, "Get Sarah…and the kid. Where's the kid?"

"Jesse? Don't worry, Dad. I'm going right now to get them. I'll be right back."

When she returned, she feared sitting on the bed might hurt him so she pulled a chair up as close as she could.

"Daddy, they're on their way, okay? They're coming as fast as they can. Hey, Dad. Remember when we were little, and you used to throw your change on the floor. Remember that?"

The old man smiled and spoke in a cracked whisper.

"Yeah. You liked that, didn't you, when I used to throw that money?"

His breathing was labored and it was difficult for him to talk.

But Terri wanted him to talk. She thought about her Aunt Nilda, her Uncle Vinnie, the names that would always get Chick riled.

"Daddy, Aunt Nilda called. She was asking for you."

"Oh she was, was she? That woman is a pain in my ass. But..."

"What, Dad?"

"I never told you this, but...Aunt Nilda had a good side. She was good to your mother. Ya' know, Aunt Nilda was the oldest sister. When your grandfather came home drunk, he was mean. They had to hide when he came home, and they couldn't make any noise or he would beat 'em. And your Aunt Nilda, she'd take them all in a room and keep the little kids quiet. She'd protect them. She was good to her brothers and sisters. She knew. Aunt Nilda knew what he'd do. When he beat your grandmother, she kept them all quiet, read them stories. She was good that way."

"Dad. Shhh. Rest okay?"

"Oh shit, Terri. Where is she? Where's Sarah?"

Terri patted his hand. "She's coming soon. Listen I'm still here."

"Damn it. I know *you're* still here, but I want Sarah."

Terri took it as a compliment. Being there for him these past months had been difficult. His words meant she'd done well.

* * *

Terri watched from her chair in the corner of the room as Chick reached his thin arms up toward Sarah. She bent down to kiss him. Jesse stood on the opposite side of the bed.

"Sarah, you came," Chick whispered. "Ya' know yer daddy loves you."

"I love you too, Dad. Of course I came. Did you think I wouldn't?"

Sarah gently released Chick's thin body from her embrace and carefully placed his head back on the pillow. He smiled as he looked at Jesse.

"Thanks for everything, kid. Ya' know, you're a good boy—my Irish son."

Jesse leaned closer to hear Chick's softly spoken words.

"I didn't do anything, Chick."

"Yeah, ya' did, kid. Ya' listened to an old man and ya' helped me out. I don't forget it when somebody helps me out."

Jesse bent down and spoke again. "Chick, you scared?"

"Nah. You kiddin'? What the hell do I got to be scared about? Watch it, kid. I might still bounce back yet."

Terri and Sarah looked at each other and smiled, as if they really believed he would.

They stayed until Chick fell into a silent sleep. Terri already missed the sound of his cocky, booming voice.

* * *

The following day the three of them sat around his bed, watching the hesitant rise and fall of his chest. With each labored breath, the sisters expected Chick to throw off the covers and start cursing and hollering.

"Maybe if I start talking about Uncle Vinnie," Terri said.

Jesse rolled his eyes. "He's in a coma for Christ's sake."

Sarah chimed in, "I can't believe this. I can't believe Daddy isn't gonna talk anymore."

Terri shook her head. "Me either. This is too much. He looks so awful."

Jesse raised his hands to quiet Terri. "Shhh. Don't say that. He can hear you. People in comas can hear, ya' know."

"What?" Sarah exclaimed.

"Yeah. That's right. I heard stories where people come outta comas and tell off all the relatives that were talkin' about them. So don't say anything about the way he looks. It's only gonna make things worse."

Terri threw her hands up. "Jesse, you're nuts! You think he's gonna come out of it too? We're all nuts! We can't just sit here staring at his chest like a bunch of assholes."

They stood up and quietly looked at each other.

Terri and Sarah bent down and kissed their father goodbye, finally accepting the inevitable.

Terri waited in the doorway and listened as Jesse leaned over Chick—the man he'd grown to love. She watched them both, thinking they'd seen the worst of her—and maybe the best. Jesse wiped his eyes with the back of his hand. Terri moved closer to hear his whispered words.

"Hey listen, Chick. When you get to where you're goin', say hello to Valentino, okay?"

* * *

Terri waited for the call. It came at eleven at night. She left the warmth of her bed and Jesse's body and grabbed the phone.

"Uh huh. Okay. Thanks"

She got back into bed and began to sob. It was a cry that came from deep inside her, a flood of emotion she'd held back for years.

Jesse held her close. "Go ahead, babe. It's okay."

She took a deep breath before she could speak.

"You loved him too, didn't you?"

"Yeah, I did. He kinda grew on me."

Terri held Jesse tight and realized these tears she cried for Chick Micelli were long overdue, like a debt finally settled.

About the Author

Say Hello To Valentino is Miranda Marin's first novel. She grew up in the riverside city of Beacon, New York, in the beautiful Hudson Valley. Her loves as a child were taking ferry rides across the mighty Hudson to shop in the great city of Newburgh, riding the trolley to the top of Mt. Beacon, exploring the woods, listening to rock and roll music, and writing. Then came the loud clanging each day as the Newburgh-Beacon bridge was being built—a structure that would soon divert traffic and commerce away from the center of her small hometown, leading to the decades of its demise.

Having survived Woodstock, the 60's, the tumultuous 70's, and a brief time in Northern California, she now lives back home in the Valley and is happy that Beacon is thriving again.

Music has always been a huge part of her life and most days you'll find Miranda hanging out in her music room singing and playing the guitar or ukulele. She listens to live music as much as possible, supporting local musicians. A natural storyteller, writing a novel was always one of her dreams. Miranda is married with two grown children

Photo Credit: Natalie Kane   natalie@jamesferrara.com

ALSO BY WORDS IN THE WORKS
Available at Amazon.com

Fiction & Poetry:

Remains To Be Seen
By Edward H. Essex

Love Poems We Love
By Edward H. Essex

Children's Books:

Max The Flying Sausage Dog—Chapter Book Series
Illustrated by Arthur Robins
Stories by John O'Driscoll and Richard Kelley

That Day in September—*Rhymes for the Times*
By Liz Lime

Memoir:

Courtney's Quest
By Courtney King Dye

Entertainment

Vocab-Du-Ku
By Arleen Phypers & Laurie Niederhauser

Made in the USA
Middletown, DE
06 June 2016